A DARK SKY

By

KATHERINE
PATHAK

A DCI Dani Bevan novel

© Katherine Pathak, All Rights Reserved, 2014

© Front Cover design, All Rights Reserved, Catacol Bay Images, 2014

The Garansay Press

φ

Books by Katherine Pathak

The Imogen and Hugh Croft Mysteries:

Aoife's Chariot

The Only Survivor

Lawful Death

The Woman who Vanished

Memorial for the Dead
(Introducing DCI Dani Bevan)

Short Stories:

Full Beam

DCI Dani Bevan novels:

Against a Dark Sky

φ

The Garansay Press

This is a work of fiction. Names, characters, businesses, places, events and incidents are either the products of the author's imagination or used in a fictitious manner. Any resemblance to actual persons, living or dead, or actual events is purely coincidental.

All rights reserved. No part of this publication may be reproduced in any form or by any means - graphic, electronic, or mechanical, including photocopying, recording, taping or information storage and retrieval systems - without the prior permission in writing of the author and publishers.

The moral right of the author has been asserted.

© Katherine Pathak, 2014

φ

The Garansay Press

Chapter One

The Trossachs National Park, Loch Lomond.
Scotland.

'Can we stop for a second, whilst I take off my fleece?'

'Sure, no problem.' James Irving stood still and surveyed the landscape. The sun was very bright. It beamed down upon them from its highest point in the sky. The group had been hiking for a couple of hours already and despite the fact it was mid-October, the walkers were beginning to feel hot. James turned his gaze towards Joanna as she pulled the sweater over her head. Her t-shirt lifted up along with it and revealed a brief glimpse of the smooth bare flesh underneath. His eyes lingered there for a moment before she tugged it back down again.

'Okay,' Joanna declared. 'Are we ready to carry on?'

'Is this where the path gets steeper?' Philippa Graves asked.

'Yes, there's something of a scramble as we approach the west ridge, but then we'll see the burn cascading down the mountainside next to us as we climb. It's pretty spectacular. You don't get anything nearly as impressive along the tourist path.' Joanna Endicott smiled, with the easy confidence for which she was renowned amongst her friends and colleagues.

The other two men in the group remained silent. James noted the expression of sheer determination on the face of Amit Batra whom he knew was itching to 'bag' his first Munro. Daniel Goff, on the other hand, he couldn't really read. Goff was a friend of Joanna's from her university days and James had only met him once before. The man appeared to be kitted out in all the latest gear. Irving suspected this ascent wouldn't pose too much of a challenge for him.

The group had set out that morning from the converted bothy they'd rented for the week. They intended to climb Scotland's southernmost Munro, Ben Lomond. Joanna had organised the trip, bringing together some of her workmates and a few likeminded pals who fancied a walking holiday in the Scottish hills. James worked with Joanna as a corporate lawyer in the City of London. When she suggested the idea of an autumn break, he found himself keen to agree. Irving didn't often get the chance to return to the country of his birth.

The views from the Ptarmigan path did prove to be outstanding. There had been a significant amount of rainfall over the past few weeks and the burn gushed down the hillside in a series of dramatic waterfalls. Daniel Goff surprised James by bringing a slim-line digital camera out of his rucksack and proceeding to snap away at the sights. Philippa Graves took the opportunity to pause for a rest-break, breathing heavily and placing a hand on the small of her back.

'How're you doing?' James asked her lightly.

'I wasn't expecting the pace to be quite so brisk,' the young woman replied. 'I must be really unfit.' She managed a weak smile.

'Hey, Jo!' James called ahead. 'Philippa and I might drop back a bit. We're finding the going fairly tough on this steeper section.'

'Fine!' the blond woman shouted in return, giving her friend the thumbs-up.

'That was very gentlemanly of you, thanks,' Philippa said as she fell into step beside James and the others strode off in front.

'Well, I'm here to enjoy the scenery. Not take part in a bloody race.'

At 2,000 feet, James and Philippa found themselves ascending into a thick mist. Previously, they had been able to see the outlines of the other three in the distance. Now, they couldn't make out anything at all up ahead.

'Is this what it's always like at the top of a mountain?' Philippa enquired tentatively.

'It can be. If the weather's not great and the cloud cover is lying low. We're only at the top of the ridge, I'm afraid. The summit is still over a thousand feet away.'

Philippa looked crestfallen. James had to admit he was disappointed too. From this point, they should have been able to see Loch Lomond in the west and the Arrochar Alps to the north of them. But with this level of visibility, James thought he'd be lucky to see his hand in front of his face if they climbed any higher.

'It's getting cold,' Philippa complained, before reaching into her rucksack to locate a rain jacket.

James put his on as well, zipping it up tight under his chin. He wondered if it was purely a figment of his imagination that the clouds were growing steadily darker, so they now resembled a blanket of thick, swirling smoke, billowing from some kind of huge, industrial chimney. The wind seemed to be getting up too. He considered whether or not he'd remembered to put his gloves into the bag when they set off that morning from the cottage.

'Shouldn't we all be sticking together?' Philippa said, trying to peer further along the ridge. 'I can't see Jo anywhere.'

James furrowed his brow, annoyed that the rest of

the group hadn't stopped to check on them. It was one of the first rules of hill climbing - you went at the speed of the slowest walker. If he hadn't decided to drop back, would the other three simply have allowed Philippa to get left behind? James gazed about him at the gathering gloom. 'The weather's closing in. I don't think we should carry on.'

The woman beside him let out an unattractive snort of relief. 'Gosh, I'm so glad you said that.'

Irving retrieved his mobile phone from a trouser pocket and flicked on the screen. 'Shit. No reception.'

Philippa tried hers but found the same. 'Can we head back without them?'

James thought for a moment. 'If we proceed down the ridge, we may pick up a signal at a lower altitude. Then we can try to get a message to the others.' He sighed heavily. 'Jo can see what's happening with the weather, just as well as I can. It must be even worse up there. Why the hell is she continuing up the mountain?'

'You know what she's like,' Philippa commented quietly.

James did know. His colleague and friend was clever, kind and damned attractive, but she was also incredibly bloody-minded and stubborn. 'Come on,' he ordered. 'Let's go. We can do more good by getting off this hillside and fetching help rather than standing here catching our deaths of the cold.'

*

Chapter Two

The two walkers descended the ridge rapidly. James sent a text to Joanna and Amit's mobile phones, letting them know he and Philippa were heading back down. He had no idea if either of them received it.

By the time the pair had passed through the valley between Tom Fitich and Tom Eas, rain had begun to fall in sheets from the leaden sky, driven into their faces by a sharp, southerly wind. James glanced over his shoulder every five minutes. He wanted to see if he could spot the rest of their group, coming off the mountainside to join them. He saw nothing except the black silhouette of Ben Lomond, becoming ever distant as Irving and Graves beat their hasty retreat.

Finally, James felt the buzz of an incoming message on the phone in his pocket. He almost dropped the handset in his eagerness to summon it up onto the screen. It was a text from Joanna, which simply read:

We're in trouble. J x.

James tried calling her number and then Amit's, but the calls cut out before they'd even had a chance to ring. He briefly considered what he should do next. Within an instant, James had dialled 999. This time, he got an immediate connection.

Philippa set about lighting the wood burning stove in the sitting room of their pretty little rented bothy. She had already put the kettle on and gone into the room she shared with Joanna Endicott to change out of her wet clothes. When she returned to the kitchen to make coffee, James was still pacing up and down the floor, his sodden socks creating a series of damp footprints on the flagstones.

'I should have let you go down alone and carried on along the ridge to catch up with the others – maybe I could have persuaded Jo to return with us.'

Philippa laid her hand on his arm. 'Then you would be missing too,' she said levelly, setting about preparing them both a hot drink.

'I'm going to get changed and go back out there. The mountain rescue guys will need some help.'

Philippa glanced out of the tiny kitchen window at the rain being blown against the thick glass. 'They told you to wait until the weather clears, then they'll be happy to have your assistance.'

James stopped pacing and looked at her. Philippa was back to her sensible and practical self now that they were off the mountain. He knew she was right. If he went out into the hills now he would simply become a liability. James slid onto the sturdy wooden bench in defeat. Philippa placed a mug of steaming coffee in front of him, into which she had added a generous slug of single malt whisky.

'Here, take a sip of this,' she urged.

James felt the heat warming his mouth and throat. 'Thanks. I just feel bloody useless, you know?'

Philippa nodded in agreement and then a thought struck her. 'Shit. Do we need to call Amit's wife and tell her what's happened?'

'I think we should wait until we know more. The Central Scotland Police said not to panic. Apparently, folk get lost all the time in the national park. The Lomond Mountain Rescue team respond to these call-outs a lot. If we ring Tanisha now it will only give her a sleepless night and she's got the kids to look after.'

'Okay, if you say so,' Philippa replied, looking sceptical. 'But I think if it was me I'd like to be informed. Perhaps we could wait a couple of hours and see what the situation is by then?' James grunted his assent but Philippa could tell he hadn't really been listening to what she said. 'Go and get out of those wet things,' she added, in her most commanding voice. 'You won't be much good to the search team if you make yourself ill.'

James looked up, momentarily shocked by her assertiveness. 'Yeah, you're right,' he answered. 'I'm going to take a hot shower. I'll leave my phone here on the table. If there's news of any kind, then give me a shout, okay?'

'Of course,' she replied, helping him up from the seat and guiding him firmly in the direction of the stairs. 'I'll let you know straight away.'

They spent the rest of the evening working through the bottle of single malt, finally deciding to get some sleep in the wee small hours. As soon as sunlight streamed into James' room the following morning, his eyes immediately flicked open. The cottage felt worrying still and quiet. Irving splashed water on his face, pulling on a sweatshirt and his spare pair of walking trousers. He glanced briefly in the bathroom mirror. He was unshaven and looked pretty tired, but his handsome features were otherwise unaffected by the trauma and exertion of the previous day.

Philippa was placing a couple of slices of bread into the toaster when he came downstairs, her dark brown hair lying loose to her shoulders. She appeared fresh and rested.

'So they aren't back yet?'

Philippa spun around. 'No. I just called the Mountain Rescue Headquarters. The team gave up at eleven last night. We're meeting them at the base of the Ptarmigan Ridge at 8.30 to resume the search. A group of local people will be joining us. Most of the volunteers are from Ardyle village. Do you feel up to it?'

'Of course.' James glanced out of the window, where the clouds had completely lifted and the sun was beating down. 'Maybe they found somewhere to shelter,' he muttered to himself.

'I'm certain they must have done,' Philippa replied in a light and jolly tone that James imagined she used regularly to pacify the children in her Reception class.

He looked at his watch. 'We'll need a hearty breakfast, but as soon as we've finished eating I reckon it'll be time to head off.'

There was a mild easterly wind, but the strength of the sun meant it was still warm. James was assigned to a group of three men. One was called Jeff and a member of the mountain rescue team. The other two were young lads from Ardyle, who James would say were no more than 18 years old. The boys seemed to know the territory very well, certainly better than he did.

They'd been allotted an area west of the ridge to search. Spreading out in a line across the hillside, the four of them scanned the landscape from left to right, calling out the names of the missing walkers in turn. Mountain Rescue could pick up no signal from their phones. GPS was useless as they had no position to fix onto.

After half an hour, James was becoming hoarse. He gave his voice a rest whilst the search and rescue helicopter flew in low over their heads, temporarily flattening the bracken and grasses in a broad circle around them. He noticed something in the distance.

It looked like polished metal glinting in the sun.

Jeff had spotted it too and started to jog across the heath, with his walkie-talkie held up to his mouth. As they grew nearer, James could see it was Amit. He was staggering through the scrubland just a few metres up ahead. James broke into a sprint and caught his friend under the arms, helping to support his weight.

'Where's Jo?' He demanded.

Amit's body was shuddering and his teeth chattered uncontrollably. James could see he was trying to shake his head. 'I don't know. We got separated last night. I haven't seen either of them since.'

Conversation was no longer possible as the helicopter landed several yards away from them. James stood well back as the rescue team surrounded his friend, wrapping him in heat conserving blankets and securing him onto a stretcher. Within a matter of seconds they were gone.

Jeff stayed on the ground. As the two men stood and watched the chopper disappearing over the mountain, Jeff's walkie-talkie crackled into life.

'What's up?' He asked, nodding slowly as he registered the reply. 'Okay. We'll be there as soon as we can.' He turned towards James. 'They've located another member of your party - a woman this time.'

James gasped with relief. 'Oh, thank God.'

But the other man's expression remained fixed. 'Come on,' he said gently. 'I'll take you to where she is.'

Chapter Three

Rain was lashing down onto the grey pavement outside. Detective Chief Inspector Dani Bevan polished off a single measure of finest Scotch whisky in one gulp.

'I thought you didn't drink, Ma'am?' Detective Constable Andy Calder commented.

'Only on occasions like this,' she responded dryly.

Their seats faced the entrance to the pub, so Bevan had the opportunity to watch Detective Sam Sharpe storm down the steps of the Glasgow High Court opposite and make his way over. The man was tall and well-built, so as he shouldered the glass-panelled door open, the entire building seemed to shake.

He turned towards his British colleagues. 'Could you please explain to me what the hell just happened in there?' Sam's face was scarlet with rage.

'We're as disappointed as you are,' Bevan said quietly, lowering her head. 'Take a seat and Andy will get you a beer.'

'Forget that, I'll have a Scotch,' Sam retorted, sliding along the bench beside the DCI who immediately placed a conciliatory arm around his shoulders.

'It's total crap, I know. But we always thought there was a risk the jury would have no sympathy for Mackie Shaw as a victim. You have to admit, Erskine's barrister did a fantastic job.'

Sam shook his head of thick sandy hair. 'No offence, but it's Erskine getting off for Gordon

Parker's murder that really bugs me. I can't believe Richard Erskine was allowed to change his statement like that. In court, he claimed that Parker had attacked *him* and he only pushed the man off the headland in self-defence. You and I both know that's bullshit.'

Andy set down Sam's drink on the dark wood table, lowering himself onto the stool opposite. 'But there were no witnesses to contradict Erskine. Not with Shaw dead.'

'I'm hoping we'll be able to demand a re-trial on the Mackie Shaw case,' Dani added decisively. 'The jury ignored some highly compelling forensic evidence. It doesn't matter what they thought of Mackie personally, the facts pointed to Erskine as his killer. That was all they needed to reach a judgment on. I'm afraid it's unlikely we'll get a guilty verdict on Parker's death now. I'm really sorry Sam.'

The American nodded, 'my department aren't going to be happy about this. The Virginia papers will be slamming the so-called British justice system by tomorrow morning.'

'Oh, we'll get that here too, don't you worry.' Dani stared at the bottom of her empty glass.

The newly trim Andy Calder, only back at work for a matter of weeks since suffering a massive heart attack last year, polished off his mineral water and offered, 'it was Erskine's story that really won the jury over. I was watching their faces as he told it. They were full of sympathy for his grandmother. When Murray White delivered his character assessment of Mackie Shaw, the jury members were totally impassive. It hadn't moved them at all.'

'Since when did the justice system become like a reality T.V show – where we vote for our favourites and completely ignore the cold, hard facts?' The DCI sighed heavily.

'I think it's always been like that Ma'am, this is just the first time we've been on the wrong side of the outcome.'

Sam had been silent during this exchange but then he banged down his empty glass. 'I'm going to head back to the flat, okay?' He looked at Dani as he stood up and grabbed his coat.

'Fine, I'll see you back there later.' Dani gave the man's arm a squeeze but he didn't respond. The American detective simply marched straight out of the pub and allowed the door to slam shut behind him.

Dani Bevan's flat was in Scotstounhill, a residential area lying to the north west of the city. It comprised the ground floor of a late Victorian, mid-terraced house, of the type which dominated this historic district. Dani chose the property because of the kitchen-diner at the rear of the flat which opened out onto a small but un-overlooked garden. This space was her safe-haven from the demands of her job and the frenetic energy of the city.

Returning home that evening, Dani found the place in near darkness. The last of the daylight was spilling into the kitchen by way of the French doors, but the atmosphere was gloomy. 'Sam?' She ventured, leaving her briefcase and jacket in the hallway, kicking off her low-heeled shoes and padding down the corridor, glancing momentarily at her face in the mirror, checking that her sleek crop of dark hair was in place.

'I'm in here,' he called back from the dining area, where he was seated in front of a half-empty bottle of Scotch.

Dani immediately flicked on the lights. Sam seemed to shrink from the unexpected brightness.

'Have you eaten?' She asked.

'Nope,' he replied sulkily.

Dani opened the large fridge and rummaged around inside, pulling out a bowl of pasta sauce and a plastic container filled with salad. 'There wasn't anything else we could have done, you know.' She closed the door, sensing Sam's presence behind her. Dani smelt the whisky fumes on his breath as he hooked his arms around her and buried his face into her neck. He ran a hand down the slim contours of her boyish form, resting it on her stomach, the one area of softer, more rounded flesh. 'Aren't you hungry?'

Sam chuckled, turning her around and pressing his lips onto hers, perhaps a little too hard. Dani knew he was drunk and pissed off about the trial, but she also knew Sam was a good man and a decent detective. They'd both worked hard to create what they thought was a water-tight case against Erskine. She understood his frustrations and hoped it wouldn't drive a wedge between them. There were already enough odds stacked against the two of them making a go of things without any more being added to the pile.

Dani was tired and not particularly hungry herself so she allowed Sam to lead her by the hand to the bedroom just off the hall, where they could banish all thoughts of Richard Erskine walking out of that courtroom scot free, for a couple of hours at least.

Chapter Four

It was a perfectly respectable hour when Dani's phone began to ring. She and Sam were enjoying a relaxed breakfast. The American was nursing a mild hangover and had scorned his bacon and eggs for a strong coffee and a litre carton of orange juice. The atmosphere was less tense than it had been the previous day.

Dani lifted the receiver and listened in silence as the Detective Chief Superintendent outlined the case to her.

'Why do Central Scotland Police need a DCI for a mountain rescue death and a miss-per?' Bevan finally asked.

'At first it seemed as if the woman, Joanna Endicott, had fallen to her death from the Ptarmigan ridge in bad weather. But when the pathologist reached the scene, she pointed out the evidence of bruising around her neck. Apparently, she'd been strangled,' explained DCS Nicholson.

'And the man who's still missing – this Daniel Goff?'

'He's our chief suspect.'

'Right. I'll be there in a couple of hours Sir, and I'll bring Calder.'

'Do you think he's ready?'

'Yes, I do.'

'Then it's your call, Detective.'

Dani returned to the kitchen and laid a hand on Sam's shoulder.

'I'll get a flight home to Richmond later today. No point in me sticking around now, you could be gone for days.' He said this matter-of-factly, without any trace of bad feeling.

Dani leant down and kissed him on the lips. 'It's been great to see you. I really am sorry about the court case.'

'I know,' Sam replied, giving her the benefit of his unsettlingly attractive smile.

The two of them finished their breakfast without undue haste, but neither made a comment on when they might be able to see one another again.

Calder drove his senior officer along part of the route taken by the West Highland Way, into the Queen Elizabeth Forest Park and past the banks of Loch Lomond.

'We're in Rob Roy country now,' Bevan commented idly, staring out of the passenger window at the endless rows of densely packed trees, which fell away every so often to reveal an impressive expanse of clear blue water.

Calder looked puzzled.

'Did you never read Walter Scott at school?' Bevan enquired, shooting a sideways glance at her colleague. Every time she took in Andy's appearance these days, since his hospitalisation and the post-heart attack regime that had seen him shed at least three stone in the space of a year, she was momentarily shocked. Andy was one of those people who when they lose a considerable amount of weight, seem suddenly like a totally different person. She wondered how Andy's wife had reacted to the change.

'I wasn't a great one for reading when I was younger, Ma'am. I'm still not, to be honest.'

'My Dad is a big fan of Scott. "The Lady of the Lake" was set around here too, I think. We walked this section of the West Highland Way together about five years back. Dad insisted we take a detour up to Loch Katrine. There's a steam boat which does day trips called the S.S Sir Walter Scott, if you can believe it.'

'You know the area well then? That could be a real advantage to us,' Andy noted.

'Aye, a little. But we never climbed Ben Lomond. I'm hoping the mountain rescue guys can provide us with all the expertise we need there.'

Calder pulled up outside the main hotel in the small town of Ardyle. It was a pleasant place which lay on the banks of Loch Lomond, just on the outskirts of the Ben Lomond National Park. The main footpath up to the mountain started from Ardyle. Its economy revolved around the walkers who came to stay here in their droves each year in order to conquer the Munro.

The two detectives checked in and deposited their bags before setting off for the Town Hall, where the local constabulary had set up their incident room. They were greeted by a smallish man in his early fifties, who introduced himself as DS Dave Driscoll of the central division. He seemed relieved to see them.

Several trestle tables lined the centre of the hall, with items of clothing and personal effects laid out neatly upon them. Driscoll led the two detectives in a solemn procession up and down the rows of evidence.

'We've got Joanna Endicott's possessions on this side, including the clothes she was wearing when she was killed. This other table is for Goff. It's all the stuff he'd left at the bothy they'd rented for the week. I've got a couple of DCs doing a background check on the guy. To see if someone nearby might be sheltering him.'

'Are we certain Daniel Goff didn't die out there on

the mountain with Joanna?' Bevan inquired.

'We can't be certain of that Ma'am, no. There are still men out searching the hills. He could have got lost and wandered miles off the designated walking routes. We're talking about maybe fifty or sixty square miles of incredibly tough terrain. His body could be lying at the base of a rock face somewhere.'

'In which case, we're wasting valuable time and resources on a man hunt which is leading us nowhere.'

Driscoll shrugged his shoulders, as if to suggest, 'that's where you come in'. Instead he said, 'we've taken statements from the mountain rescue volunteers who found the body. They didn't disturb Joanna in any way. The white coats took a raft of photographs *in situ*, but we had to move the body out, I'm afraid. There was too much of a risk from wild animals to leave her.'

'That's fine. I'd like to speak to the other members of the walking party. They're still in the area I take it?'

'Aye, the chap who spent the night on the hillside, Amit Batra, was discharged from hospital this morning. They're all back at the bothy now. I told them they couldn't return home until they'd got your say so.'

'Very good. Andy and I will head over there now. Continue looking into Goff, will you. But put a couple of the team on Joanna Endicott. I'd like to know everything I can about her. Have her family been notified yet?'

'Yes, the next of kin have; an aunt and a couple of cousins. Her parents are no longer alive but I'll see if we can find out anything else. Oh, have you brought a 4X4 Ma'am?'

Dani shook her head.

'Then I'll get a uniform to drive you both to the

holiday cottage. You'll find it's a little bit out of the way.'

Chapter Five

Driscoll wasn't exaggerating. From a distance, the tiny stone building looked derelict. Only as they bumped and juddered closer along the rocky track could they make out the wisp of smoke snaking from a chimney and the glint of expensive, thickened glass at the small windows.

Calder banged loudly on the door. A tall man, with dark hair and a muscular build, whom Dani placed in his mid-thirties, opened up. She immediately evaluated him in her mind: professional, well-off, south of England, possibly private school educated. So it surprised her when he used a reasonably broad Scottish accent to invite them in.

The interior of the bothy had been kitted out to the highest spec. Staying here was an opportunity to get closer to nature for only the most sophisticated of clientele. A wood burner was pumping out heat in the open plan kitchen-diner. Dani had to take off her suit jacket straightaway and was tempted to suggest they open a window.

'My name is James Irving.' The man held out his hand. 'I worked with Joanna. She and I are lawyers – *were* lawyers, in the same office in London. Sorry, I'm still getting my head around the situation.'

Andy brought out his notebook and signalled for James to take a seat. 'Could you tell us a little about Joanna and the reason why you were holidaying here at Loch Lomond, Mr Irving?'

'Yes, of course. I'd known Jo for about three years. We hit it off as soon as we met. Not romantically, but as friends. We had a similar sense of humour. We both enjoyed walking and climbing. It gave us something to talk about other than corporate deals and the London property market.' He tried a smile but it died, half-formed on his face. 'Jo was great, really good fun and independent. That's the kind of woman chaps like me are drawn to. They aren't going to start getting all clingy on you.' He looked up at Andy. 'Is this the kind of thing you want to hear?'

Andy nodded, not interrupting the man's flow.

'Jo had her own flat, near the Barbican. I don't think there was a man on the scene right now. I can give you a list of the guys she'd been involved with in the last few years. Not many, just a handful, really. Jo never gave the impression of being the settling down type.'

'Was the holiday Jo's idea?' Andy prompted.

'Yes, definitely. Jo planned the whole thing. I was the first on board because it's my kind of trip. Jo invited her flat-mate, well – lodger, Philippa Graves. And it was Jo who asked Daniel Goff along. He'd been to university with her. Exeter, they both went to. Goff was now living in London. He and Jo had hooked up a few times for drinks. I invited Amit, because I knew he wanted to climb a Munro and doesn't often get away from home. His children are very young.'

'Did Amit Batra know Joanna well?' Dani asked.

James considered this. 'Yes, a little. Amit is a really good friend of mine. We've all been round for dinner at my place, along with Amit's wife, Tanisha. The person who none of us really knew was Goff. I don't even think Joanna knew him all that well either.'

At this point, a young woman stepped timidly into the room. She was pretty, with dark brown hair worn straight to her shoulders and large, hazel eyes under heavy lashes.

'Philippa Graves?' Bevan enquired.

The girl nodded cautiously.

'I am DCI Bevan and this is my colleague, DC Calder. We need to ask you some questions.'

Philippa slipped onto a chair next to Irving, beside whom she looked almost childlike. Bevan wondered if the woman could possibly be as meek as she appeared.

'I was just about to explain your relationship to Jo, but as you're here, you can do it yourself,' Irving stated flatly.

'Jo was my landlady, I suppose. But we were also friends. I needed somewhere to stay whilst I studied for my teacher training at the University of London. I went to school with Jo's cousin and she suggested renting a room to me. It worked out pretty well. I finished my training a couple of years back. I've done a term's maternity cover but haven't found anything permanent yet.'

'I thought they were crying out for teachers in London?' Andy asked, a note of scepticism in his tone.

'Oh, that's Secondary. I teach Reception, you know, the tiny ones. I wouldn't be able to handle them any older than that.' The woman snorted out a chuckle.

'What happened on the day you planned to climb Ben Lomond?'

James took the lead again. 'We'd checked the forecast and it was good. Jo wanted to avoid the tourist path, which she said would be packed with men in flip-flops and girls in high-heels. There's a trail that leads into the National Park from along the glen just behind the cottage. It takes you up Ben Lomond via the Ptarmigan Ridge. It's a perfectly well-trodden and safe route. But it can be arduous in places. Philippa was finding the going tough. I dropped back with her, just at the point where we passed between Tom Fithich and Tom Eas. By 2,000 feet, the weather had begun to close in on us. It really came on without warning. I tried to call ahead to Jo on my phone but there was no signal. We decided to move to lower ground, where we might find a better reception.' James cleared his throat and looked a little awkward.

'So you had become separated from the rest of the group, even by that early stage?' Andy probed, 'and what time was this, exactly?

'The others were still visible up ahead, right until the last moment,' Philippa chipped in. 'The mist just seemed to suddenly descend and then we could barely see a thing. It all happened so quickly.'

'It must have been about quarter to three,' James answered, as if the young woman next to him hadn't spoken. 'We'd set out in plenty of time to reach the summit and get back down again. Jo and I are experienced climbers.'

'Then why didn't the group stick together?' Bevan queried acidly, 'you aren't supposed to leave the slowest one behind.'

James' cheeks flushed pink. 'I've no idea why Jo didn't lead them back down the mountain, especially when the visibility became so poor. I was a little angry with her for charging on ahead, if I'm perfectly honest.'

'Perhaps Mr Batra can tell us some more about the reason for that,' Andy added, letting his eyes sweep through the ground floor of the cottage, spotting no other signs of life.

'Sure, I'll go up to the bedroom and fetch him,' James offered. 'But look, go easy on Amit will you? The night he spent out there on the moors really shook him up. He's fairly jittery. I haven't been able to get much out of him myself.'

'Don't worry Mr Irving,' Bevan replied dryly. 'We'll be very gentle.'

Chapter Six

It took several minutes for Amit Batra to join them. By which time, Philippa Graves had fixed up a pot of coffee.

From the briefing that Dani Bevan had received, she already knew Batra was 36 years old and lived in Loughton, Essex with his wife and two young daughters. He worked as an IT manager for a bank in the City of London. The Asian man who was shambling down the narrow flight of stairs towards them now was quite noticeably overweight. Bevan was immediately surprised he was able to keep up with Endicott and Goff during their ascent of the mountain. On first impressions, Dani would have put money on Batra being the one who trailed behind.

As soon as he'd lowered himself into a seat, James Irving placed a protective hand on Batra's shoulder and Philippa slid a cup of strong coffee under his nose.

'Perhaps we could have a word with Mr Batra in private?' Andy suggested.

'Oh, of course,' James replied, and the pair promptly carried their steaming mugs to some other part of the tiny building, where if they wished to listen in, there wasn't much the detectives could do to stop them.

Bevan eyed Batra closely. His face was glistening with sweat. The room *was* incredibly warm but nonetheless, Dani sensed the man's discomfort was caused by stress. She went over to one of the thickly glazed windows and wrenched it open.

'Mr Batra,' Andy began. 'Could you describe to us

exactly what happened after your group became separated from James Irving and Philippa Graves?'

'None of us were talking much. I didn't really know Jo and Daniel all that well. I was just determined to make it up the mountain.' He caught Andy's eye. 'It was my first Munro, you see. I'd kind of told everyone back home that's what I was going to do this holiday. I was planning to post a photo of me on Facebook, once I'd reached the summit.'

Andy showed no indication that he recognised this concept.

'Anyway, that was why I was pushing myself. It was Joanna who was taking the lead. She seemed totally confident. Even when the mist came down her manner was unchanged, Jo kept up the exact same pace. When it started to get really dark, I was nervous about where to put my feet 'cause I was genuinely concerned I'd go over the edge of the ridge. That's when I sensed there was something else going on.'

'What do you mean?' Andy asked.

'Well, I couldn't understand why Jo hadn't mentioned the fact the weather had turned so awful. I knew it wasn't right. Then I suddenly got it – she and Goff were playing some kind of game. Like, who was going to crack first and mention how bad things were.' Amit paused to sip his coffee, peering at the detectives to see if they were showing signs of getting his drift.

'Why didn't *you* say anything, Mr Batra? You could easily have suggested turning back. Did you think to check that Irving and Graves were okay?' Bevan subjected him to her best schoolmistress glare and then immediately regretted it. Batra looked as if he might be about to cry.

'The conditions were really worsening by then. I *tried* to call James, of course I did, but there was no signal.' He sighed heavily and rested his head in his hands. 'I should have spoken up but I was scared. I knew I needed Jo and Daniel to get me off that mountain alive. They kept glancing at one another – teasing, almost sexual looks. I didn't know how to break into that silent understanding they seemed to have developed. Then, at about 3,000 feet up the ridge, it was suddenly as dark as night. I had to lean right into the mountainside to stop myself being blown off by the wind. That's when I shouted to Jo that I wasn't going any further. She acted like I'd never even spoken.'

'Did Joanna and Daniel Goff carry on without you?' Andy said.

'Oh yes. The two of them just strode off ahead, into that black fog. We had no idea if it was solid rock or thin air that we were about to set our feet down onto. For them to keep going was utter madness. Within minutes, I could no longer see them at all. From that moment, I was on my own.'

The man shivered, hugging his cup for warmth. 'I edged my way back down the ridge, pressing myself up against the rocks and just praying I didn't lose my footing. There was a section where the wind wasn't quite so strong. I stayed there for maybe twenty minutes. The cloud was gradually lifting but by then I was completely lost. By nightfall, I'd reached lower ground but knew it wasn't the same place we'd started out from. I found a dip that provided me with some shelter and hunkered down for the night. Not that I really slept. I was wandering around this huge area of featureless scrubland from first light. That was where James and the search team found me.'

'And you didn't see Joanna or Daniel Goff again, after they left you on the western face of Ben Lomond?' Bevan clarified.

'No. I saw no sign of human life out there until I was rescued the following morning.'

'Thank you, Mr Batra. You've been very helpful.'

'What do you think?' Bevan asked Calder, as the police 4x4 took them along the winding trail back to Ardyle.

'My first thought is that Joanna Endicott and Daniel Goff were a couple of over-privileged thrill-seekers who, like so many before them, believed they could take on the Scottish mountains and the Scottish weather and win. Perhaps, when he realised they were in real trouble, or that the whole game was just a tease and Jo had no intention of succumbing to him, Goff turned on her, venting all his anger and frustration, wringing her neck with his bare hands.'

'That's our most likely scenario, I agree. Goff then disappeared into the wilderness, finding somewhere to lay low for a few days. If that's the case, we'll flush him out eventually. But did you believe the others?'

Andy paused to consider this. 'I did wonder why Irving hung back with Philippa Graves. He looks far more the outward bound type than Batra. Do you think he fancies her?'

'She's not his type,' Bevan responded; quick as a flash.

Andy eyed her curiously.

Bevan chuckled. 'I haven't got any kind of insider knowledge. It's just he said he liked Joanna so much because she was independent and self-reliant. Irving hinted that was his sort of woman. Graves, on the other hand, has the word 'needy' practically tattooed across her forehead. I got the sense she irritated him.'

Andy nodded. 'So why did Irving hang back?'

'I think he's just more sensible than the others.

Irving had grown up in Scotland and was an experienced mountaineer. He understood the need to respect the weather conditions. Besides, he had less to prove than the rest. Batra wanted to bag a Munro and Goff wanted to bag Joanna. I think James Irving just wanted a quiet holiday.'

Chapter Seven

The Carraig Hotel in Ardyle was part of the Great Glens chain. A tour party of over-fifties were currently staying on the premises, meaning that the dining room and lounge were packed out at all times of the day. But Bevan and Calder counted themselves lucky to have got rooms there at all.

Bevan quickly assessed there would be no chance of them battling the crowds to the breakfast buffet in the mornings. She spied out a local bakery instead, where they could pick up a cappuccino and a pastry to take with them to the Town Hall.

The detectives reached the mocked up incident room by 9am. Driscoll was already there, leaning over a couple of young DCs who were sifting through papers on what looked like an old school desk. Dani strode across the zigzagged parquet flooring to check on their progress.

'Any sightings of Daniel Goff?' Was her first question.

'Not yet, Ma'am,' Driscoll replied. 'I've stood some of my officers down from the search. The mountain rescue guys say Goff couldn't have survived three cold nights out there in the National Park, so if he's alive, he must have found proper shelter. We've got an all ports warning activated and officers at every train and bus station in central Scotland.'

'So if he *is* still out there in the hills somewhere, it's a dead body we're looking for.'

'That's right.'

'What have you got on Goff's background?'

Driscoll gently nudged the young DC sat beside him.

'Daniel Goff is 34 years old,' the lad began falteringly. 'He was born in Coventry, England, in 1980, attended his local Comprehensive and went to Exeter University to study History in 1998. He stayed on post-graduation to gain an MA in Medieval Studies.'

Bevan pulled up a chair next to the DC, looking closely at his neatly transcribed notes. 'So Goff is highly educated. He must be intelligent then.'

The lad nodded. 'Aye, but he seems to be one of those permanent student types. Following his MA, he gained a qualification to teach English to foreign students. He remained in Exeter to do it. After that, he taught in various cities around Europe for a decade. He never settled long in any one place. Goff's been in London for the last two years.'

'Had he ever lived in Scotland?'

'Not that I've discovered so far. These Language Schools tend to employ people on temporary contracts, making it difficult to pin them down on who was working where, when.'

'Okay, keep at it and good work.' Dani glanced back up at Driscoll. 'What about Joanna?'

'Her background was more conventional. She was born in '83 and was an only child. Her parents were called Charles and Mandy Endicott and lived in Chiswick, West London. She attended a fee-paying girls' school and read History and Politics at Exeter. That's where she must have met Goff, who would have been studying for his MA when Joanna was an undergraduate.'

'Where did Joanna Endicott do her legal training?' Bevan interrupted.

'At the College of Law in London. It's near Gower Street, I believe. My niece studied there a couple of years back,' he added for clarification.

'Joanna was from a different social class to Goff. I

wonder if that affected their friendship in any way.'

'I wouldn't have thought so these days, Ma'am. Youngsters mix with all different types at college. My daughter's going out with an Asian lad at her university. No one bats an eyelid anymore. My old dad would have hated it, but I don't dare mention that. It's just not acceptable, is it?'

Bevan was impressed by the Sergeant's candour. 'No it isn't - especially not for a serving police officer.'

But at the same time, she thought to herself how this group; Joanna, Irving, Goff, Batra and Graves, were closer to her own age. They were mid-thirties or thereabouts, not in their early twenties as Driscoll's daughter must surely be. Dani knew full-well that class tensions still existed when she was a student. It was an issue she wasn't fully prepared to dismiss at this stage.

'Mandy Endicott died of ovarian cancer in 2009,' Driscoll continued. 'Joanna's father passed away from a liver disorder two years later. Joanna inherited her parents' property in Chiswick which she still owned and rented out. The rest of the bequest she used to pay off the mortgage on her flat.'

'We're talking about a tidy sum there. Who will inherit it?'

'Joanna's aunts and uncles are her next of kin. I assume it will be split between them. I bet the girl hadn't made a will.'

'I really can't see the money being a motive for murder here. But I'm willing to wager you're wrong about a will. Joanna was a lawyer and a canny type. We should check with her family solicitors.'

'I'll get onto that immediately, Ma'am.'

'If you don't mind, Driscoll, I'm going to ask my Sergeant back in Glasgow to do some digging into the lives of Irving, Graves and Batra. I don't want to tread on your toes, but he's a wiz at that kind of thing.'

'Not a problem,' Driscoll said with a laid-back smile, which Bevan thought was genuine.

'Good. I'll give Phil a call now.'

Sergeant Driscoll insisted on taking Bevan and Calder for a drink in one of the local pubs at the end of the day. Dani was tired and would rather have retired to their hotel, but she didn't want to upset the regional force. Bevan needed to show the DCS that she could pull together a team, generating loyalty between different divisions. This was almost as important as getting a result.

The bar was old-fashioned and full of middle-aged men. It wasn't one of the family-friendly gastro-type establishments which now dominated these little tourist towns. The three detectives took their drinks over to a corner table. Driscoll leaned towards them conspiratorially.

'There was something I wanted to tell you about, away from the local lads,' he said quietly, holding a full pint glass level with his thin lips.

'Oh, aye,' Andy responded with interest, having allowed himself the rare luxury of a half of 70 shilling ale.

'This case, it's going to shake up some bad memories around here.' Driscoll glanced about him. 'You may recall the incident. Your parents certainly would. Thirty years back, a party of kids from the Primary School here in Ardyle had a day trip into the Lomond National Park. It was their last year before going up to the High School. Most were aged ten. The expedition was very well organised and took place just after the Easter break, at the beginning of April. There were twenty kids out there on the hills and five staff. They'd split into groups and each one was collecting a different kind of data. Then, all of a sudden, about mid-afternoon, the weather took a turn for the worst. Within the half hour, sleet was falling and the temperature had dropped by a least fifteen degrees.'

'I think I've read an article about it, although I hadn't clocked on it had happened here,' said Dani. 'Some of the children got lost, didn't they?'

Driscoll sighed. 'Aye. Three of the groups were rounded up almost immediately, but one lot had wandered away in the wrong direction. The teacher lost his bearings in the low cloud. The search continued all through the night and into the following morning. Police, townsfolk and parents were all involved. By midday, the party were finally accounted for. Three were dead; a girl and two boys, all ten years of age. They perished in the terrible cold of that night.'

'It must have had a profound impact on the town,' Andy added gravely, thinking about his own wee girl, only a year old.

'In many ways, Ardyle is still grieving. One of the DCs on this case, Sammy Reid, lost his older sister that night. You'll find that most people in the town have a connection to the children who died in some way or another. It's a small place.'

Bevan took a gulp of her orange juice. 'Going out to search for the missing walkers the other day must have brought back painful memories. No wonder so many locals offered to help the mountain rescue guys.'

'The legacy hasn't been all bad. Local groups run talks in the nearby schools to teach safety on the hills. It's the tourists now who tend to get into trouble. Everyone's an expert in outdoor activities these days. As soon as they've bought the kit, they think they can take on a Munro.' Driscoll shook his head, downing the remainder of his pint. 'Another?'

'No, thank you, David. I'd like to head back to the hotel and think this through. It looks like the case is going to be a tricky one. I'll have to come up with a pretty good strategy if I'm going to keep the people of Ardyle happy during this investigation. Let alone catch the killer of Joanna Endicott.'

Chapter Eight

'Thanks for coming out here again,' James Irving said smoothly, standing back to allow Dani to pass over the threshold.

The cottage was much cooler than when Bevan had last been here. It was no longer reminiscent of a nineteenth century sick house, where patients sweated out unidentified contagions in poky, sealed-up rooms and all who entered were doomed.

As if reading Dani's thoughts, James explained, 'we've cleaned up the place and given it an airing. Amit is feeling a little better now.'

The detective followed the man into the cosy sitting room where she sat down on a leather armchair beneath the window. James perched on the edge of the sofa, leaning forward so that his elbows rested on his knees. 'I expect you know what I'm going to say.' His handsome face cracked into a half-smile. His slate grey eyes gazed piercingly into hers. 'We all want to know when we can return to London. Amit's wife is going spare, as you can imagine. I could really do with getting back to the office myself.'

'This is a murder inquiry, Mr Irving. It's only been a couple of days.'

'Of course.' He looked sheepish. 'Well, it isn't just that. We wondered if it was actually safe for us to be out here, what with Goff still missing and everything. Philippa got herself into a real state last night-'

'Do you have any reason to believe that Daniel Goff will come after any of you?' Bevan interrupted, sitting forward in the seat herself, suddenly intrigued.

'No, nothing specific, I suppose. It's simply that if he did kill Jo then Goff might be some kind of homicidal maniac. He may come back for the rest of his gear and discover us still at the bothy. We're pretty isolated out here. You can appreciate how the imagination starts to play tricks, especially at night, when the wind's howling down the glen.' James flushed a rosy pink with embarrassment.

Bevan's face broke into a smile. 'The hotels and guesthouses in town are all booked out. I can send over one of our officers to spend the night on your couch if you like?'

James beamed with relief. 'That would be great. Look, I know I'm a Scot, but I grew up in the suburbs of Edinburgh. I'm not a country type. Holidays and hill-walking are one thing, but tiny cottages on the moor with a murderer on the loose are something else.'

'Yes, I can understand that. We aren't made of stone, Mr Irving. Whilst I'm here, can you give me that list of Joanna's ex-boyfriends? If you could recall their addresses and workplaces it would be a great help too.'

'I'll do my best.' James picked up a pen and sheet of paper from a desk in an alcove, where somebody had set up a laptop computer. Dani remained silent, allowing the man time to think.

'If you don't mind me saying, you're quite young to be a Detective Chief Inspector. It's sort of like the equivalent of making Silk for a barrister,' he commented suddenly, glancing up from his list.

'I think I'm a little older than you.'

'Really? Oh well, you know what they say about policemen starting to seem younger.' James handed her the sheet, keeping hold of the corner after Dani had taken it, as if he wanted to maintain a physical connection with her. 'Jo was the opposite type to you. She was old for her years. Clients thought she was our most experienced advocate but actually, Jo was the youngest. I'm not sure if it was to do with the way she dressed, or just an air she had about her.'

'Were Jo and Daniel Goff having a sexual relationship?'

James looked momentarily startled. 'Not that I was aware of. Jo was sharing a downstairs room with Philippa. Daniel was in the bedroom next to me and Amit. If the two of them were together, none of us would have objected to them bunking up. I never thought Daniel was Jo's type.'

'What do you mean?'

'Well, he's sort of lanky and skinny. He wears his hair long and is a bit of a hippy. Jo always went out with smart city boys, pumped up muscles under tight, tailored shirts.'

'Men like yourself, Mr Irving?'

'Touchè. Jo and I were just mates, honest. But I could never have said anything absolutely with Jo - she liked to generate an aura of mystery. Jo would never have admitted to you that she was frightened to stay in this bothy, for instance. She'd have used it as a trial of strength. As for me, I'm a new man, quite happy to let you know when I'm scared witless.'

'I'll send an officer over in a couple of hours.'

Bevan allowed him to see her to the door. 'It's very quiet here,' she commented.

'Amit and Philippa went for a walk. Not far, just for some fresh air.'

Bevan nodded and smiled, pacing back to the police Land Rover with the list in her hand, wondering exactly what to make of James Irving.

For once, the bar of the Carraig Hotel was quiet.

Bevan and Calder ordered coffees and compared their notes.

'DC Clark is going to spend the night at the bothy,' Dani began, swirling a sugar lump around her cup. 'Of course, this request could all be a ruse, to give us the impression that Irving, Graves and Batra are a group of cowering, innocent victims.'

'Do we really have those three in the frame?'

'The PM report suggested that Joanna was strangled sometime after 4am. Her body was discovered at 10.45am. She'd been dead for several hours. Batra could certainly have done it. He'd been out there on the mountain unaccounted for since the previous day. As for Irving and Graves, they alibi each other, claiming they spent the entire night at the bothy and didn't set out until 8am the following morning to join the search team.'

'But either of them could have left the bothy without the other one knowing,' Andy suggested.

'Irving is the only one out of those two who I could picture navigating around the National Park on his own at night.'

'Unless Philippa Graves' helpless routine is just a put up job. Maybe she's a lot more capable than we think.'

Dani looked at her colleague carefully, knowing he possessed good instincts. 'Could you get back onto the pathologist in the morning? Ask if it's possible Joanna was strangled by a woman.'

'Will do.' Andy thought for a moment. 'She's quite petite too though, don't you think? Philippa is what, 5'4 max? Joanna Endicott was 5'8 and athletically built. My hunch is if Graves was involved in this crime, she didn't act alone.'

Dani nodded her head slowly. 'I agree. At this stage, I don't think we can rule out any of those three at all. Let's keep them on the suspect list. I'll get onto Phil tomorrow. I want to find out everything there is to know about Miss Philippa Graves.'

Chapter Nine

Detective Sergeant Phil Boag was in his late forties, lean and with a head of thick, grey-streaked hair. His wife was the Headmistress of a sprawling Glasgow inner city comprehensive. Her career took priority in the Boag household. Dani tried to utilise Phil's policing skills in a way that allowed him to look after his two teenage daughters. Phil was Bevan's IT man and had a great eye for detail. He wasn't infallible, but she'd rather use him than anyone else.

Knowing he'd be at his desk early, Bevan gave her sergeant a call before heading to the incident room. 'Have you got anything for me, Phil?'

'I'm faxing some printouts over to the local station this morning. In the meantime, do you want a précis?'

'Aye, fire away.'

'James Irving is completely clean. Not so much as an unpaid parking ticket to his name. He attended The Scott Academy in Edinburgh and his parents have a house in Leith. He's lived in London for eight years, no convictions, no debts.'

'Okay.' Dani was expecting that.

'Amit Batra is a bit more interesting, but not much. He got married five years ago. The Batras' have two little girls; the eldest is two and a half and the other just six months old. He grew up in Croydon, South London and has a Computer Science degree from Southampton University. The only blot on his copybook is that a couple of years back he lost his job and couldn't make the mortgage payments on their house for a few months. He ended up on a credit blacklist. Batra is in employment again now and seems financially secure. However, their mortgage is still huge. It must put him under pressure.'

'Everyone's mortgage is huge, especially down in London. It sounds like a fairly typical tale of the recession.'

'Philippa Graves is a curious lass. She grew up in Brentford, West London.'

'Not far from Joanna Endicott.'

'But not in nearly so nice an area. Philippa is the youngest of three children and turned thirty in March. She's got a qualification to teach in primary schools but hasn't managed to complete her induction year yet. Graves covered a maternity leave in a school in north London. The contract ended last Christmas. I managed to have a word with the Headmistress there. She was rather cagey about Philippa.'

'Oh yes,' Dani listened with interest.

'I think the woman was being careful to cover herself. She said Philippa did a decent job but that some of the parents hadn't been happy about her manner with the kids. I had to press her on what they meant by this. Apparently, Philippa spoke harshly to the children and some mums found it 'inappropriate'. There'd also been the occasional 'unfortunate choice of words', the Headmistress said, although she was quick to point out there was absolutely no suggestion of physical violence against the children.'

'Sounds like a bunch of euphemisms if ever I heard them.'

Phil chuckled. 'I asked Jane her opinion about the Headmistress's comments. She said it sounded like the girl didn't know how to deal with that particular age group appropriately. Jane said that if she'd been Philippa's Head, she would have subtly suggested a change of career.'

'It's interesting, but I don't see how it ties into the murder of Joanna Endicott. Graves doesn't gain anything by Joanna's death, does she?'

'No, on the contrary, Endicott's flat will be sold and Graves will have to find somewhere else to live. It looks like she wasn't paying much rent. She'll probably have to leave London if she can't find another job pretty quick.'

'Anything else?'

'I'm still looking into Joanna's boyfriends, but not having much luck at this stage. London's a big place. I'm sending you over copies of the newspaper reports from 1983 about the Ardyle tragedy. You should get those shortly.'

'Great work Phil, thanks.'

DC Clark was hanging around the entrance to the Town Hall as Dani mounted the steps. 'How was your night in the house of horrors?' she called ahead.

Clark gave a smile that was part grimace. 'Quiet, Ma'am.' The young man shifted from one foot to the other. 'I can't do tonight, though. It's my mother-in-law's birthday. The wife's got reservations for dinner.'

'Of course, not a problem. I'll find somebody else.'

The man looked mightily relieved and stepped aside to allow her to enter the building.

Andy Calder was sorting through papers on one of the trestle tables. Dani thought he was looking pale. His improved physical appearance made her forget how close he came to losing his life just a few months ago. Dani felt reluctant to ask him to stay up all night at the bothy. She knew he would want to be treated the same as everyone else but as Dani was the one who'd seen him in that terrible state, in the grips of a massive heart attack during the search for Richard Erskine, she wasn't sure she could do it, which probably meant that for the sake of his career, Andy should really be working for somebody else.

Dani adopted a beaming smile, striding towards the team of young policemen who were processing the minutiae of the evidence they'd already collected. She knew it could be a soul-destroying task.

'Okay,' Dani called out decisively. 'Gather around for a briefing.'

Driscoll signalled to his troupe of detectives. The men shuffled over to form a semi-circular shape in front of her. She gave them a run-down of Phil's findings. Looking at the young DC from yesterday, Bevan asked if they'd discovered anything more about Daniel Goff.

The lad's cheeks flushed deep red, but he puffed himself up and said, 'the Registrar at Stirling College just got back to me, Ma'am. She believes that a man named Daniel Goff worked at the language school there in the summer of 2007. They run English courses for overseas students before term starts, in order to prepare them for their degree.'

'Fantastic!' Dani exclaimed. 'So the man's got a link to the area. Did she tell you anything more?'

The DC nodded his head. 'The Registrar said that although she wasn't working there at the time, the records indicated there was an incident involving Goff in which the police were involved. One of the students, a Spanish girl, accused Goff of assaulting her after lessons were over. Goff claimed they were having a sexual relationship and the girl had become upset when he ended things so had made a false allegation. There wasn't enough evidence to take it any further. Goff left at the end of his contract and never worked at the College again.'

'Do we have the details of this assault?'

'Not yet, I've only just received the tip-off.'

'Sergeant Driscoll, can you organise the investigation of this lead? We'll need the police report from Stirling and the name of this Spanish student, if possible.'

Driscoll nodded his head.

Dani addressed the room. 'I also want to know if Goff has a contact in the area. If he lived around here for a few months in 2007, maybe he's got a friend who's sheltering him. I know it's a long time ago but this is a strong line of enquiry, let's make sure we've examined it thoroughly.'

The group broke apart and scattered to the various desks and tables around the hall. Andy stepped forward to join Dani. 'I've spoken to the pathologist, Ma'am. She's faxed over the PM photos.' Calder led Dani over to the table where the blurry prints were laid out in a long line.

Dani looked carefully at the images of Joanna's body, taken from multiple angles and graffitied with a mystifying range of arrows and scrawls. 'Explain what I'm looking at.'

'There was no sign of recent sexual activity or sexual assault.' Calder pulled across a shot of Joanna's head and torso. 'Here's the bruising around the neck.' He ran a finger across the greenish line on the woman's pale skin. 'Dr Murphy thinks she was throttled with just one hand. She can only make out a single thumb print, not two.'

'There's no way Philippa Graves could have done that to Joanna.'

'No. Dr Murphy says she cannot swear to it, but her professional judgement would dictate this was a male assailant, strong and at least as tall as Joanna.'

'Was there a struggle - skin under the fingernails, that kind of thing?'

'Not much of one,' Calder selected another photo, this one being of Joanna's once elegant hands, the chipped remnants of a pinkish varnish still evident upon the long nails. 'Murphy believes it happened very quickly. Joanna was taken by surprise and completely overwhelmed by her attacker.'

'The woman would also have been weak. She'd been out on the hillside for hours and hadn't eaten since the previous day. Joanna was tired and cold. Could she have been asleep when he attacked her?'

'Murphy didn't rule it out. She said Joanna was perfectly healthy and physically fit. In normal circumstances, she should have been able to put up a strong defence.'

'Perhaps he threatened her with a weapon of some sort?' Dani said, considering all the possible scenarios. 'We found nothing at the scene or within a two mile radius of it.'

'He might have taken it with him.'

'Or dumped it somewhere else in the National Park. Let's face it, there'd be no chance of us ever recovering the thing.'

'If Goff's motive was sexual,' Andy said levelly, pushing the stark photographs around the table to create an even square. 'Then why didn't he try to rape her? Joanna's clothing was undamaged and left in place.'

'There's more than one kind of sexual, Andy. Perhaps Goff enjoyed squeezing the life out of Joanna Endicott, especially as she was such a feisty and self-assured woman. I'll be particularly interested to hear what Goff did to that student in Stirling back in 2007, very interested indeed.'

Chapter Ten

James Irving opened the door and looked surprised. He ran a hand over the stubble on his chin, thinking that he'd have made more of an effort if he knew it wasn't going to be DC Clark who was kipping on their sofa tonight.

'To what do we owe this pleasure,' he asked with a grin, stepping back and allowing Bevan to enter.

'I've got paperwork to catch up on. My team deserve a decent night's rest. It's been a busy couple of days.'

James was impressed, although he suspected that the DCI would be observing them all very closely over the course of the evening. 'We've already eaten, I'm afraid.'

'Don't worry, so have I. Just let me have a quiet corner to work in and you'll barely notice I'm here.'

Bevan took up a position at the kitchen table, setting down a file which contained the documents sent by Phil earlier in the day. Philippa Graves was moving about in the preparation area, filling the dishwasher and making coffees. Dani sensed the woman was fidgety and a little nervous. As the natural light gradually receded, Philippa flicked on the overhead spotlights, solicitously ensuring the detective could see what she was doing. Dani assessed Philippa as someone desperate to please others. She wondered to what lengths the girl would go in order to please a person she really cared for.

Amit and James were seated next to one another on the sofa in the sitting room, impassively watching the TV, with glasses of red wine in their hands. Irving noticed her glancing over. 'You're welcome to have something stronger than a coffee, Detective Chief Inspector. I realise you'll say no, but it would be rude not to offer.'

Dani smiled. 'A coffee is fine, thanks, but the offer is duly noted and appreciated.'

About halfway through the evening, Batra stepped outside the kitchen door to call his wife on a mobile phone, explaining the signal was better out there. From what Bevan could observe of his body language through the window, the conversation wasn't an easy one. Dani imagined that Tanisha Batra was becoming exasperated by her husband's absence, left to look after a toddler and baby on her own. Whenever Andy Calder was called away on a case, Carol's mother came to stay in their west-end flat to help with the baby. Bevan had become quite used to appreciating the ins and outs of a household in which there were young children. She knew there could be extreme stresses and strains, especially if both parents were working. Dani believed she would crack under the pressure if it were her. She was surprised more couples didn't.

The man eventually stepped back into the kitchen, his mouth set in a grim line. 'The baby's got a cold. Tan hasn't slept in two nights.'

Bevan nodded, resisting the urge to point out that a young woman was dead and perhaps they should be counting their blessings. She knew it would be unfair.

The household had all retired to bed by half past eleven. Philippa Graves had now taken the bedroom which used to be occupied by Goff, not wishing to be the only one sleeping downstairs.

In her quiet solitude, Bevan read carefully through the reports of the schoolchildren's deaths in April 1983. There were photographs of the unfortunate three, in their school uniforms, looking sweet and innocent. It was a heart-breaking accident, made much of by the tabloid press at the time. The coverage continued for weeks afterwards, the image of those poor weans staring out from the front page obviously shifting thousands of copies. Family members and local residents were interviewed, but the articles were blissfully free of thinly veiled attempts to attribute blame. The teachers all did what they could. The parents were broadly satisfied with the actions of the police and mountain rescue. It was simply a terrible tragedy.

Dani felt herself beginning to doze off, her eyes were losing focus on the words and her head was resting more heavily on her hand. Then, she sensed a presence behind her and this made Dani jolt upright again.

'I didn't mean to startle you,' whispered a male voice. 'I couldn't sleep.'

She turned around to see James Irving, in a T-shirt and pyjama trousers, standing at the foot of the staircase. He padded across the room and filled the kettle. 'Do you want one?'

'Yes, please.'

'What's that you're reading?'

Dani hesitated before replying, but then decided it had no real bearing on the case and was information entirely within the public domain. 'These are copies of newspaper reports about an incident that happened here in the glen, thirty one years ago.'

James moved across and scanned one of the articles over Dani's shoulder. 'I hadn't realised something like this had happened here before. Well, obviously it isn't quite the same, but you know what I mean.'

Dani did know. 'Climbers get into trouble on Ben Lomond every year. It's important not to read too much into the two events.'

James set a couple of mugs down on the table. 'We were only very young when those schoolchildren were killed, but I bet our parents remember it.'

'It happened at a similar time to the death of my mother. Our family were still living in Wales.'

'Oh, I'm really sorry, I didn't realise your mum had passed away when you were so little.' James looked at Bevan closely, an expression of genuine sympathy on his face.

'It was a very long time ago. My father and I moved to Scotland not long after. I grew up on Colonsay.'

'Oh well, you really are a country lass, then.'

Bevan smiled, taking a sip of the pleasantly hot tea.

James pulled the papers across the table towards him. 'I suppose it shows how easy it is to get lost in the National Park in bad weather and how quickly it can set in. It doesn't matter how experienced you are, Nature always has the potential to catch you out.'

'In the case of Joanna, there was also human wickedness at play. I'm just not sure yet whether her death was a spur of the moment thing, or this whole murder was carefully pre-meditated; the trip, becoming separated from the rest of the group and then getting trapped on the mountain.'

'If anyone had been guilty of planning it, it would have been Jo herself. She was the one driving this entire adventure. Jo couldn't have been scheming to murder herself.'

'Did you ever get the sense Joanna was being led by somebody else - that there was a force behind her decisions?'

'Some sort of passive-aggressive side-kick you mean?' James sighed and thought about this carefully. 'Joanna was probably the most single-minded individual I ever met. She was definitely a leader and not a follower.'

Dani was about to ask another question when they both heard a noise outside. They remained absolutely silent. Then there was a loud clatter, which sounded like a bin being kicked over by a person moving about in the darkness.

Dani rose to her feet. She stalked across the room and pressed herself flat against the wall next to the kitchen door, slowly turning the key in the lock. 'Stay here,' she whispered to Irving, who was frozen to the spot.

The sky wasn't completely black. A half-moon illuminated the hillside behind the bothy, but in the passageway between the stone cottage and the ruins of a small outbuilding, it was difficult to make out anything at all. Then Bevan spotted a flicker of movement. Someone had disappeared round the side of the building. They were definitely trying to get in. Dani doubled-back; not wanting the intruder to reach the kitchen door before she did.

As she careered around the corner of the bothy, a large form charged at her from out of the shadows, knocking her to the ground. She instinctively sent a strong kick upwards towards her attacker and caught him somewhere on the shin. He stumbled backward against the stone wall.

'Stop, police!' she called out firmly, springing to her feet and standing her ground. The dark figure lunged forward once again, barging into her shoulder and pitching her off balance. This time, he sprinted away up the hillside. Bevan watched his retreating form, knowing she had no hope of chasing him down in the darkness. Besides, she couldn't leave the others unprotected.

Dani re-entered the cottage. Amit Batra and Philippa Graves were standing in the centre of the living room, looking as if they had hastily dressed. James was leaning against the door frame with his arms crossed over his chest, a look of anger and confusion on his face. The atmosphere between the three of them was decidedly chilly.

'I went upstairs to warn Amit we had an intruder,' James explained. 'But when I went into our room, he wasn't there. So I thought I'd check on Philippa instead. Low and behold, there was Amit. The two of them were doing the wild thing in Philippa's bed. They didn't even notice I'd entered the room for a good five minutes.'

Dani looked at Batra. She was disgusted to note the man actually had tears running down his cheeks. 'Put the kettle on again would you Mr. Irving? I think this is going to be a very long night.'

Chapter Eleven

A police van was outside the bothy. Uniformed officers were busy searching the surrounding countryside. Beams of torchlight occasionally flashed through the windows of the kitchen, briefly illuminating the tired faces of those seated around the table, as if an interrogation lamp were being randomly directed at them. The effect was strangely disconcerting.

'Just how long has this been going on?' James Irving's face was red with rage.

Bevan sat back in her seat and allowed him to continue, the man was doing a pretty good job of questioning Batra on his own.

Amit hung his head in shame. 'A few months.'

'Right, a few months eh?' James did some sums in his head. 'Don't tell me you were sleeping with Philippa at the time your wife was having a baby?'

Amit looked straight at his friend. 'No, it started after that, I promise.'

Bevan observed Philippa Graves during this exchange. She sat silently next to Batra with her hands clasped in her lap, almost as if she was at prayer. Dani could have sworn there was just the tiniest hint of a smile on her face.

'Do you know what really rankles?' James continued, 'is that you used me to set up this dirty weekend for the two of you. I happen to like Tanisha a great deal and I'm truly pissed off that you involved me in your plan to royally stitch her up.'

Bevan decided to intervene. 'Did either Daniel Goff or Joanna Endicott know you were having an affair?'

Amit shook his head vigorously. 'No, we'd played it really cool this holiday. Just spending time together rather than actually having sex.'

James snorted. 'That's not what it looked like to me!'

Bevan shot him a warning glance.

Philippa shuffled forward slightly in her seat, not uttering a word until all eyes were upon her. 'Actually, Joanna did know about it.'

Batra's mouth dropped open. 'What?'

'I told her, a few days before we came here. I thought she could help arrange for me and Amit to have some time alone together. I knew Joanna wouldn't judge us.'

'What *was* Joanna's reaction to this news?' Bevan asked the young woman, watching her face closely.

'At first, she laughed. Joanna said she'd always suspected most marriages to be a sham. It kind of vindicated her life choices. Then, Jo offered to let us use the bedroom. Under the cover of darkness, she'd go out and sleep on the sofa, while Amit slipped into my bed.'

Dani immediately wondered if Jo was really planning to spend a cramped night on the couch or if she envisaged herself creeping into Daniel Goff's bed instead. By James' reaction, she was pretty certain he wasn't in on the sordid little arrangement. Clearly no one had been sneaking between *his* sheets this week.

Amit appeared confused. 'But you never told me this – and we didn't actually do that, Philippa. Tonight is the first time we've been together since we got to Scotland.'

'I'm saying that's what Jo and I *discussed*, I'm not suggesting we'd got around to putting it into action just yet.' The woman looked indignant.

James put his hand up, as if obtaining permission from the teacher to speak. Dani humoured him by nodding her assent. 'I'm sorry, Philippa, but that doesn't sound like something Joanna would do. I know she'd had a few different boyfriends over the years, but she was actually quite moralistic in lots of ways. A married client of ours, very good-looking and well-off, was coming on to Jo for months. He sent flowers and chocolates almost every day. Jo was very definite about not getting involved with him. She said cheating on your wife was the pits. It gives me no pleasure to tell you this, but Jo didn't actually like you very much. You were her lodger and she felt sorry for you not being able to find a job after qualifying. I simply don't believe she'd have orchestrated this set-up on your behalf.'

Philippa sprang to her feet, pushing the chair back so that it scraped across the stone floor. 'Well, that's where you're wrong!' She declared, storming up the stairs. Several minutes later a distant door slammed shut.

'You do realise that this changes everything?' Bevan's question filled the silence.

Batra stared down at his lap. 'I just didn't want my wife to find out.'

'Do you think it could have had something to do with Jo's murder?' James asked.

'I certainly can't rule it out.'

As Bevan stepped outside the cottage, to check on the progress of the search, she left James Irving gaping at Amit Batra with a mystified expression on his face. The reality was obviously dawning on him that he wouldn't be able to trust his old friend ever again.

*

DS Driscoll was jogging down the hillside towards

her as she crunched across the gravel drive.

'Any luck?' Bevan called ahead.

Driscoll shook his head. 'No sign of him, Ma'am. We'll get the helicopter out at first light.'

'Damn it!' Bevan exclaimed with considerable feeling.

'You were right not to go after him. It wasn't feasible without back-up. Do you think it was Goff?'

'I didn't see the man's face but he was tall and strong, I think we have to assume so.'

'What was he doing back here? It was a huge risk for him to return.'

'Maybe he thought his stuff would still be at the bothy. Or perhaps he knows there's something still here that belongs to him.'

'You should get some rest, Ma'am. We'll need you to give a detailed statement about what happened.'

'Oh, the intruder's only the half of it, Dave.'

The man looked puzzled.

'Leave a pair of uniforms to guard the place and send the remainder of the search team home for a couple of hour's kip. We'll meet back at the incident room at 8.30am for a briefing. I'll fill you in on all the sordid details then.'

Chapter Twelve

Andy Calder was the only member of the team who looked fresh the following morning. He also looked pissed-off. Bevan had expressly requested that her DC not be required to take part in last night's search. Calder was clearly very unhappy about this. It was fairly obvious every other officer had attended the call out but him. In the heat of the moment, Dani suspected she'd made an error of judgement.

Taking a deep breath, she outlined the events of the previous night, including the revelation of Batra and Graves' affair. 'So, what are we thinking?' Bevan asked the group, scanning each of their faces in turn and inviting their feedback.

Andy stepped forward, his tone brusque. 'If Joanna Endicott possessed information that could have ended Batra's marriage, it gives him a motive to kill her.'

'Yes, but that all depends on whether Philippa Graves actually told Joanna about the affair. I'm not sure we can trust anything the girl says. I think she's a fantasist,' Bevan responded.

'The sexual relationship between Batra and Graves was real enough,' Driscoll pointed out. 'I sense that Joanna was a clever and perceptive type of woman. Whether Philippa told her about it or not, she may already have known.'

'That's a valid point,' Bevan conceded.

'But the fact Daniel Goff came back to the bothy for something, still makes him our prime suspect, along with his evasion of the police. If the feller's innocent then why hasn't he come forward, why all the cloak and dagger?' said DC Kendal, the young man who had been researching Goff's background.

'He might be frightened,' Andy suggested grumpily, refusing to elaborate on the point.

'Have we got any more information on the assault allegation made against Goff in Stirling?' Bevan demanded.

'The police records of the incident were very vague, but we've managed to track down the woman involved. Her maiden name was Imelda Cabello. She married last year and is now known as Imelda Watson. She's 26, and lives in Glasgow with her husband.' Driscoll handed the sheet of paper to Bevan.

'Great work. I'll get Sergeant Boag to pay her a visit. Any luck with old friends or workmates of Goff who still live in the area?'

Driscoll shook his head and frowned. 'Nothing yet, Ma'am. It was seven years ago and no one seems to remember the guy. Kendal had the idea of posting a query onto the College's Facebook page to see if someone out there recalls him. We're going to try that this morning.'

'Excellent idea, Kendal.' Bevan looked directly at the lad. He squirmed with embarrassment. 'Let me know straight away if you get a result.'

Dani allowed Andy to drive the police jeep over to the bothy. They were going to inform the three witnesses that they were free to return home. Dani didn't have the resources to protect them 24 hours a day. She was pretty sure none of the group would attempt to leave the country.

Andy jumped inside and started up the engine before Bevan had even opened the passenger door.

Once they were half-way to their destination, Dani broke the awkward silence. 'I should have got Driscoll to call you last night Andy, I'm sorry. It was an insult to your rank.'

Andy kept his eyes glued to the route ahead. 'Why did you exclude me, Ma'am? It undermined my position in the team.'

Dani sighed. 'I'd taken the job of guarding the bothy so that one of us could get a good night's sleep. I need a partner who can be on the ball even if I'm not. I rely on you.'

'Is that really the only reason?' He turned to look squarely at his colleague.

Dani paused for a moment before replying. 'No, it wasn't. It's your first active assignment since the heart attack. I didn't want you to overdo it.'

Andy bashed the steering wheel hard with both hands. The jeep lurched violently over a line of loose rocks before he regained control. 'With respect Ma'am, it sounds like you're talking about one of your elderly relatives.'

'I wanted to ease you in gently. I realise now that may not be possible in a murder investigation.'

'It's not fair to dismiss me as unfit for proper service. You aren't a doctor, Dani.'

The words stung her. She and Andy were good friends, but he'd never shown her disrespect on the job before. 'Perhaps it would make more sense for you to be assigned to another senior officer, someone who isn't so emotionally bound up in your wellbeing. A person who didn't see you lying there in agony on the ground; a young man with his life ebbing away from him...' Dani turned her face towards the passenger window, determined that he would not see the tears that had formed in her eyes.

'I think you may be right,' he replied stonily.

Chapter Thirteen

It was a crisp, sunny day, as Phil Boag made his way towards the Gallery of Modern Art in Royal Exchange Square.

Imelda Watson-Caballo, as she was now known, worked as an assistant curator there. Phil had arranged to meet the woman during her lunch-break, in the public cafeteria situated on the second floor. The room was flanked by windows, each displaying an impressive vista of the sun-drenched city. Phil placed his warrant card in an open wallet on the table. Imelda strode straight towards him with her tray, sitting down in the seat opposite.

The young woman before him was petite and very dark in colouring. Her clothes were chic and she wore a pair of impossibly high heels. Phil wondered how on earth she remained on them all day. Her lips were painted a deep plum and she separated them slightly in a pained smile.

'Good afternoon, Sergeant Boag. How may I help you?'

'I'm a member of the Major Incident Team investigating the murder of Joanna Endicott and the disappearance of Daniel Goff.'

Imelda grimaced. 'I thought you might be. Am I in trouble?'

Phil leant forward. 'Why do you ask that?'

She fiddled with a serviette, her burgundy nails contrasting sharply with the white material. 'Because I have information about Goff, but I never came forward to tell the police.'

'Well, you can tell me all about it now,' he replied gently.

'It's rather embarrassing, really. My husband doesn't know it happened.'

'There's no specific reason why he needs to find out. Your case is unrelated, but it may give us an insight into Goff's character and behaviour traits.'

Imelda nodded her head. 'Daniel Goff was my tutor in English when I first came to Stirling. I was 18 years old and in a class of about twenty other students. I knew fairly early on that Daniel found me attractive. He gave me a great deal of attention and we often chatted about other stuff, like music and the cool places to go out in the city. I was very young, Sergeant Boag, and a long way from home.'

Phil considered how back then Imelda was only a year older than his eldest daughter was now. It made his skin crawl. 'What was Daniel Goff like? We don't have a very strong sense of his personality.'

'Oh, Daniel was quiet. He was an intellectual type who enjoyed playing guitar and composing songs. I'd go as far as to say he was sensitive. But he had this other side to him.' Imelda looked up and caught Phil's eye, as if to make sure he was following her meaning. 'Daniel was insecure, I think. He was 27 years old but still living a student life; he didn't own a property, have a steady girlfriend or even a permanent job. I believe he shied away from those things but at the same time knew it was what society expected of him.' Imelda lowered her gaze once again. 'We began a sexual relationship after a month of me being in his class. We always met at his rented flat, never on campus. I was naïve and thought I was in love with him. A couple of weeks before the course was due to finish, Daniel told me we couldn't continue seeing one another. I was angry with him, realising I'd been used, I suppose. In the final week, after one of the lessons, I hung back. Daniel tried to pretend I wasn't there. It made me furious. I said that I loved him and how could he turn his back on me so easily. Very calmly, he went to the classroom door and shut it. He walked slowly back towards me. Daniel took me by the arms and said, 'if you really love me, then prove it." Imelda had begun shredding the napkin. Little white feathers of paper filled the table in front of her. 'I let him have sex with me, against the desk. But it was not pleasant. Daniel was angry and he was being very rough. I ended up with nasty bruises on my arms and thighs. At one point, he pinned me back by my hair and I had no way of getting free of him. When he had finished, Daniel released his grip on me. I ran from the room.'

'You reported the incident to the university?'

'Yes, I was in a terrible state when I returned to my dorm. One of my friends persuaded me to go to the welfare officer. She referred the case to the police.'

'But charges were never brought?' Phil prompted.

Imelda smiled ruefully. 'I consented to the sex, Sergeant Boag. There was absolutely no hope of taking things further. The police officers were very kind and they let me down gently. He got into trouble with the College, though. He left almost immediately. I don't think Daniel even taught another lesson.'

'Did Goff have any friends, on the staff or in the surrounding area?'

'During the time we were seeing each other I don't recall meeting any of his friends. He was involved with a local band. They were a group of musicians who played gigs in some of the city pubs. Daniel practiced with them occasionally. I'm afraid I couldn't tell you any of their names.'

'I'm sorry to ask you this Imelda, but could you describe for me again the way in which Goff restrained you. It could be important for our current investigation.'

The woman thought carefully for a moment. Phil experienced a flicker of hope as Imelda unconsciously placed a protective hand at her neck.

'He used his body weight to keep me pinned against the desk. That was really enough. Daniel was much taller and larger than me. He grabbed at my upper arms and my thighs, sometimes digging his fingernails into my skin, which really hurt.' She paused, seeming to be experiencing the pain all over again, squeezing her eyes tight shut. 'Towards the end, he took hold of my ponytail with his left hand and with his right, he pressed down on my neck. That was when I thought he might actually kill me. When he was spent, he released his hold. I was able to shove him away and get out of the classroom.'

'Are you absolutely certain he held your neck?'

'Yes, but it wasn't a hold so much.' Imelda leant forward and demonstrated on Phil. 'He sort of pressed down on my windpipe with the flat of his palm, see?'

Phil nodded. 'I get it. Would you be willing to make a formal statement to that effect, Mrs. Watson-Caballo?'

The young woman sighed. 'Yes, of course. I'd been debating about whether or not to inform the police ever since I saw his name on the news. Tell me Sergeant Boag, do you really think Daniel killed this poor woman?'

'I don't know for certain, Imelda, but it's looking increasingly likely that he did.'

Chapter Fourteen

'You realise that if I hadn't had the heart attack, I'd be a sergeant by now,' Andy stated levelly, swilling the remainder of his Merlot around the long-stemmed glass.

'Yes,' Dani replied, slowly chewing her lamb and washing it down with a sip of mineral water. She'd decided to ask her partner out for a meal in one of the restaurants in Ardyle. Bevan was amazed when he actually agreed.

'The funny thing is, I wasn't even all that ambitious before. Now, it's all I think about. I'm absolutely determined to move up through the ranks.'

Dani didn't wish to get into another argument with him, but at the same time felt as if he wanted her advice. 'Give it time. It will take the management that bit longer to accept you're ready for it now,' she gave a half-smile, 'a bit like being a woman, in fact.'

To her great relief, Andy grinned back. 'It didn't take you long to progress though, did it?'

'I'm a fast-track graduate in her mid-thirties with no husband and no kids. I've devoted everything to my career and it's been duly noted upstairs. You've got Carol and Amy and were always intent on getting the balance right between work and home. I don't want to see you lose the perspective that you used to have. I always thought it was incredibly healthy - excuse the irony.'

'If you ignore the beer and the greasy takeaways, you're probably right.' Andy pushed away his empty glass and reached for the water jug, as if to emphasise his change of lifestyle.

'Don't become like one of those people who suddenly lose a lot of weight, learn how to make more of their looks and immediately become attractive to the opposite sex. They always make bloody fools of themselves, because they're not used to the attention. I knew so many girls like that at college. Half of them ended up pregnant and stuck with some lad with no prospects. They didn't understand when to say no.'

'I'm not intending on having an affair!' Andy looked quite put out.

Bevan shook her head vigorously, chuckling at the same time. 'I didn't mean it that way, it was just an analogy. I meant, now you're fit and clean-living and feel like you can take on the world, don't make the mistake of thinking that the world is worth having.'

Andy looked at his boss as if she'd lost her marbles.

'Just focus on Carol and Amy, the rest will follow at its own pace,' Bevan clarified.

'Good. Because I thought for a moment there you were actually trying to give me relationship advice.' Andy lifted an eyebrow archly.

Dani laughed.

The restaurant Bevan had chosen was a bistro facing the market square which boasted an impressive menu of local produce. Mid-week it was quiet. An older couple were sitting a few tables away from them. After paying their bill, the pair approached the two detectives.

'Excuse me, but are you the police officers working on the case of the woman killed up on Ben Lomond?' The man asked politely.

'Yes, that's correct,' Dani replied. 'I'm Detective Chief Inspector Bevan and this is my colleague, Detective Constable Calder.'

The man nodded and gave a faint smile. Dani thought he was probably in his early sixties. His hair was almost completely gone, just a few wisps at his temples remained. 'We're staying at the Carraig and have seen you both in there. You always seemed in such a hurry. My wife and I used to live in Ardyle. Now we just come back to visit every so often.'

Dani invited them to take a seat, sensing there was something the couple wished to talk about. She ordered coffees for the table. 'When did you move away from Ardyle?'

'Twenty years ago now,' the woman replied. 'My name is Joy Hutchison, this is my husband Bill. We lost our son here in 1983. It became difficult then for us to stay.'

'Was he one of the schoolchildren lost on the mountain?' Dani enquired gently.

'Aye,' Bill continued. 'Neil Hutchison. Ten years old. When we heard about the woman found dead on Ben Lomond on the local news, we decided to come and stay nearby. We aren't ghouls Detective Chief Inspector, but it somehow felt appropriate.'

Joy added a dash of milk to her coffee. 'We were upset, you see. It will sound very odd, but we like to think that Neil and the others help to protect people who climb the mountain. There hasn't been a single death out there in the National Park since that terrible night. People have got lost, certainly, but they've always been located alive and well. This time it was different, which is why we needed to come back.'

'This case is quite unlike the situation with your son, Mr and Mrs Hutchison. Joanna was murdered by somebody. It wasn't simply a case of getting into difficulties on the mountain. Sadly, there wasn't a great deal that anyone could have done to save her. I can assure you both we are doing everything we can to catch her killer.'

'Oh, we know it's not the same,' Bill responded quickly. 'But we believe we may be needed, nonetheless. I think we could help you in some way.'

Dani desperately wanted to make this poor couple feel as if they could contribute something to the investigation. 'Did you take part in the original search – when the schoolchildren first went missing?'

'Yes,' said Bill. 'As soon as we heard they were in trouble we headed out. The mountain rescue chaps were in charge. We couldn't fault them. The conditions made the landscape almost unrecognisable. It was frightening how altered everything was by the weather. People don't realise the dangers. It was impossible to get your bearings in the thick fog.'

'The records indicated that your son's teacher led his group in the wrong direction?'

'That is true,' Joy said. 'But we were out there too that afternoon and could never possibly have blamed him for it. You could barely make out the hand in front of your face. Mr Ford did the best he could. If we were going to attribute blame, Bill and I would have looked to the Headmaster at the time, Samuel McAlister. He was the one who planned the expedition and was in overall charge.'

'Although, we never harboured any grudge,' Bill swiftly clarified. 'The schoolchildren had been out on the hillside before. We'd taken Neil and Louise to the National Park often enough ourselves. If we'd felt it was too risky, we'd never have given permission for him to go.'

'What happened to Mr Ford and Mr McAlister - were either of them found to be at fault?' Andy asked.

'There was an inquiry, yes. The Procurator Fiscal

was involved too. It was ruled as death by misadventure for all the three children. McAlister remained as Head of the Primary until his retirement maybe five years later. Jack Ford was never quite the same afterwards. He still taught, but he didn't do all the football training and outward bound stuff he'd done before.'

'It was a shame, really, because Jack was good for the local children. But I understand why he stopped.' Joy finished her drink. 'We'll be heading back to the hotel now.'

As the couple stood to leave, Bill Hutchison suddenly added, 'my wife and I will be here in Ardyle until your investigation is over. If you do ever need our help, you know where to find us.'

Chapter Fifteen

During their briefing the following morning, Dani read out the transcript of Imelda Watson-Caballo's statement to Strathclyde Police. When she got to the section about Goff pressing his hand down on Imelda's throat, a ripple of excitement was palpable throughout the assembled group.

'I want to know if Goff assaulted any other women when he was working his way around Europe. Kendal, any luck on finding out where Goff taught for the decade he lived abroad?'

'I'm getting there, Ma'am. I'll go back to my notes and contact the relevant colleges and police forces to find out if he committed any offences during those years.'

'Good. Anything else to report?'

'You were correct about Joanna Endicott making a will, Ma'am,' said Driscoll. 'She left all her property and savings to her uncles and aunts. The house in Chiswick is worth 2.5 million pounds.'

Several whistles went up from the men.

'That's more than enough to kill for,' Driscoll added.

'You're right. We definitely need to check it out. Can you gather together statements from all of the principal beneficiaries? We'll need alibis for the night of Joanna's murder. I still don't think money is our motive here but it would be remiss not to investigate it. Driscoll, can you and Clark get the train down to London today to interview the family?'

The Sergeant nodded his head, pleased to be given the responsibility.

'Isn't all property in London worth that kind of

money these days? If it were a motive for murder, there'd be no one left alive in the south-east of England,' Andy Calder said dryly.

Driscoll shot him a sideways glance, not sure what to make of the comment.

Dani smiled. 'If my wee hoose in the west-end were worth that much, I wouldn't be standing here in front of you guys, that's for sure. But seriously, Andy, I take your point. However, it could have meant a great deal to a member of the Endicott family who needed it desperately enough. *That* would be our motive.'

DC Kendal jumped to his feet. Dani thought he was about to take issue with her. Then he announced, 'I've just had a reply to my post on Facebook! A guy who says he used to play in a band with Goff, in Stirling, about seven years ago.'

'Reply to him straight-away please, and get us an address.'

It took Andy and Bevan just over an hour to drive to Stirling. The man they'd come to see lived in Cornton, a district on the north bank of the River Forth. Craig Douglas's house lay within a sprawling new estate. Andy made several wrong turns before finally locating the address. It was after six by the time the detectives parked up. Dani hoped Douglas would be home from work by now.

The house was only about ten years old but already appeared tatty. The letter box was broken and the front garden overgrown. Andy pressed on the bell. Eventually, the man opened up. Craig Douglas was in his early thirties and possessed a mop of dark greasy hair pulled back into a ponytail. He led them through to a cluttered sitting room. Musical instruments seemed to fill every free surface.

'Just move something aside if you want a seat,' Douglas suggested unhelpfully, taking up position by the window. 'Can I make you a brew?'

'No thank you, Mr Douglas. We'd like to ask you a few questions, that's all.'

'You're still into the music then?' Andy commented, squeezing himself onto the sofa next to an acoustic guitar.

'Aye. My band play gigs in town. Mostly at 'The King and Castle' on the roundabout, do you know it?'

Andy shook his head. 'Can you tell us what you remember about Daniel Goff?'

'Not a great deal if I'm honest. I only go on Facebook to promote my band, that's why I noticed your request on the College site. We sometimes do concerts at the campus during Freshers' week. I hadn't heard the name in years. Dan played guitar with us for a few months about seven years back. He saw an advert I'd put in the student magazine.'

'But Goff wasn't a student at the time,' Bevan added.

'No, he was teaching English at the summer school. Dan was a couple of years older than us and was pretty cool. He'd played in all kinds of places, like Madrid and Rome. It seemed glamorous to us boys at the time.'

'Do you recall Daniel Goff having any girlfriends during the months you associated with him?'

Craig furrowed his brow. 'Girls kinda liked him. The pretty ones always came up to Dan after we'd finished a set. He took lassies home from time to time.'

'Do you remember a girl called Imelda from the college, she was eighteen years old back in 2007?'

'No, I don't. Dan didn't introduce us to any of his

mates. He came to practice, usually at my place, which was at the Top of the Town in those days. He'd turn up for a gig and that was it. By the end of the summer he simply disappeared. We were due to have a session on the Saturday night but Dan never showed. I've heard nothing from him since. So when I saw the message on the college Facebook page I was quite excited. I thought we might be able to get back in touch.'

'So you've had no contact with Daniel Goff in the last two weeks?' Andy asked carefully.

Craig Douglas looked surprised. 'As I said, I've no' seen Dan in years.'

'Do you follow the news at all, Mr Douglas?' Dani enquired gently.

The man now appeared embarrassed. 'Aye, when I can, but life's busy, you know? What with work and the band. When I'm no' writing new material, I'm asleep.'

'Could you give us the names and addresses of the other band members who knew Goff back in 2007? And if the man does try to get in touch with you, please inform us straight away.'

Dani handed Craig Douglas her card.

The man examined it carefully before asking, 'so is Dan in some kind of trouble then?'

Chapter Sixteen

'Do you think Craig Douglas is hiding Daniel Goff somewhere?' Dani asked this only semi-seriously, as she and Andy finished their dinner at the hotel.

'I had a good shifty round the house when I went to use the toilet - definitely no sign of him there. If Craig Douglas *is* helping Goff to hide from the police, he deserves an Oscar.'

Dani chuckled. 'We'll check out the other band members in the morning. My suspicion is that Goff could have another girlfriend in this area. Someone he's been cultivating for all these years. I think it is women he has a skill at manipulating. Sadly, he kept that side of his life very secret. If there is a woman out there protecting him, she'll be totally in his thrall. It will be very difficult to persuade her to turn him in.'

'We can't get Joanna's parents to make a television appeal, because they're both dead.'

'And there's no grieving husband, either.'

Andy suddenly shifted forward in his seat. 'What if we released the details of Goff's attack on Imelda Caballo? That might make this woman have second thoughts about him. It would at least shake her up a bit, which might encourage her to make a mistake.'

Dani became alert. 'It would be even better if Imelda talked about it in person. Phil says she's very sympathetic.' The DCI shook her head. 'Imelda's husband isn't aware of the relationship the girl had with Goff. Phil promised that her testimony could remain anonymous.'

Andy shrugged his shoulders. 'It's your call,

Ma'am. But bear it in mind. I'm sure you could talk her into it. This guy will probably go on to kill somebody else if he isn't caught. He'll disappear back abroad, where it will be easier for him to target vulnerable women.'

Dani stared at her half-eaten dessert, her appetite gone. She glanced back up at her companion. 'There's something about Imelda's testimony that has been bothering me, ever since Phil sent the details over.'

'What is it?'

'Well, Goff is a sexual predator, right?'

Andy nodded.

'He gets his kicks out of dominating women during the sexual act. I read Imelda's account very carefully. It seemed to me that Goff's attack on her was centred on him reaching climax. Once he'd been satiated, he let her go. She was of no further use to him. It's like an exaggerated form of a primitive male attitude towards woman - that once the sexual act is completed, the fascination is gone. He then moves onto another prey.'

'You've obviously been going out with the wrong kinds of men, Ma'am.'

Dani ignored the comment. 'Therefore, I would've expected the murder of Joanna Endicott to have a sexual element to it. There was none. Her clothes hadn't even been loosened. There was no evidence of semen anywhere on or near the body.'

'Perhaps the motive was different this time. Goff killed Joanna out of expediency. He needed her dead because she knew something about him and he had to silence her.'

'Or, the environment was wrong. Goff was exhausted and tired after getting lost on the mountain. He simply couldn't perform in that state. But to me, that would mean the impetus to commit the murder would no longer be there. *If,* it really was a sexually motivated crime, that is.'

'Let's get some sleep. It's an angle to consider when our minds are fresher.'

The pair exited the dining room. Dani's eyes were suddenly drawn to one of the corridors leading off to the left, where there were a number of ground floor rooms. It was dimly lit, but Dani had seen a figure standing about half-way along, watching them intently as they passed. Dani raised her hand to acknowledge the man, when she realised it was Bill Hutchison. He remained entirely impassive, as if in a trance and Dani wondered just how long he'd been waiting there.

By the middle of the following day, Driscoll and Clark were back in Ardyle. Dani called them into one of the side rooms at the Town Hall she was using as her office. There was only just enough room for the three of them to sit down.

'As we might have expected, they've all got pretty solid alibis. Most of the relatives were amazed to discover the house was worth that much and even more amazed that Joanna had left the money to them. I didn't sense the family were all that close. One of Joanna's cousins is off travelling the world on his gap year. His mum gave us a print-out of the e-mail she received on the day Joanna was killed. He was in Kuala Lumpur.'

'Okay. It was worth pursuing. Dave, could I have a word with you in private for a moment?'

'Certainly Ma'am.'

Clark left the room, pulling the door closed behind him.

'Have you ever heard of the Hutchisons? They lost their son in the Ardyle tragedy.'

Driscoll screwed up his face and then shook his

head. 'I really don't recall the name. I was a young copper in Fife back then, I didn't have any connection to the town.'

'Could you send DC Reid in to speak with me, please?'

The older policeman nodded, but his body language suggested he wasn't overly enthusiastic about the idea.

DC Sammy Reid was about the same age as Dani, perhaps a year or two younger. He was tall and good-looking. A fresh-faced type of character with neatly styled hair. Dani gestured for him to take a seat.

After asking him to update her on his current assignments she said, 'I hope you won't find this intrusive, Sammy, but I wondered if I could ask you a couple of questions about your sister?'

The man cracked a wistful smile. 'I thought this might come up, Ma'am.'

'Do you mind?'

'Not at all. It happened a long time ago.'

'Did Katrina's death have a bearing on your decision to become a police officer?' Dani thought for a moment about her own mother's death, which occurred at a similar time to the Ardyle tragedy.

'I suppose it must have. You find yourself forever searching for the answer to something. Sorry, it's hard to explain.'

Dani nodded, she understood only too well.

'Do you recall the Hutchison family? Their son died on the mountain along with Katrina and William.'

'Aye. We knew each other well. Mum and Joy remained friends for a long time. But they moved away from here a good few years back.'

'They're staying at The Carraig right now. The couple approached Andy Calder and me at dinner the other evening. They seemed to believe they could assist us in solving our current inquiry.'

Sammy grimaced. 'Permission to speak off the record, Ma'am?'

'Of course.'

'The Hutchisons took Neil's death very badly. Well, we all did, but Bill and Joy went a little peculiar. They became devoutly religious afterwards. Joy was always trying to get Mum to go with her to the Kirk to pray for the souls of the children. Mum didn't think it was healthy. In the end, she used to avoid her like the plague. It sounds mean, but Mum and Dad had their own way of coping with Katrina's death and the Hutchisons really didn't help. When they moved away, they kept sending us cards, with clippings folded up inside. We assumed they did the same with the other family who lost a child that night.'

'What did the cards say?'

'The clippings were excerpts from local and national press reports of walkers who'd got lost in the Ben Lomond National Park. The cards always had a religious image on the front and inside they said, 'our angels have kept them safe'. Mum knew the Hutchisons were trying to gain something positive out of their loss, but to be honest, it just freaked us out.'

'I can see that,' Dani replied gravely.

The Detective Chief Inspector thanked Sammy for his time and allowed him to take his lunch-break. She sat back at the cramped desk and thought for a while. For some reason, the Hutchisons' angels hadn't kept Joanna Endicott safe. This was why the couple had felt compelled to return to Ardyle. They were determined to find out why not.

Chapter Seventeen

Dani's mobile phone began buzzing on the bedside table a few seconds before the alarm clock went off. She'd been in such a deep sleep that this brutal wrench into consciousness left her disorientated. It took her a little while to interpret what the caller was saying.

'Okay, so you're ringing from the Met, to inform me about a house breaking and a GBH. Are you sure you have the correct number, Detective Sergeant?'

Dani levered herself up onto an elbow, becoming more alert as the Sergeant provided the additional details. She grabbed for a pad and pen, jotting some information down. Bevan glanced at the clock.

'Thank you for letting me know. I'll be in London with you by early afternoon.' Dani ended the call, swinging around to sit on the edge of the bed, resting her head in her hands and rubbing at the temples.

Amit Batra was in hospital. Someone had broken into his family home in the middle of the night. Batra had disturbed the burglar, confronting him with a baseball bat. But the intruder had got the better of Batra. The man had been very badly beaten. He'd suffered a fractured skull and had not yet regained consciousness. The rest of the family hid upstairs during the attack. They were unharmed. The intruder made off with a backpack full of valuables. The police have not yet been able to find him. All of this Dani had scrawled in note form on her pad.

Taking a deep breath, Dani went into the en-suite bathroom and turned on the shower, returning to the bedroom to call Andy. If they were really going to reach east London by this afternoon, she'd have to get a move on.

Calder and Bevan caught a flight from Edinburgh to Stansted Airport in Essex. They reached the town of Loughton, on the outer borders of the east London suburbs, by mid-afternoon. Dani had arranged to meet the senior investigating officer at Whipps Cross Hospital, where Batra was in the Intensive Care Unit.

DI Long, a stocky man in his early forties, greeted them in the waiting area. 'When I put Batra's name into the NEXUS system, your case came up. I hope you didn't mind the wake-up call from my Sergeant. This assault is probably unrelated, but these days you've got to cover all the bases.'

Bevan nodded with understanding. 'Has Batra woken up yet?'

The Detective Inspector pulled a face. 'The specialist has just finished running a few tests. He reckons there might be brain damage.' He swept a hand through his thinning, silvery hair. 'I haven't told his wife the bad news yet.'

'Can we see him?'

Long gestured towards the room next door. Batra was visible through a glass partition. Bevan and Calder didn't ask to go inside. They simply stood by the window directly opposite the bed, observing the myriad of machines and tubes currently doing the job of keeping Amit Batra alive. His face was puffed up and unrecognisable due to the multiple lacerations and oedema.

'Someone did a real job on him, poor sod,' Andy commented quietly.

Bevan suddenly heard a movement behind them. She turned to see James Irving sitting on one of the plastic seats that lined the corridor. He had his head buried in his hands and didn't appear to have noticed their presence.

Dani moved across and sat down next to him. She laid a hand on his shoulder. 'Mr Irving, are you alright?'

The man immediately looked up, his eyes swollen and bloodshot. 'DCI Bevan, what the hell?'

'We need to find out if there's a connection between the assault on Mr Batra and Joanna Endicott's death.'

'Might there be?' Irving seemed utterly bemused and lost. 'I just don't know what to believe anymore.'

Bevan gestured to Andy, indicating that he should buy them all a coffee. She mimed the addition of multiple sugars. Andy raised his eyebrows, but obediently shuffled off along the corridor, having apparently got the message.

'Did Amit ever give you the impression that he might be frightened of someone?'

James stared at her face intently. 'He'd been jittery ever since the night he spent on the mountain. I thought that was pretty understandable under the circumstances. I assumed he was in a state of shock.'

'There was an intruder at the bothy and now Batra's house has been turned over and your friend left for dead. I'm afraid it is too much of a coincidence to ignore. Did Amit Batra have anything on his person when he was discovered on the hillside – an item that he didn't set out with perhaps?'

James screwed up his face in thought. 'There was a glint in the morning sun, like a metal object momentarily reflecting the light. That's how we found his position amongst the scrubland. As soon as we reached him, I thought no more about it. I was just so glad he was alive. I wanted him to tell me where Jo was.' The words trailed away as tears rolled down his cheeks. 'Amit and Jo were my best friends.'

Dani put her arm around his shoulders, just as Andy arrived with the drinks. She levered James' fingers around the paper cup, blowing on it for him and manoeuvring it up to his lips. 'Come on, have a sip and you'll feel better.' The man took a tiny mouthful.

James automatically coughed, spitting the hot liquid straight onto Andy's trousers. 'Bloody hell! There must be about twenty sugars in there!'

Calder stormed off to the gents.

Bevan put a hand up to her mouth, but she couldn't prevent a chuckle from escaping. James turned towards her and started to laugh too.

'My friend's lying in a bed in the ICU, close to death, and I'm sitting here in hysterics,' he managed to say between guffaws. 'You're definitely the bad cop.'

This made Dani laugh even more but she took several deep breaths and willed herself to calm down. Thankfully, they were both fairly composed by the time Andy returned from the toilets, a steely expression on his face.

'Sorry, mate,' James mumbled quietly.

Andy nodded but Dani could tell he was still cross. It made her sad. A few months ago, her partner would have been laughing along with them. It had been Calder's grumpy reaction to getting sprayed that made the situation so comical. The heart attack had really changed him.

She made no comment on it. Instead, Dani scribbled her mobile number onto a business card and handed it to James. 'We'll be staying in town for the next couple of days. Call me if you remember anything significant.'

Chapter Eighteen

The Batras' house was a fairly ordinary-looking semi on one of the leafy back roads leading away from Loughton High Street. It was positioned halfway along a row of properties facing directly onto Epping Forest.

Bevan knocked at the door. A pretty Asian woman in her early thirties answered almost immediately. She had a baby held in her arms. The face of a little girl poked out between her mother's legs.

'Tanisha Batra?' Bevan showed her warrant card.

The woman nodded, automatically standing aside to allow them both to enter. The house was a mess. Dani glanced through to the kitchen, where the panels in the door leading out to the garden had been boarded up. The living room was marginally tidier. Tanisha set the baby down into a bouncer and perched on the edge of the sofa, with the little girl clinging steadfastly to her leg.

Dani thought there was something spaced-out about the woman. Her eyes had an unfocused look to them. 'Mrs Batra, we'd like to ask you a few questions about the break-in.'

'Okay,' she said carefully, holding her daughter to her tightly.

'Did you hear or see anything at all during the burglary?'

'Yes. I heard the glass in the back door being broken. Amit had woken too. He went to the wardrobe and took out a baseball bat that he keeps in there. Then he went downstairs to see what was happening.'

'Did you not think to call the police first? Most people have a mobile phone close to hand these days.'

'It all occurred very quickly. All we knew was that there was an intruder in the house. Amit wanted to protect the children.'

'What happened next?'

'I went into the children's rooms and brought them into the main bedroom with me. I closed the door. There was lots of banging and shouting downstairs. It lasted for about five minutes and then there was silence. I waited for a while, then I left the children upstairs and went down to see what was going on. Amit was lying in the hallway, with blood all over his face. He was unconscious but I found he was still breathing. I called an ambulance.' Tears were streaming down Tanisha's cheeks. Her words had become slurred.

'So you never saw the intruder at all?' Andy asked.

She shook her head vigorously.

'Did your husband give any indication that he was frightened or nervous in the days leading up to this attack, Mrs Batra. Did you receive any threatening phone calls or letters?' Dani enquired.

'No. He'd been very quiet ever since he returned from Scotland. All he wanted to do was stay home with us. I assumed he was sad because Jo was dead. It is a terrible shock when somebody so young dies.'

Dani sat forward in her seat. 'Have you been drinking, Tanisha?'

The woman looked agitated. 'That is none of your business,' she retorted.

'It certainly *is* my business when you are responsible for the care of a baby and a young child.'

Andy quickly intervened, 'have you got a relative or a friend who could come and help you out, just whilst your husband is still in the hospital, perhaps?'

'My mum has been dropping in,' Tanisha said faintly, looking now as if she might be sick.

'I think your mother should take the children for a few hours and give you a proper break. We could arrange for a WPC to come round and check on you?' Andy suggested.

'Do you often drink alcohol this early in the day, Mrs Batra?' Dani demanded.

Andy shot his superior officer a puzzled look.

Tanisha became angry again. 'What is this? My husband may not live because he confronted a burglar in our house and now you're trying to imply that I am an unfit mother!' She suddenly jumped up, pushing the little girl towards Andy. Tanisha rushed out into the hallway, where they heard her retching violently into the toilet bowl. Dani observed Tanisha's daughter closely, as she stood calmly beside Andy, holding his hand. In that moment, the Detective Chief Inspector was quite certain that this was a scenario the child was perfectly used to.

'If you don't mind me asking, Ma'am – what was that all about?' Andy swung their hire-car onto the driveway of the hotel.

'Tanisha Batra is an alcoholic,' Dani said levelly.

'We can't be certain of that, surely?'

'The little girl wasn't at all shocked or frightened by her mum's behaviour. She was entirely used to it.'

'I'll get onto social services and see if there's a file on the Batras.' Andy sighed heavily. 'The woman might just be struggling to deal with what's happened to her husband. Perhaps we should cut her some slack. It's bloody hard looking after young kids, especially on your own.' Andy turned to face Bevan, who refused to meet his eye.

'The baby is only six months old, Andy. It isn't our job to 'cut her some slack'. It's our *duty* to look after the kids.' Dani climbed out of the passenger seat and slammed the door shut behind her, leaving Andy sitting behind the wheel, thinking that he'd never seen his boss react quite so strongly to an interview before.

Chapter Nineteen

Detective Inspector Long showed Bevan and Calder into an open plan office area on one of the upper floors of New Scotland Yard.

'Social Services don't yet have a file on the Batra family, but they're sending out a social worker today to do an assessment,' Long informed them, gesturing towards a coffee machine in the corner of the room, indicating they should help themselves. 'We were already onto the problem, DCI Bevan, even before you mentioned it. One of the officers who took Mrs Batra's original statement could smell alcohol on the woman's breath. This was at 9.15am.'

Dani nodded. 'Have you got an up-to-date list of what was taken from the house?'

Long eased onto a swivel chair and opened a file on his desk. Dani and Andy took the seats in front of him, waiting patiently for the information they needed.

'It appeared that Batra's attacker took some jewellery; a gold necklace and a couple of bracelets, a smartphone and purse which had been lying on the kitchen table and a small digital camera. Obviously, Mrs Batra is not the most reliable of witnesses. We were depending upon her to notice what was missing.'

'And that was worth battering a man nearly to death for?' Andy added with feeling.

'You know as well as I do, that some folk would stab you for a bag of sweets,' Long responded soberly.

'Were the smartphone and camera Tanisha's or Amit's?' Bevan suddenly asked, letting her eyes run down the list.

'The phone and purse were Tanisha's and the camera was Amit's. Mrs Batra said the camera was practically brand new. Amit had bought it especially for his trip to Scotland. He wanted to take plenty of shots of himself at the top of some mountain or other.'

'Ben Lomond,' Dani said absent-mindedly, her thoughts elsewhere.

'How is Amit Batra, has he woken up yet?' Andy enquired politely.

'Not yet, I'm afraid. The docs won't know the extent of the brain damage until he's out of the coma, poor bugger. But we'll send in an officer to interview him as soon as he does wake. It looks as if Batra was the only one who actually saw this intruder. The neighbours didn't hear a thing.'

'Any luck on tracking him down?'

Long shifted uncomfortably. 'There were no prints in the house or on the baseball bat. He must have been gloved up. We've got absolutely no witnesses. Tanisha Batra was so late calling us in that the bloke was long gone by the time we got there. He must have taken off into the woods, but there was no sign of him.'

'Well, I don't think there's much else we can do from here, Detective Inspector. Thank you for your time. Please let us know about any developments in Amit Batra's recovery.'

Bevan and Calder had already packed their bags and were ready to drive to the airport. As they walked towards the car Calder commented, 'what would make an intelligent young woman like that become an alcoholic?'

'Post-Natal Depression may have triggered it, or boredom being at home with small children all day.

Having an unhappy marriage wouldn't help. She may always have suffered from mental health problems and used the alcohol to self-medicate. Didn't Phil say they'd had financial problems a couple of years back? That could very easily have made Tanisha start drinking. The strain of money issues on top of looking after a little one may have proved too much.'

Andy was amazed at how much Dani seemed to know about the subject. 'It makes you wonder what came first.'

Dani looked puzzled.

'Well, whether Tanisha drank because her husband had affairs, or Amit found another woman because Tanisha drank.'

'It's a miserable situation either way,' Dani paused, as the mobile in her pocket began to ring. She spoke briefly to the caller and then turned to Andy. 'That was James Irving, he's remembered something. He wants to meet me and discuss it.'

Dani waited for Irving in a large, soulless pub next to Bank tube station. This was the nearest place they could both reach at short notice. Dani didn't want to have to get a later flight. James Irving pushed through the huge, glass and metal doors a few moments later. She watched as he approached her at the bar. He was dressed very smartly, every bit the young urban professional.

'Is the Detective Constable not with you?'

Dani shook her head, 'he's driving around in the car. There aren't many parking opportunities in the City of London.'

'As long as he wasn't worried I was going to spit my drink at him again.' James gave a wry smile, ordering an orange juice.

Dani smiled, determined not to allow herself to be charmed. 'What information do you have for me?'

Irving hopped onto the stool next to her, their knees dangerously close to touching. Dani unconsciously reached down to lower her black skirt, suddenly aware of revealing a reasonable amount of thigh. The action simply resulted in James' vision being drawn in the direction of her legs, which made them both blush.

'It came back to me in a kind of flash,' he began. 'I recalled that as we were climbing the mountain, with the burn cascading down to the side of us, Daniel Goff brought out this little slim-line camera. I was surprised, because I didn't have Goff down as the type to take holiday photos. It struck me last night that this is what I'd seen in Amit's hand when we found him the next day. Well, I can't be sure, but that it might have been. Because the camera had a dazzling silver coating and when Daniel had been snapping away at the scenery, it reflected back a piercing beam of sunlight, similar to that which I'd seen when we were searching the heathland and discovered Amit. Sorry, I hope that helps, it sounds a bit silly now I've said it out loud.' James took a sip of his juice.

'Not at all, that's extremely helpful. Mr Irving, did you ever think that Tanisha Batra drank too much?'

James stared down into his lap, as if examining the hand-stitched seams on his trouser pockets. 'She did used to knock it back a bit at parties.' He looked up. 'Amit had to practically carry her home sometimes. But we all enjoy a drink occasionally, don't we? Amit said Tanisha became quite depressed after Sunetra was born. I probably noticed her drinking more after that.'

'Okay, thanks. I don't believe it's got any bearing on the case. Look, James, I'm going to have to dash off. Our flight's in an hour and we've still got to get to Stansted.'

Irving nodded. 'Sure, of course. Just, erm, keep in touch, yeah?' he said.

Chapter Twenty

It was late by the time the detectives returned to the Carraig Hotel. The large party who'd been staying there the previous week had now departed, leaving the place strangely quiet. Andy had asked Dani if she fancied an after-dinner drink. She could tell he was keen to discuss the latest developments in the case. But Dani was exhausted and told him she was retiring straight to her room.

The DCI kicked off her shoes and lay back on the duvet. Her heavy eyelids were just closing as the mobile phone at her side began to chime. She barely had the energy to flick it open.

'Were you still awake?'

Dani shook herself into alertness at the sound of Sam Sharpe's transatlantic drawl. 'Of course,' she replied.

'How's the new case?'

'Becoming increasingly complicated – how's life in the fair city of Richmond, Virginia?'

'We've had a couple of homicides, drug-related we think.' With the pleasantries over, Sam's tone became more serious. 'Have you seen the papers?'

Dani sat up straight. 'Not in the last twenty four hours, no.'

'Perhaps you should have a look. The US media haven't taken too kindly to Gordon Parker's murderer being found innocent. I've mailed you a link. I just wanted to say that none of the information they've used came from me. I've no idea where they got it from.'

Dani was really worried now. 'Okay, I get the

message,' she said warily.

'I'll let you get back to sleep. I know how hard you're working right now. Goodnight.' With that, he was gone.

Dani quickly checked her inbox. It didn't take her long to discover what Sam meant. Several of the US nationals had covered the story. It would just be a matter of time before it broke over here. On the front page of the New York Times was a photograph of her and Sam walking up the steps towards the High Court. The headline read: 'The special relationship?' with the byline: 'Did the secret romance between two detectives allow the killer of a US citizen to walk free?'

Dani didn't want to read on, but she forced herself. The reporter accused her of making crucial mistakes in the gathering of evidence, errors which had allowed Erskine's lawyers to get him off. The implication of the entire article was that Dani was a sad, single woman who was too busy romancing an American cop to concentrate on nailing a killer. The accusation really stung. It was exactly the kind of reputation she had worked so hard to avoid. Added to that, it was all her own bloody fault.

Dani tossed the smartphone to the other side of the bed, wriggled out of her clothes and climbed under the covers, reaching out a hand to switch off the light. Her last thought before drifting away into blissful oblivion was that whatever the outcome of this debacle, as far as she and Sam Sharpe were concerned, things were well and truly over.

Bevan was still reeling from her phone conversation with DCS Nicholson when she stood up to take the morning briefing. Dani hoped her discomfort wasn't too obvious. Andy Calder did seem to be looking at her oddly, but she dismissed it as simply her imagination. Dani outlined the Met's investigation into the attack on Amit Batra and invited comments from the team.

DC Reid was the first to offer a response. 'Do we think Daniel Goff is now in London, then?'

'Good question. If we believe that the camera stolen from the Batras' house was Goff's and there was something on it that might be incriminating to him, we've got to assume he's our prime suspect for the break-in and the assault on Amit,' Dani explained.

DS Driscoll stood up to speak. 'How can it be possible for Goff to move around the country so easily? We've got alerts out for his arrest in all the airports, train stations and motorway services in the UK.'

'He must have an accomplice. A friend who is driving him around and giving him a place to hide,' Andy suggested.

'Then we need to check the CCTV on the motorways between Scotland and London.' Dani looked towards Driscoll. 'Can you arrange that please, Dave?'

'We'll just have to hope they didn't travel via the back routes, if they did, we're screwed.' Andy crossed his arms defensively.

'I cannot believe it's possible to drive into London without getting caught on camera somewhere. The man isn't superhuman. He's bound to have slipped up.'

DC Reid stepped forward again. 'Maybe you're right and Goff isn't superhuman.'

'What do you mean?' Dani listened with interest.

'No one saw or heard this intruder except Tanisha and Amit Batra, right? Well, Amit is in a coma and can't tell us what actually happened that night, which leaves Tanisha as the only source of information. The neighbours didn't hear a thing. What if there never was any intruder? Tanisha Batra could be making the whole thing up. She discovers that her husband was having a fling with Philippa Graves, right? They have a blazing argument and Tanisha's drunk, which skews her judgement. She goes up to the bedroom, where she knows Amit keeps a baseball bat in the wardrobe. Tanisha goes downstairs with it and beats him around the head. The guy wouldn't have stood a chance.'

Dani took up the mantle, 'when she calmed down and saw what she'd done, the woman panicked, deciding to make it look like a break-in. She smashes the back door and disposes of the few valuable items she finds to hand. Tanisha had no idea the camera was significant. It may prove to have no bearing on Amit's attack at all. Then the woman wipes the place free of prints.'

'Tanisha *was* very late in calling the police. By the time she got around to it, there would be no chance of them catching up to any thief who'd fled the property,' Andy added.

'It's certainly worth investigating. I'll ask DI Long to take a look at the forensics on the house and see if it's possible the whole thing was an inside job.'

'It might be an idea to check the back garden and the neighbours' bins,' Reid chipped in. 'If she had to get rid of the valuables in a hurry, there wouldn't have been many places she could have stashed them.'

'Excellent work, Reid. It would certainly be a bonus to be able to get hold of that camera and see what's on it. Let's hope Mrs Batra cracks under pressure and tells us where it is. For the time being, however, we focus on two possible scenarios. Firstly, that Goff somehow travelled to London in order to get his camera back from Batra. Amit disturbed him in the process and ended up receiving a beating which left him in a coma. And secondly, that Tanisha Batra attacked her husband after finding out about his relationship with Philippa Graves. She staged the burglary to cover her crime. Andy will assign tasks. The rest of you can return to concentrating on the Joanna Endicott case.'

Andy knocked on the door of Dani's makeshift office. He entered more hesitantly than usual and appeared to be holding something behind his back. Bevan couldn't interpret the strange expression on his face. He took the seat opposite her.

'Have you seen today's Informing Scotland?' He asked carefully before placing the folded newspaper down in front of her. 'I think you should take a few minutes to read it, Ma'am.'

Having been given the heads-up by Sam, she already had a fair idea what it would be about. After smiling grimly at the dated photograph of her on the front cover, Dani scanned the piece, stopping dead when she got to the half-way point. The story was pretty much taken word-for-word from the American press, until the section she was currently staring open-mouthed at, which provided an account of Bevan's early life and career.

Somehow, the journalist had found out about the death of Dani's mother. She supposed it wouldn't have been difficult. But here were all the wretched details, laid out in black and white before her. Dani immediately worried that her father might have seen it. Although she knew the daily papers wouldn't have reached the island of Colonsay quite yet. She'd have to call him sooner rather than later.

Andy's voice snapped her back to the present. 'I didn't realise your mother had committed suicide,' he said quietly. 'I'm very sorry.'

Dani cleared her throat. 'I was eight years old when it happened,' she began. 'Mum had suffered from depression ever since I'd been born. I don't believe Dad really knew how bad it was. Mum had been drinking to cope, but it was in secret. She covered it up pretty well. Until one day, when I was seven and a half.

It was the end of school and I was waiting for Mum to pick me up from the gates of the village Primary, where we lived in the Welsh valleys. She didn't come, so I decided to walk back home by myself. It wasn't too far, just a mile or so. But it involved taking the country road which snaked up to our cottage on the side of the steep valley. There was no pavement for much of the way. As I was walking, it had begun to get dark. Somewhere along a winding section of the road, a car must have hit me. It knocked me into a ditch that bordered the small stretch of forest which lay on both sides of the track.'

'Did the car stop?'

Dani shook her head. 'No. It's possible the driver never even saw me. I was unconscious for a while. When I woke, it was properly dark. The police thought I'd been down there for several hours. Mum never noticed I was gone. She'd fallen asleep and was out of it until Dad got home at about half past six. Of course, when he realised I wasn't there he panicked. A full search of the village and surrounding areas was instigated. No one had seen me since the end of class at three thirty. Dad was beside himself. One of the villagers discovered me in the ditch at around nine o'clock. I spent the night in the local hospital, with Dad by my side. I had a mild head injury and a broken ankle, was terribly cold and in shock. I remember very little about it to be honest.'

'What happened to your mum?'

'Dad sent her to a special clinic to get help, where she finally received the right medication to treat her depression. But she couldn't forgive herself for what had happened to me. Once she'd sobered up, Mum was horrified. When I'd been released from hospital, Social Services wouldn't allow me to go back home. I spent a year with a foster family in a nearby town. They were very good people, kind and loving. Dad visited every day, but he had to work, so couldn't look after me full-time. When I was taken into care, Mum really declined. She took an overdose of tranquilisers one morning after Dad had left for school. It was a serious attempt to end her life. Mum knew that no one would find her for at least eight hours.' Dani turned and stared out of the tiny window, catching a glimpse of the Lomond mountain range in the distance.

'Poor woman,' Andy muttered.

'Without Mum at home, Dad was allowed to have me back. He employed a child-minder to pick me up from school and make me tea. But Dad couldn't bear to stay on in the village. He must have been on the lookout for jobs elsewhere because within three months we'd left. Dad became the Headmaster of the primary school on Colonsay and we began a whole new life.'

'No wonder you don't drink,' Andy said, almost to himself. 'Don't worry about this article,' he added, more stridently this time. 'The people who work with you will understand. Nobody blames you for Erskine getting off the hook. We'll nail him on a re-trial.'

Dani managed the flicker of a smile. She could shrug off most things, but her mother's death was different. She was going to have to work hard not to let this knock her off course. DCS Nicholson had given her a dressing down earlier this morning, telling her not to allow her private life to compromise her work as a police officer. She couldn't have agreed with him more. Sam Sharpe could easily be banished from her heart. Moira Bevan, on the other hand, was a more difficult ghost to exorcise. But if Dani was going to continue to do her job properly, then she'd have to do it, once and for all.

Chapter Twenty One

It was late by the time Dani got back to the Carraig. She didn't fancy going into the dining room to eat and decided to order room service instead. Andy had driven home to Glasgow for the evening. Hearing the tale of Dani's mother must have left him with the pressing need to see his wife and baby, she thought.

As Dani was passing the desk in the lobby, a receptionist in a smart tartan blouse called her over. 'Detective Chief Inspector!' she announced, with a knowing smile on her perfectly made-up face. 'A bouquet of flowers arrived for you this afternoon.'

The woman bent down beneath the counter and brought out a pretty spray of white and yellow roses, a small envelope protruding conspicuously from the centre of the foliage. Bevan took the bouquet from her in a business-like way, feeling more apprehensive than pleased to receive them; such was the effect of today's unwelcome developments.

She waited until reaching her room, closing the door firmly and kicking off her shoes, before plucking out the card and reading the message. Dani felt a prickle of excitement mixed with confusion as she realised who they were from. James Irving. Apparently, he had seen the newspaper reports about her on the web and felt compelled to express his moral support.

Dani placed the flowers on the dressing table and positioned the buds into the most attractive arrangement possible, stepping back to survey her handiwork. It was a lovely gesture and one which Dani felt was made in the spirit of friendship. For that, she was immensely grateful. Anything else would have put her in an awkward situation professionally. She'd already got on the wrong side of DCS Nicholson and didn't fancy doing it again.

After eating, Dani made herself take a long bath. Then she slipped into a comfortable, full length nightdress before sliding between the cool crisp sheets, relishing the size of the hotel's king-size bed. She mustn't have been asleep for very long when something woke her. Dani automatically swung her legs across to the side of the bed and reached for her mobile phone. The sound came again. It was a soft and unsure knock on her bedroom door.

Dani put on the hotel's complementary bath robe and peered through the spy hole. Standing on the other side of the door, his face oddly obscured by the convex lens, was Bill Hutchison. Dani immediately opened up.

'Mr Hutchison, how may I help you? It's very late.'

The man appeared jittery. 'Yes, I apologise. I just couldn't sleep. Can I speak with you for a moment?'

Dani opened the door wide and allowed him to enter, pulling across a chair for him to sit on. Bill glanced at the flowers on the table but made no comment on their presence in the room.

'I read the piece about you in the Scottish press,' he began awkwardly. 'I'm very sorry for your loss.'

Dani dipped her head in recognition. 'I lost my mother a very long time ago.'

'As we did our son, Detective Chief Inspector, and it doesn't lessen the pain.' Bill leaned forward, his face crinkled in concentration. 'It suddenly struck my wife and I, as we read the newspaper report this afternoon, how your mother had died in the exact same month and year that our Neil did.'

Bevan experienced a tiny jolt of surprise at receiving this news, but tried not to show it. She hadn't before made the connection. 'It's a strange coincidence, certainly.'

'It means there must be a reason why you are here, DCI Bevan. My wife and I knew we had to come to Ardyle, as soon as we heard the news of the lady's death on the mountain. Now, we discover that the detective leading the case suffered a similar loss to us, at one and the same time. It is very significant, Ms Bevan. It suggests the two cases are connected. Don't you see? God has called us all here for an important purpose.'

Dani looked closely at the man's drawn and grey features, feeling an immense pity for him and his wife. 'I'm sorry, Mr Hutchison. I really can't agree with that assessment. I am here investigating Joanna Endicott's death because it is within my rank and jurisdiction to do so. Coincidences exist everywhere in life if we choose to highlight them. I think you'd better go back to your room and get some sleep.'

Bill's face seemed to crumple. 'At least bear it in mind, Detective,' he pleaded.

'Of course. I always keep an open mind during a murder inquiry. But I cannot operate on signs and portents, Mr Hutchison. My team need solid evidence.'

He nodded resignedly, standing up and making his way towards the door. As Dani watched him depart, Bill suddenly turned and said. 'You worked on the Richard Erskine case, did you not?'

'Yes, I did.'

'He is a very evil man, Detective Chief Inspector. He will undoubtedly kill again. Next time, you must ensure he goes to prison for life.'

Dani was taken aback. 'Do you know Richard Erskine?'

'No, I do not. But Neil has spoken with Erskine's

unfortunate victims, Ms Bevan. Our son tells us everything.' With that, the man was gone.

Chapter Twenty Two

Early the following morning, seated at a desk in her tiny office in the Ardyle Town Hall, Dani received a phone call from DI Long at the Met.

Amit Batra had died during a surgical procedure to treat a blood clot on his brain three hours previously. The case was now one of murder. Dani asked if his forensic team had made any progress on the theory that Tanisha Batra could have been responsible for her husband's death.

'It's certainly possible,' Long explained. 'The murderer wiped the weapon clean of prints. But the back door was definitely smashed from the outside in and the lock broken with considerable force. If it was Tanisha who did the job, I'd be incredibly surprised. This was a sober and methodical break-in. If it involved Batra's wife, then in my opinion there'd have to be an accomplice involved - a boyfriend or a hit man. Tanisha doesn't have an independent source of income, so that pretty much rules out the latter.'

'It's too much to hope that she might confess to her part in the attack, I suppose?'

Long chuckled. 'Yes, Detective Chief Inspector, it *is* too much to hope for. We've had her back in for questioning. The woman's a mess. Currently, she's more concerned with the prospect of losing custody of her children than in the fate of her husband. But I'm not taking that as a sign of guilt. She's not changed a single word of her statement and made no attempt to cover her tracks.'

'I'm assuming her daughter is too young to be

able to tell you anything about the night of the assault?'

'Sunetra Batra is only two and a half. The girl certainly isn't acting as if she recently witnessed her mother murdering her father. The children are comfortably placed with a local foster family. I'm not keen to upset the apple cart by getting a child psychologist in to interview the girl.'

'No, you're quite right, that would be unnecessary.'

Bevan informed the detective that her team were still checking the CCTV cameras for signs of Daniel Goff on the motorway routes into London from the north but had so far drawn a blank. Long ended the call with the promise he would keep her updated on any new developments.

Dani made her way towards the incident room. She found Andy leaning over a monitor where DC Clark was scanning through CCTV footage. Andy straightened himself up as she approached. Dani felt as if he looked much fresher as a result of his trip home. She informed the officers present about Batra's death. The team maintained a respectful silence for a few moments.

'We're not having much luck finding motorists who resemble Daniel Goff,' Andy finally supplied. 'Let's face it, if he's got an associate, Goff might be lying low under the back seat or crouching inside a van for all we know. So we've decided to focus only on vehicles with Scottish plates. There are fewer of those than you might think. For each car, we are performing a thorough check, to see if the owner has any links to the Stirling area.'

'Excellent work. Which routes are you examining?'

'The M1, A1 and M11 for now, which is more than enough to keep us busy. We are aware though, that he could easily have entered London from the south or the west. I just don't have the manpower to look into those possibilities just yet.'

Bevan led Andy out of Clark's earshot. She told him about the visit she'd received the previous night from Bill Hutchison.

'That's just what we need,' Andy sighed, 'a pair of certifiable crackpots hanging around the investigation.'

'We've got to tread carefully, make them feel involved in our inquiries.'

Andy raised his eyebrows. 'That's not going to be easy, Ma'am.'

'Then you'll just have to try harder.' Dani adopted a steely tone. 'The couple lost their son under tragic circumstances and are searching for some answers. We know they'll never get them, but we need to remain sensitive to the feelings of the local community. That's as important these days as catching the bad guys.'

Andy nodded. 'Message received, loud and clear.'

Bevan stepped out of the town hall and into the market square, where the piercing autumn sun was lying low in the sky. She took a few moments to examine the quaint stone buildings of this neat little town. There were a good number of independent shops and busy cafés leading away from the main square. A Celtic cross stood proudly in the centre of the thoroughfare. Dani could easily imagine what this place would have looked like a hundred years ago, let alone thirty, when the schoolchildren went missing on the mountain.

She found a quirky looking gift shop and nipped inside to buy a condolence card. Dani swiftly wrote down a message and copied the address she had stored on her smartphone. Sticking on a stamp, she thrust it into a post box, before there was time to have second thoughts about sending it.

For some reason, she decided to enter the nearest café and stay for some refreshment. Dani had no intention of shying away from her workload, but simply had a sudden desire to get more acquainted with the locals. The woman serving was a few years older than herself and rather plump. Frizzy curls were pinned back in a severe bun, but her warm smile helped to soften the harsh effect.

'I'll be with you in a moment,' she said, whirling past the table Dani had chosen by the window.

Bevan took the opportunity to survey the establishment and her fellow customers, none of whom appeared to be under the age of 55. The décor was old-fashioned. But a brand new, shiny black Italian coffee machine dominated the cramped area behind the counter. The sight of it filled Dani with optimism.

The friendly waitress finally reached her table, fishing a pen out of an apron pocket. She paused, with the ballpoint hovering expectantly over a pad. 'Now, what can I get you?'

'Just an Americano, please.'

'Milk?'

'On the side, thanks.'

A few minutes later, the lady returned with the steaming cup, after a reassuring amount of noise had been generated by the huge machine in the corner. She lingered for a second. 'Are you one of the Glasgow detectives here to investigate that woman's death, up on Ben Lomond?'

Bevan sipped the strong coffee, nodding her head slowly. 'Am I that conspicuous?'

The lady smiled. 'Not really, it's just that we mostly get old folk in Ardyle off-season like this. Coachloads come from all over Britain to tour the

Trossachs. Everyone else is a local.'

The policewoman put out her hand. 'I'm Detective Chief Inspector Danielle Bevan.'

'I'm Charlotte Wallace. I run this place with my husband. He and I went out with the search party at first light on the morning after the climbers were reported missing.'

Dani gestured for Charlotte to join her. The woman pulled out a chair and told one of the girls loitering behind the counter to start taking the orders.

'Which part of the hillside did you search?' Dani asked.

'The mountain rescue boys sent us up the tourist path, towards Sron Aonaich. We didn't see a single soul that way. Stuart and I carried on searching until mid-afternoon. Our rescue leader was still looking for the other fella in the group, Goff was it?'

'Yes, that's right.' Dani savoured the bitter tang of her rather excellent cup of coffee, allowing Charlotte to elaborate.

'You think he's the man who killed that girl?'

'We can't be sure, but he's certainly one of our principal suspects.'

'The police can't truly believe he's still alive out there?' The woman's face was incredulous.

Dani instantly got the feeling that Charlotte Wallace was expressing a view held by the entire populous of Ardyle.

'Well, we don't think he's actually living out in the national park somewhere, if that's what you mean, but we're fairly confident he may be lying low in a neighbouring town or village.' Dani placed her empty cup into its saucer with a clatter. The sound seemed to echo around the now near-empty café.

Charlotte's face became fixed in a grim line. 'I don't know why the police never confer with us locals. It's always the same, even when the school kids went missing all those years ago. They must just think we're a bunch of country bumpkins, without the brains we were born with.' She crossed her arms indignantly. '*Ardyle* is the nearest settlement to Ben Lomond, and your fugitive certainly never turned up here, because one of the residents would have clocked him straight away.'

Dani sat forward in her seat. 'Go on,' she urged.

'To the north of Ben Lomond, the lochs provide an impassable barrier between a walker and the nearest proper village. To the south and east lie thick forest and steep mountain ranges. If Goff had been out on the hillside all night in that weather, he'd *never* have got past those obstacles. The man is clearly dead, Detective Chief Inspector, and if anyone had thought to ask the opinion of us locals, we would have informed you of that fact over a week ago.'

Chapter Twenty Three

When Dani asked Mrs Wallace to expand upon her theories, the detective was immediately hustled into a back room of the café, where Stuart Wallace was sitting at a desk in a tiny office space.

The man looked up from an accounts ledger, peering at Dani through small, round glasses. Charlotte introduced them both and encouraged her husband to bring out his seemingly exhaustive collection of Ordnance Survey maps, before leaving them to it, returning to her duties front of house.

Mr Wallace laid out two or three of the maps on top of the already cluttered worktop, creating a bumpy terrain reminiscent of the mountain ranges themselves. He plucked a pencil out of a pot and drew an imprecise circle around Ben Lomond.

'The mountain rescue lads are fantastic,' he began. 'But most of them hail from Stirling and Aberfoyle. They don't know the hills quite as well as us folk who've been climbing them since childhood.' Stuart used the pencil as a pointer, to highlight the areas he was referring to. 'The dead woman was found here. Just beneath the western edge of the Ptarmigan ridge. If her companion had been within the same vicinity, he may have wandered outside of the national park, into the wooded area which borders Loch Lomond, just here.'

Dani examined the area closely. 'Didn't the mountain rescue team already search there?'

Stuart ran a hand through his silvery hair. 'It's a huge area, Detective Chief Inspector, they may well have touched upon it, but a number of us locals know that forest extremely well. I think you should look again, this time focussing on the band of territory running along the eastern banks of the loch, right here.' He outlined a narrow strip of hill and forest with the tip of his pencil.

'Okay,' Dani responded carefully. 'If I go ahead and authorise this, will you agree to join in the search with us?'

DCS Nicholson took a great deal of persuading to release the funds necessary for another major man hunt. Dani had to put her reputation on the line to assure him it was a worthwhile exercise, so she sincerely hoped it would be.

It was damp first thing, but mild and muggy, with the forecast suggesting brighter skies as the day progressed. Dani had scraped together a party that was thirty strong, including Stuart Wallace and a few of his hill-walking friends. Bevan had the idea, late last evening, of asking Bill Hutchison to join the search. She thought it might give him a sense of purpose and a feeling he was involved in the investigation.

Bill was in fact, the first to arrive. His tall, lean figure, in waterproofs and hiking boots, could be spotted at the head of the forest track as soon as she and Andy pulled up in the police van.

'He looks creepy, stood there,' Andy commented quietly, as they trudged along to join him.

'We need all the help we can get,' Dani replied.

Once they were all assembled, Bevan split the volunteers and police officers up into groups, with an experienced walker leading each one. Stuart gave them a brief talk about the terrain before they set off across the forest. Bevan ordered her men to check in with the base back in Ardyle every thirty minutes.

Dani decided to keep Bill in her group, along with a handful of folk from Ardyle village. As the morning wore on, she became quite impressed by Bill's knowledge of the geography and history of the area. It began to feel like one of the hikes she liked to take with her father, when she had the free time that was.

Bill suggested they take a detour in the direction of Rob Roy's prison. Dani felt this might be too far out of their search area, but finally agreed, knowing they had to cover all possibilities.

Dani was surprised by how steep the eastern banks of the loch were. In some places, a sheer rock face shelved straight into deep water. The DCI decided to ask her team to search the jagged inlets and tiny, naturally occurring islands that populated the banks of Loch Lomond itself.

Bill Hutchison strode off ahead, seemingly comfortable with the continuously undulating landscape. After another mile, Bill appeared to have stopped to look at something. Dani watched him carefully as the rest of the group grew closer. The man's progress had been halted by a gushing burn, which was cascading down the hillside and dropping into a cove, smoothed out of stone, which lay about thirty feet below. Bill turned to look at her, slowly beckoning the team over. When she was by his side, Bill pointed silently downwards into the plunge pool at the base of the waterfall.

An object was caught in the circular swell. Dani could make out an occasional flash of dark blue material which she took for a waterproof jacket of some kind. Then she noticed the hair. For a fleeting moment, the body bobbed up enough so that the scalp was clearly visible from their vantage point on the cliff top above. She promptly reached for her mobile phone and called off the search.

Chapter Twenty Four

'Why wasn't the body discovered first time around?' DCS Nicholson demanded, with a clipped tone which revealed his frustration and anger.

'We took the advice of Central Scotland Mountain Rescue when we drew up the original search parameters, Sir. They focused us on the Ben Lomond National Park. It was only as a result of Mr Wallace thinking outside the box, that we even considered searching the banks of Loch Lomond itself. We're talking about hundreds of miles of terrain.' Dani felt herself shifting uncomfortably in her seat. She knew Nicholson hailed from the Highlands and just hoped he understood the limitless nature of the task.

'Okay. I'll emphasise to the press that we're extremely lucky to have located Goff's body at all.' The DCS's voice had noticeably softened. 'What condition is the corpse in Danielle?'

'We've not got the PM results yet. The pathologist performed a preliminary examination at the scene. Thankfully, the water in the loch is very cold. This has helped to preserve the body to a certain extent. The man had definitely been dead for several days at the very least. The pathologist would guess a week or more but after this long, it isn't going to be possible for him to give us an absolute on the time of death.'

Nicholson sighed heavily. 'Just make sure you're a hundred percent sure it's Goff before notifying the next of kin. This development will mean a complete change of tack for the investigation. Send me an update on fresh strategies by end of play today.'

Dani only just had the chance to answer before

her boss abruptly ended the call.

Bevan took a deep breath and straightened her suit jacket. She strode confidently out of the little office and into the Town Hall, where her team were gathered around expectantly, talking in excited whispers, waiting for her to tell them what on earth to do next. Dani was aware that not all of the men had taken part in the search. Many were hearing the news about the recovery of the body second hand. She knew this needed to be remedied, fast.

'At 11.45am, the body of an adult male was discovered on the banks of Loch Lomond, two and a half miles west of the Ptarmigan ridge, at Rubha Curraichd. The cadaver had been in the water for a few days at the very least. I'm betting it's been there since Goff went missing. The body was in a fairly advanced state of decay. The PM will take place tonight. We should have an identification and a cause of death by first thing tomorrow morning.'

Hands began to shoot up around the hall. She glanced over at her DC. 'Andy.'

'Do we still have Goff in the frame for Joanna Endicott's murder?'

'It depends on the time of death, which, unfortunately, the pathologist isn't confident that he can pin-point with any great accuracy.'

DS Driscoll spoke next. 'It's conceivable that Goff killed Joanna and then got into difficulties himself. I had a long chat with Stuart Wallace this morning. When he heard where the body had washed up, he suggested that if Goff had continued following the Ptarmigan ridge around from the point where we found Joanna, it would have eventually led him into the forest. If it was dark, or the visibility was bad, the man could have stumbled straight off the side of a cliff into the water. It's possible to completely lose your bearings out there at night.'

Andy furrowed his brow. 'How come Bill Hutchison knew exactly where to look, Ma'am. He deliberately led you along the eastern banks of the loch, didn't he?'

Dani had been expecting this question. 'Hutchison had lived most of his life in Ardyle, just like Mr and Mrs Wallace. Bill told me he had a feeling that Goff may have fallen off one of the rocky outcrops into the loch. The man certainly didn't have a motive to kill Daniel Goff, if that's what you're driving at.'

'It's just that he's your textbook psychopath, Ma'am. The first opportunity he gets to be involved in the investigation, he discovers a body. The guy gives me the heebie-jeebies.' Andy shivered theatrically, earning a few sniggers from his fellow officers.

DC Sammy Reid stepped forward. 'Bill and Joy Hutchison always claimed the children who died up on Ben Lomond thirty years ago spoke to them from beyond the grave; particularly their son, Neil. They said the kids told them if someone was lost or injured on the mountain and where to find them.'

The room fell absolutely silent, with no one knowing quite what to say. Some of the men stared resolutely at their shoes.

'Are you suggesting this was how Bill knew where Daniel Goff was?' Dani asked levelly.

Sammy smiled and shook his head. 'No, of course not. I just meant that people handle their grief in odd ways. The fantasy that the Hutchisons have created, where the dead children act as guardian angels for folk out on the mountain, is very important to them. It's crucial for the couple to be able to maintain it. I reckon Bill must have studied the maps for hours on end and racked his brain to think of all the places where a body might have wound up. Then, when he steered you in the right direction during the search, it seemed to prove his story correct.'

'I can see exactly what you mean,' Dani added. 'It makes perfect sense.'

Andy still looked concerned. 'Yes, I can totally buy that theory, but now I'm wondering just how far Bill Hutchison would go to prove that these spirits from the dead really are communicating with him and his wife. Would he go to the lengths of killing Goff and dumping the body in a place that only he could locate?'

Dani sighed. 'Okay, I don't think we can discount Bill as a suspect. Let's find out when he and Joy arrived in Ardyle and check their alibis for the 12 hour window in which Joanna Endicott was killed and Daniel Goff went missing. Andy, you can handle that.'

Sammy Reid raised his hand. 'I know we've got to investigate them, but just for the record, I don't believe the Hutchisons could do something like this. They might be delusional and weird, but they're both pretty harmless.'

Dani nodded. 'Point taken and duly noted, Constable.'

Then she turned on her heels and headed purposefully back towards the wee office, where she needed to draft a new strategy proposal for the Detective Chief Superintendent, perfectly aware it had to be one that didn't make it appear as if she'd completely taken leave of her senses.

Chapter Twenty Five

The body laid out on the slab had a recognisably human form. The arms, legs and head were all intact. To Detective Sergeant Phil Boag, this made the state of the cadaver even more disturbing.

The face and stomach were horribly bloated, with a criss-crossing of thick blue veins clearly visible beneath the paper-thin skin. Decomposition was evident in a number of areas, along with several gruesome indications of where water-borne creatures had been feeding off the corpse.

Phil automatically put a hand up to the mask attached to his face, just to make sure it remained firmly in position. 'Can you extract a DNA sample?' He asked.

Dr Culdrew grimaced. 'It's going to be tricky after the amount of time he spent in the water. I'll try, but it won't stand up in a court of law. There are too many expert witnesses out there now who will testify to the ambiguity of DNA evidence extracted after this long in fresh water.'

Boag nodded. 'Would it be enough to satisfy us that this is Goff?'

'I believe we can be pretty sure of that already.' The doctor pulled back the lips to reveal a set of yellowed but thoroughly intact teeth. 'I examined Daniel Goff's dental records and compared them to the set we have here. It's definitely Goff. I'm a hundred percent certain of that.'

'Good, that's something to tell the boss. What about cause of death?'

'I can't be quite so unequivocal there, I'm afraid.' Dr Culdrew gently shifted the head to one side.

'There's a nasty wound to the base of the skull just here. It damaged a significant amount of the man's brain tissue. My opinion would be that this is what killed him. However, the blow could have been received when his head hit a rock on the way down. Goff was certainly dead when his body went into the water. There are no signs of defensive wounds, so either this was accidental or as a result of being hit from behind without warning.'

'Can you give me a time of death?'

Dr Culdrew sucked the putrid air in through his teeth. 'Goff's been in the water for a week at the very most. I can't give you a more specific time frame than that. The core body temperature has been completely distorted by the coldness of the water. But then you knew I was going to say that.'

Boag nodded again. 'What would your opinion be, Dr Culdrew, entirely off the record, of how this man died?' Phil knew that this particular pathologist was a keen theoriser and wasn't absolutely slavish about sticking to the scientific evidence.

Culdrew stood back and placed a hand on his chin. 'I very rarely have a body on my slab recovered from a remote loch that hadn't been dumped there deliberately. Goff wasn't weighted down, which precludes pre-meditation in the act. There's a slim possibility the man fell in by accident. But most likely he was killed and the body deposited in the water by his murderer. The loch was the nearest available disposal site. The killer cannot have had the time or the necessary equipment to dig a grave, which would have been a more thorough method of disposal. This is either a crime of passion or a spur of the moment thing.'

Boag thought this was an interesting choice of words. 'Might Goff have been murdered by a woman?'

'As he was attacked from behind and no attempt was made to shift the body away from the murder scene, I'd say yes. This person was either physically unable to do it or didn't have the time. However, Goff was tall and the blow delivered with considerable force, so I'd say the woman would have to be 5'7" or over.'

'Could Goff have been killed by the same person as Joanna Endicott?'

'Don't push your luck Sergeant,' Culdrew chuckled. 'I couldn't say one way or the other. The methods of killing are quite different, yet neither appeared to have been pre-planned. The murder weapon in each case was either bare hands or something found nearby, like a rock or a tree branch. Yet two people are dead, within close proximity and during a similar time frame. If I were you, I would certainly be looking for one killer.'

Dani read through Phil's report in silence. The logs were crackling in the grate and the warmth from the flames made her sleepy. Andy sat in the armchair opposite, a glass of whisky cradled in his hands.

'So it's definitely Goff.' She declared.

'Which puts us pretty much back at square one. It also begs the question who it was that tried to break into the bothy that night, if Goff was already swimming with the fishes by then.'

'I still believe we've made some progress.' She shifted up straighter in her seat. 'I think we're forming a better picture of the killer. This wasn't planned. Something happened out there on the mountain to trigger these deaths. Nobody deliberately brought along a murder weapon.'

'I know that Dr Culdrew suggests there was only one killer, but I can't help thinking the two victims were treated really quite differently. Joanna was left out in the open, with no attempt made to cover her up or even obscure her body. Yet the killer disposed of Daniel Goff very carefully. He was placed in the Loch. We weren't supposed to discover that he was dead at all.'

Dani thought about this for a moment. 'Perhaps the murderer was being clever. With Joanna dead and Daniel Goff unaccounted for, the police would single in on Goff as their chief suspect, which is exactly what we did. This has given our man a full week to cover his tracks.'

'So has our killer got anything at all to do with the death of Amit Batra?'

Dani shook her head in frustration. 'I don't know, Andy, I just don't know.'

Chapter Twenty Six

Dani Bevan had pretty much discounted James Irving as a suspect in the murders of Joanna Endicott and Daniel Goff. So she didn't feel too concerned about agreeing to meet with him in Edinburgh the following day.

Irving was visiting his parents for a weekend and had called Dani late the previous evening to suggest they get together whilst he was in Scotland. Bevan needed to stop in Falkirk anyway, to question the Hutchisons' neighbours, so it didn't seem like much of a diversion.

Andy had confirmed that Bill and Joy Hutchison arrived in Ardyle two days after Joanna Endicott's body was found. Dani wanted to check the Hutchisons were actually at home in Falkirk before that time. The couple's house was exactly as Dani would have envisaged. It was a new-build, detached but small. The front garden was immaculate, even though the Hutchisons' had been away for several days. Dani wondered if someone came over to tend it.

Luckily, this was the kind of estate populated by stay-at-home mums and retired folk. Bevan was guaranteed to find somebody at home in the middle of the day. She tried the Hutchisons' closest neighbour first. There was no reply, so she walked across to another house which stood on the corner of a quiet junction. She spotted an elderly lady at the kitchen window as she strode up the driveway.

Dani showed the woman her warrant card and encouraged her to look at it closely, pointing out the details which indicated it was genuine. The DCI knew full well that many ladies of this age would open the door to any old chancer flashing a photo driving licence.

Dani allowed the lady, who introduced herself as Rita McCulloch, to make them both a cup of tea. She didn't particularly want one but sensed that Rita was keen to make an occasion of it. The living room was spacious and warm. Dani removed her rain jacket and folded it neatly on the sofa next to her. She glanced at the photographs lining the mantelpiece and noted that Rita was a grandmother several times over.

'I wanted to ask you some questions about the Hutchisons, Mrs McCulloch. Do you know the family well?' Dani took the cup from Rita's tray and winced at how hot it was.

'Are Joy and Bill alright? There's been no one at home the last few days,' the woman asked with alarm, lowering herself into an armchair.

'They're absolutely fine, don't worry. Mr and Mrs Hutchison are in Ardyle, consulting with us in the Joanna Endicott murder inquiry. Their knowledge of the local area has proved to be extremely valuable.'

Rita shook her head and tutted. 'I'm really not sure that's a very good idea, Detective Chief Inspector.'

Dani was intrigued. 'Why not?'

'Because Bill and Joy haven't really been able to move on from the death of their son. This whole business will bring it all back up again.'

'The Hutchisons came to us voluntarily. They wanted to help.' Dani took a tentative sip of tea, wondering if it would ever cool down.

Rita sighed. 'Aye, I expect they did. It's such a shame. Their eldest daughter Louise has a couple of wee boys herself. They live in Glenrothes. I've told Joy countless times that they need to move up there to be closer to her. See the grandchildren every day and be a proper part of their lives, that's the only way to get over it.'

Dani nodded, thinking this was sensible advice. 'When was the last time you saw Joy and Bill?'

'It would have been Wednesday morning of last week, because Bill brings my wheelie bins back up the drive after collection. I waved at him from the window.'

'Do the Hutchisons ever talk to you much about what happened to their son?'

Rita gave a wry smile. 'I've had to work hard to *stop* them talking about him over the years.' The lady gestured towards a photograph of a handsome young man, taking pride of place on the mantelpiece. 'My grandson Chris was killed in Afghanistan a couple of years ago. Joy and Bill got me through it. I had to be strong for my son and daughter-in-law you see, but when I came home I would collapse with grief. Joy recognised the state I was in straight away. They took care of me for months. During that time, they talked about wee Neil a great deal. I talked about Chris too, mind, but once I'd passed through the worst of the grief I knew I needed to stop. I had to let the lad go. Bill and Joy have never been able to do that with their Neil.'

'Do you think there's a reason why they haven't been able to let him go?'

'He still haunts them.' Rita smiled a little and explained, 'I know my Christopher was killed serving his country, doing the job he always wanted to do. He knew the risks and still decided to follow his dream. I'm quite aware Chris is at peace. That knowledge allows me to move forward with my life, even at my age. But Joy and Bill think Neil's still got something to tell them. They believe the wee bairns' spirits are still out there on that mountain. I've tried for twenty years to get the pair to see reason, but it hasn't worked. So now we tend to avoid the subject altogether. But I know Joy and Bill still think about him and the other children regularly. They probably will right up until the day they die.'

Dani raised the cup to her lips and flinched; finding it was suddenly stone cold. 'Thank you for the tea, Mrs McCulloch, you've been very helpful indeed.'

Bevan was still feeling unsettled as she located a parking space in central Edinburgh and squeezed her car into it. Dani didn't know the city very well, so had arranged to meet James at the coffee shop in Jenner's Department Store on Princes Street, a place she used to visit with her father when they first moved to Scotland.

When she stepped out of the cramped, antiquated lift which had deposited her on the top floor, Dani immediately saw her friend seated by the window. It looked as if he'd already ordered for her. Irving's face broke into a wide grin as he caught sight of her approaching. He leapt up and placed a kiss on each of her cheeks.

'Sorry I'm late,' she said, sliding onto the seat opposite. 'I was interviewing a witness.'

James looked at little sheepish. 'I hope you don't mind, I ordered for the both of us.'

Dani glanced down at a huge slice of strawberry gateau, oozing with whipped cream and wedges of fruit and the bath-sized mug of milky coffee next to it.

'I realise that's the kind of cake no woman would ever select for herself. But for some reason, I thought you might be in need of it.'

'Actually, I didn't have time for lunch and I really am.' Dani found herself tucking into the gateau, which was perfectly light and not at all sickly, simply allowing James to talk. She watched his face closely as he detailed his journey to Edinburgh. He then described the hysteria he encountered upon arriving at his parents' home, where they were busy preparing for his father's seventieth birthday party the following evening.

Dani felt James possessed a kind face, which was expressive and open. Dani sensed she came across as quite the opposite, her expression being often guarded and closed. It was a hazard of the job, she'd always supposed. She was trained to give nothing away. Dani took a gulp of the milky coffee, feeling it warm and comfort her, immediately deciding she would always associate that pleasant sensation with the man seated before her.

'I got your card. It was kind of you to send it. You must have been busy.'

'It only took a moment. I appreciated the flowers, too. It's been a difficult week for the both of us. You realise I can't discuss the details of the case, don't you?'

James nodded. 'Of course, but I know you found Daniel Goff, it's all over the news. I really believed he'd killed Jo.'

'Are you still in contact with Philippa Graves?'

'God, no. I couldn't bear the woman before all of this stuff happened, so I'm unlikely to be friends with her *now*.'

'How tall is she, would you say?'

James considered this carefully. 'Well, like almost all young ladies these days, she tottered about for most of the time in impossible heels. Padding about the bothy, however, I'd say she was 5'4" maybe? She was a good few inches shorter than Jo. Sorry, I would have taken more notice of Philippa's height if I'd fancied her.'

Dani laughed. 'Don't worry, that's very helpful.'

As they stood up to leave, James fished an incredibly elaborate printed card out of his jacket pocket. 'It's an invite, to Dad's party tomorrow night. I know its short notice and you're probably madly busy with the case, I just didn't want you to be able to claim I'd left you out.'

Dani was momentarily stymied. 'Oh, thanks. I'll try my best. I can't guarantee I'll be able to make it.'

'Sure,' James said with an easy going smile, 'but if it turns out you're free after all, it might just be fun.'

Chapter Twenty Seven

When Dani entered the incident room at 9am on the dot, she was immediately confronted by the unexpected presence of Bill Hutchison, sitting ramrod straight on one of the plastic chairs in the centre of the hall.

'Is everything okay?' Dani asked as she walked towards him.

'I'd like a word please, if you got the time, Detective Chief Inspector.'

'Of course, follow me into my office. We'll have a little more privacy in there.'

Dani was annoyed at being caught off guard. She hadn't even had the opportunity to settle behind her desk and enjoy the take-out cappuccino she'd just bought from the Wallaces' café. 'Would you like a coffee yourself?' Bevan offered amicably, as she gestured for the man to take a seat.

'Detective Constable Calder is already fetching me one, thank you.'

He'd be loving that, Dani thought to herself and couldn't suppress a wry grin. 'Now, how may I be of assistance, Bill?'

'My neighbour, Mrs McCulloch, told us you'd been speaking with her.'

'Yes, it's normal procedure. You were the person who discovered Daniel Goff's body. We needed to check your alibi for the time of his death.' Bevan kept her voice perfectly level, trying to assess Hutchison's mood. 'Can you confirm that you and Mrs Hutchison were at home in Falkirk during the weekend of Saturday, 16th October?'

Bill's mouth dropped open in surprise. He had

clearly expected to be the one asking the questions. 'Yes, of course. In fact, our daughter and grandchildren were visiting on the Sunday afternoon. She could verify that for us.'

'Good. One of my team will give her a call this morning.'

'Oh, fine. Only, am I a *suspect*?'

Dani smiled as warmly as she was able. 'We're simply ticking boxes, Bill, that's all.'

'I see.' He shuffled about in his chair, looking as if he was about to say something else when Andy burst into the room with a scowl on his face. He placed a cup of what appeared to Dani to be the contents of the washing up bowl down on the desk.

'Er, thanks,' Bill said instead.

'I want to keep you in the loop, Mr Hutchison, but as you can imagine, we're rather busy,' she continued.

'How did Daniel Goff die?' The man blurted out.

'I can't tell you that.'

'I think you should speak with the policeman who originally investigated my son's death. He's still alive, I've checked. His name is Ronnie Sheldon and he retired ten years ago. He now lives in Crieff. I've got the address here.' Bill reached into his coat pocket.

'Hold on a minute,' Dani put up a hand. 'Where on earth has this come from?'

'We got to know Ronnie quite well back then. His wife counselled the families of the children who died. He was a good man. The thing is, he was a fanatic fan of the 'Jags' - Partick Thistle, I mean.'

Dani wasn't quite sure what she should say to this. 'I know the team, yes.'

'Their strip is very distinctive, with a thistle set on a red and yellow background. My wife, you see, she dreamt about the emblem last night. Joy wouldn't normally be able to tell you one Scottish football strip from another, but the minute she woke up this morning, that was the image imprinted on her brain – a black thistle against red and yellow. As soon as she told me, I knew what it meant. I needed to contact Ronnie again.'

Bevan sighed in exasperation. 'Joy could have seen that logo *anywhere*, Mr Hutchison. These images imprint themselves on our subconscious mind all the time. We don't have to be footie fans to notice them.'

Bill leaned forward. 'Then why that particular team and why now? It *must* mean something, Detective Chief Inspector. Can't you see that?'

Dani took several deep breaths and counted to ten in her head. 'I will get in touch with Mr Sheldon, *when* I've got a spare moment. It might be worthwhile to see what he remembers from back then.'

Bill Hutchison finally let his tensed up body relax. 'Thank you, Ms Bevan. I'll inform Joy straight away.'

Andy Calder rocked back and forth in his chair with laughter.

'Be careful, or you'll have another heart attack,' Dani said dryly.

The DC finally managed to control his mirth. 'You know, I can't decide if the guy's a total fruitcake or if he's very cleverly trying to put us off the scent.'

'I think the couple are genuine. Bill certainly believes what he's saying.'

'They'd be better off with a few sessions of counselling than in digging up the case of the dead schoolchildren all over again. It's like they're deliberately torturing themselves.'

'I suppose it's difficult to know how people will react to the death of a child. I'm not averse to speaking with Ronnie Sheldon. He may have some tips on the best way to handle the Hutchisons. His wife was a police counsellor back then and spent a great deal of time with the bereaved families.'

'It's your call, boss.' Andy shrugged his shoulders.

'How are you and Clark getting on with the CCTV motorway footage?'

'We're working through it, slowly but surely. There's a list of names that Rick is currently checking out. It just takes time, that's all.'

'Can you spare me for a few hours this evening?'

Andy looked at his colleague quizzically. 'Yes, of course.'

'Good. If you need me, I'll be on my mobile.'

Chapter Twenty Eight

Bevan had very few items of smart clothing with her. She selected a simple, figure-hugging black dress which Dani occasionally wore with a jacket for meetings. She partnered it with a pair of simple red pumps and added a dash of crimson to her full, heart-shaped lips. The detective's dark hair was styled in a low maintenance crop which required little effort for special events beyond a wash and blow dry.

The journey didn't take long. It was just before 8pm when Dani pulled up onto the gravelled driveway of the Irving's house in Leith. It was certainly impressive from the outside. Dani parked next to a brand new Mercedes sports car, taking care not to bash the immaculate paintwork as she climbed out.

It was a mild evening and the front door was wedged open to allow guests to come and go freely. Dani knew she was going to have to fight the urge to inform her hosts that even in such a salubrious part of Edinburgh, this wasn't a great idea.

Dani took in her surroundings, partly as a wide-eyed party guest and partly in the role of an organised criminal, checking out the premises for a future break-in, deciding on entry and exit routes and totting up what was worth stealing.

James emerged from an enormous kitchen-diner into the main hallway, with an open bottle of champagne in his hand. 'Dani! Come and grab a drink.'

She brushed her lips against his cheek, allowing

him to place his free hand at the base of her spine and direct her towards the rear of the property, where most of the revelry seemed to be taking place. A conservatory with doors wide open to the dark sky led out into a patio area where numerous small groups were gathered around blethering. Little chains of fairy lights had been strewn across the trees and hedgerows in the vast garden, making the scene look magical.

A three-tiered cake sat in the centre of the dining table and an impressive collection of beautifully wrapped gifts surrounded it.

'Oh, shit,' Dani gasped. 'I haven't brought a present.'

James laughed, 'don't worry. I really didn't expect you to.' He handed her a flute of bubbly and took her out into the garden, where a handsome grey-haired man in a stripy, open-collared shirt greeted them warmly.

'This is my guest, Dani Bevan,' James explained cheerfully.

'Happy Birthday, Mr Irving,' Dani said. 'You have a very lovely house.'

'Call me Jim, please. Now, my wife, Linda, has organised some entertainment. There's a magician circulating around here somewhere and a lady in the summer house will tell your fortune, if you cross her palm with silver, of course! Perhaps you youngsters will enjoy it more than us old fogies.'

Dani smiled gratefully as James found them a seat opposite a small ornamental pond.

'I definitely approve of being referred to as a 'youngster',' Dani commented, sipping her champagne.

'Well, that's what you get when you frequent parties full of seventy year olds. Now, if we were out together having a drink at the Liquid Room, we may not be perceived in quite the same way.'

'We'd best avoid it then.'

James chuckled. 'Oh yes, my clubbing days are well and truly over.'

'Are many of your family here?'

'My sister and her husband are around somewhere. Grant is always the life and soul of any shindig. Sally's probably helping Mum with the food.' James glanced about him, but didn't appear to be making any great efforts to locate them.

'Have you got siblings?'

Dani shook her head. 'It's just me and Dad. We've never been big on parties. If there's a birthday celebration on Colonsay, we all just meet up in the pub.'

'Sounds like a wonderful idea. My mother's added ten years to her age organising this party. You'd have thought it was a royal coronation.'

'But it's really nice to be able to do something special like this. It's just so, *normal*. Believe me, in my line of work that is the greatest compliment I can give.'

Bevan started to feel chilled. She suddenly wished she'd brought a shrug or a jacket with her. James noticed her shiver. 'Come on, I'll take you back inside. Looks like the canapés are being brought out. I've been eyeing them up all day.'

Sally and Linda Irving were in charge of the food. James' sister was tall and slender and quite glamorous, but Dani would have said she was a good decade older than her brother. Linda was a more petite lady, who wore her ash-golden hair in a neat, shoulder-length cut. James introduced Bevan to them. Sally immediately shot Dani an inquisitive glance, but covered it up expertly with a beaming smile.

'Lovely to meet you. We aren't often permitted to

get acquainted with James' *friends*. You must be special.'

James' cheeks seemed to flush-up, but Dani wasn't sure if perhaps it was simply the champagne. Linda was struggling to lift a couple of trays laden with finger-food, so Dani offered to help. She took one from her hostess and proceeded to assist James' mother in handing the canapés around.

'Oh, you don't need to do that, you're a guest,' Linda argued.

'It's okay. I won't get a chance to chat with you otherwise.'

The woman looked pleased. 'What do you do for a living, Dani?'

Bevan smiled. It was the question which usually spelt make or break for every new relationship she forged; friend or lover. 'I'm a police detective.'

'My goodness. James nearly specialised in criminal law, you know. Then he decided on corporate. He'd have been too soft for it, if truth be told.' Linda appeared to have taken the news in her stride. But then the woman stopped walking. 'Are you working on the Joanna Endicott murder case?'

'Yes, that's how James and I met.'

Linda put down her tray and led Dani over to a small sofa at the far end of the dining room. They sat close to one another. 'Jim and I have been wondering if James really is alright about Jo's death. We keep asking him, but of course he puts up a brave front. You know what young men are like.'

'It's certainly been very difficult for him, especially with the death of Amit happening so soon afterwards. They were all close friends.'

Linda frowned, obviously not being completely sure if she should say anymore. 'It's just that for the last couple of years, we'd thought James was very keen on Jo. You know how sometimes you can really tell, because of the way a person speaks about someone else. I was convinced they'd get engaged, sooner rather than later.'

To her surprise, Dani felt her stomach tighten into a knot. It was a most unpleasant sensation and one she was not used to. 'I didn't realise their relationship had been a romantic one.'

'Well, James is always extremely cagey with Jim and me about the ladies in his life. We never know for certain. But he and Jo took a holiday last year, to Madeira. They said it was because work had been so frantic they both needed complete relaxation. *I* thought it was the two of them seeing if they were properly compatible. Jo was like that, you see, very business-like. After they returned, all sun-tanned and full of beaming smiles, we were on tenterhooks, waiting for them to finally tell us they were an item.'

Dani politely excused herself and walked out into the garden. She breathed in the cool air. It made her feel slightly better. Dani glanced back towards the house and saw James conversing animatedly with a male guest. To her horror she felt tears welling up in her eyes. James suddenly noticed her standing there, in the centre of the lawn, and began to make a move in her direction. Dani turned and dashed towards the summer house, determined to avoid him.

Bevan didn't notice there was anyone else in there with her until she backed against a table and some cards fell onto the floor. 'I'm terribly sorry,' she said to the woman who was sitting in the shadows, a tasselled shawl pulled tight around her shoulders.

'Close the door and join me,' the woman said. 'He won't follow you in here.'

Dani did as she was told and perched on one of the garden chairs.

'You're upset,' the lady said.

'I've found out something about a man I thought I liked. I need some time to think about what it means.'

'It isn't just that though, is it? You're feeling conflicted about your personal and private life.' The woman reached forward and took her hands. Dani found the gesture oddly comforting.

'Doesn't everyone?' She quipped.

'But it's different in your case.' The woman paused, leaning into the light. 'You do realise that she never blamed you?'

'Who? What for?' Dani was instantly on her guard.

'For deciding to walk home on your own. She never for one moment believed that what followed was your fault.'

Bevan snatched her hands out of the woman's grip, stood up shakily and wrenched open the doors of the summer house. James Irving was standing directly outside with a bemused and hurt expression on his face. Dani stormed straight past. Spotting a passageway running alongside the house, she jogged through it and out onto the floodlit driveway. Then she climbed into her car and sped swiftly away.

Chapter Twenty Nine

After arriving back at her hotel room in Ardyle, Dani had given herself a stern talking to. Only a few days ago, all the details of her mother's alcoholism and suicide had been reported in the national press, along with her photograph. Charlatans like the medium at the Irvings' party used that kind of thing to their advantage. Who in the modern world didn't have problems juggling their private and professional lives?

It was how these people operated. Only a tiny thread of their spiel had to strike a chord with someone. Then they had them well and truly hoodwinked. But Dani had always prided herself on being better than that. She was becoming as bad as the Hutchisons, for heaven's sake.

By the next morning, Dani was feeling more circumspect. As soon as she got into her stuffy office, she dug out Ronnie Sheldon's current address and phone number, which she'd printed off the police database yesterday. He'd retired in 2005, after reaching the same rank as Dani. The man was now 64 years old. She called his number straight away. He answered immediately.

'Mr Sheldon, my name is Detective Chief Inspector Dani Bevan. I'm currently working on the Joanna Endicott murder inquiry. I know that you led the Ardyle investigation back in '83. It may sound off the wall, but I wondered if you might be able to offer me some insights into the behaviour of Bill and Joy Hutchison. They seem to have attached themselves to my case.'

'In what respect, Detective Chief Inspector?'

Ronnie Sheldon possessed a broad Glaswegian accent, apparently un-softened by the years he'd spent living away.

Dani explained how Bill had helped the police to pin-point the whereabouts of Daniel Goff's body.

'I've been following the progress of your inquiry in the press myself,' Sheldon responded. 'I certainly felt there was a strong resonance between your case and the incident with the schoolchildren. I can perfectly understand why the Hutchisons wanted to get involved. They wrote to me and my wife regularly for many years after the case was closed. It was the kind of investigation that stays with you for your entire career. I had young children of my own back then, who were just bairns at the time. Although it shouldn't do, it makes it hit harder.'

'Was there anything unresolved about that case, Ronnie? Why are the Hutchisons so reluctant to let the incident go?'

'From a policing point of view, it was clear-cut. The children got lost in terrible weather that nobody could reasonably have predicted. All of the weans had suffered from hypothermia and exhaustion, but for three of them, the symptoms proved fatal. If you asked my wife Judy, she would tell you that the reactions of the parents were complex, as they are in the aftermath of any tragedy.'

'Would it be possible for me to have a word with your wife?'

'Judy passed away from breast cancer in 2011. But I might be able to find some of her notes from back then.'

'Oh, I'm terribly sorry.'

'Look, I'll see what I can scrape together. Are you still based in Ardyle? I could drive across tomorrow afternoon and speak with you about the case. Judy had piles of patient notebooks and I've got my own papers on the incident. I've not read them for decades. We could have a sort through together if you'd like?'

'That would be great, if you're absolutely certain you can spare the time?' Dani felt her heart beat faster.

The man chuckled. 'Oh aye. The golf course won't miss me for one day. To be frank, this is the first time I've been asked for my input on a live case in over ten years. I'm hardly going to pass that opportunity up!'

Dani called Andy into her office. She'd decided that honesty was going to be the best policy and explained to him how James Irving had sent her flowers and then invited her to his father's shin-dig in Edinburgh. Bevan outlined her conversation with James' mother the previous evening.

'Okay, so it's possible that Irving was in a relationship with Joanna Endicott at the time of her death,' Andy replied steadily. 'But you do realise that the way this evidence was ascertained makes it totally inadmissible? If it turns out James Irving *did* kill Joanna, his defence lawyers would have a field day with you meeting up with him off-duty like this. We'd never secure a conviction. The situation would be even worse than with Richard Erskine.'

'I've been a bloody idiot.'

'Did you sleep with him?'

Dani looked her friend in the eye. 'No, I did not.'

'Then it's salvageable. But we'll need to keep it between ourselves.'

'Would you be prepared to do that?'

'Dani, I'm perfectly aware that if it wasn't for you, I'd never have been allowed back on active service. Not to mention the part where you saved my life.'

'Yeah, that is true.' It was still a mess, but Dani

felt a sense of relief rush through her body.

'Besides, I really don't think Irving's our man. I know he's only got Philippa Graves to vouch for him on the Saturday night Goff and the others went missing, but I never had the sense he'd been lying about drinking that half bottle of whisky and flaking out. The mountain rescue lads said his hangover the next morning was genuine enough.'

Dani thought of something. 'What if it was more than a hangover? Graves could have put something in his drink to make sure he never noticed *her* going back out later.'

'It's possible, but there's no hope of proving it now. For what it's worth, I think Joanna was the type of lass who'd fooled around with plenty of fellers. The guys she'd dated over the last few years in London barely knew anything about her. They had dinner from time-to-time and occasionally had sex. Joanna wasn't searching for a man to settle down with. Maybe she did have a fling with Irving last year, but his mother was probably overstating the matter when she suggested they were on the verge of tying the knot.'

'What if James wanted more from the relationship than she did? Seeing her flirting with Goff and inviting him to come away to Scotland with them might have been the last straw for James.'

'With all due respect, that's how a woman might react, not a man. For us, if a lassie wants to have sex, no strings attached, no commitment required and we can still be mates afterwards, great.'

'I'll be sure to mention that to Carol the next time we meet up.'

Andy laughed. 'When the right time comes for a man to settle down, he chooses a woman accordingly. The next lassie he asks out will be the marrying type – homely, kind, pretty enough and someone who doesn't put it about. Believe me, James Irving hadn't placed Joanna into that category. To him, she was a great mate; fun, sexy, exhilarating and good for the occasional roll in the hay. He wasn't in love with her.'

Dani was genuinely surprised by Andy's insight.

'I'd even go as far as to say that Irving wouldn't have considered looking in London for his soul mate. When Irving finally decides it's time to settle down, he'll come back to Scotland to find his wife.'

'Are you taking an online psychology degree on the quiet?'

Andy chuckled. 'I may be an ill-educated Glasgow boy, but I know James Irving's type. He's public school with pukka parents and a respectable, well-paid career. He'll never choose a life-partner who doesn't fit the mould.'

'Do you know what?' Dani said cheerfully. 'I think you're absolutely right.'

Chapter Thirty

The next day was a Saturday and although Dani was expecting her visit from Ronnie Sheldon in the afternoon, she'd decided to go into the incident room a little later than usual. Dani felt that a slower start might help to get her ideas flowing.

She took a long shower. When she finally emerged from the en-suite, Dani picked up her mobile and tapped on the frequent contacts list. Her dad answered their home phone after several rings.

'Hi, it's Dani. Were you outside?'

'Aye, we've had strong winds overnight. The fences are down.'

'You'll have to ask Cameron to help you fix them. Don't try and do it on your own Dad, please.'

'I'll take a drive over to his place later, if the road is clear. How's the case? Are you still in Ardyle?' Her father sounded genuinely interested.

'We've been set back by the discovery of Daniel Goff's body,' Dani explained.

'I saw it on the news.'

'Did you read the stuff about me in the papers?' Dani waited nervously for his response.

'It was hard to avoid. The higher up you go in the police force, the more you'll have to expect that kind of thing. Luckily for me, I'm surrounded by folk who don't give a damn what's written in the gutter press. I just hope it hasn't caused you problems at work?'

'It will blow over. There've been far worse scandals involving senior police officers in the last few years than this. By comparison, my life is pretty mundane. I was just worried that having Mum's illness raked up again might upset you.'

Huw Bevan chuckled. 'Of course not. When you live on an island on the fringes of the Atlantic Ocean, not much that happens in the outside world does bother you. Don't waste your time fretting about me.'

Dani felt tears spring to her eyes. 'Good. I'm glad things are okay. Just do your best to refrain from shifting any heavy fence posts single-handed now, do you hear? I'll get Jilly O'Keefe to spy on you with her binoculars. She'll let me know straight away if you do!'

'Oh, I've no doubt she would, no doubt at all.'

Dani laughed gently and ended the call, before her dad had a chance to notice that her voice was wavering. As she placed her mobile down on the bed, she spotted there'd been a message from James Irving. Dani ignored it, thinking that perhaps she should delete his number.

Whilst Dani was speaking with her father, the television set on the dressing table had been tuned to a current affairs channel with the sound turned low. One of the breaking news strands rushing across the bottom of the screen suddenly caught her attention. She reached for the remote control and cranked up the volume.

'Dear God!' She loudly proclaimed, pulling on her work clothes and applying her make-up as quickly as possible.

Ten minutes later, she was in the Town Hall. The janitor had kindly wheeled out an old fashioned television set on a trolley for them to use. Dani had it switched onto the BBC News channel. The officers in her team were perched on the edge of desks and seated on every available chair, their eyes glued to the screen.

Dani laid out the facts she had so far gleaned. 'That gentleman there,' the DCI said, pointing at the grainy photograph of a middle-aged man dressed in a police dress uniform, holding up a long-service medal, 'is Ronald Sheldon, known as Ronnie. He was due to travel here this afternoon to show me his notes on the Ardyle case of 1983. He'd been the officer in charge of that investigation back when he was a DI. But Ronnie sadly won't be visiting us today, because he's currently laid out on a mortuary slab in Perth, after his home was subjected to an arson attack in the early hours of this morning.'

'Bloody hell,' Andy muttered.

'This *cannot* be a coincidence. I spoke with Ronnie yesterday. He told me there were notes and files relating to the Ardyle case that he wanted to show me. I have to assume right now that these have all gone up in smoke. According to the Crieff Force, somebody broke into the Sheldon house and started a fire in the sitting room or kitchen at roughly 2am. Ronnie was fast asleep upstairs. The poor guy didn't stand a chance. We're talking about a man who'd served in the police for 35 years.'

'Who knew that Ronnie Sheldon had spoken with you?' Andy immediately enquired.

'Well, Bill Hutchison suggested I get in touch with Sheldon, but I didn't inform him of our plan to meet up.'

'He knew that you were going to speak to Sheldon at some point though, didn't he?' Andy persisted.

'But it was Bill who was desperate for me to get in contact with Ronnie Sheldon in the first place. He was convinced there was a link between the Ardyle tragedy and the murder of Joanna Endicott. To be fair, it looks as if he's been proved right,' Dani declared.

'*Exactly*,' Andy retorted. 'Bill Hutchison's amazing supernatural powers have been shown to be correct, yet again. Funny, that.' A few members of the team snickered.

'Do you seriously believe that Bill did this? Tipped me off to the importance of Ronnie Sheldon as a witness and then burnt him to death in his bed in order to make it look like his wife has the gift of 'second sight'? Why would he do that?'

Andy shrugged his shoulders. 'I don't know, perhaps not.'

'Bill would never have harmed this man.' DC Sammy Reid stepped forward, his face red with anger. 'The Hutchisons got on really well with Ronnie and Judy Sheldon. Judy helped us all through a terrible time. Bill just wouldn't have done something like that to him.' The handsome young officer strode out of the hall, flashing Andy Calder a look of distaste as he passed.

Dani designated tasks and then walked out of the front of the building to locate her young DC. He was leaning against the wall of the Town Hall, his right boot resting on the bricks, smoking a cigarette.

'Andy can be very blunt sometimes, I'm sorry. He should have been far more sensitive to the situation,' Dani said.

'I don't want my past history to affect my performance in this investigation. I shouldn't have got angry, I was just frustrated.'

'You feel fairly certain that Bill Hutchison couldn't have set that fire. This is based on having known the man for over thirty years. That is an insight which is extremely valuable to me. It also happens to be my instinct too. But we have to be open to alternative theories. To ignore them could seriously damage an investigation. It's what makes police officers suffer from tunnel vision. We have to be open to everything, however uncomfortable it makes us.'

Sammy nodded, throwing his stub down and grinding it out on the stone step. 'I know that, but when it impacts upon you personally and your family, it isn't an easy rule to stick to.'

Dani smiled. 'Murder inquiries affect *every* police officer, regardless of whether they have a connection to the events. But now we know that the Ardyle case will have to be re-examined, I'd be within my rights to take you off the investigation.'

Sammy looked horrified. 'I really want to remain on the team, Ma'am. I was only six years old when Katrina died. I recall almost nothing about what went on back then.'

Dani knew this made no difference, but she was also aware that it was entirely her call. The connection between Ronnie Sheldon's death and their current investigation had not been made official. Bevan was inclined to keep Sammy on the team. She liked him, and sensed his knowledge would prove extremely useful. 'For the time being, I will keep you in the unit. But if the DCS decides that you're compromised, I'm afraid you'll have to go.'

Sammy nodded with understanding. 'Thank you, Ma'am, I really appreciate this.'

Chapter Thirty One

Bevan wasn't certain she wanted to speak with Andy Calder right now, so she headed straight back to her office, leaving the men to do their work. She was happy to indulge in constructive debate with her officers, but there was something about Andy's demeanour in briefings at the moment which bordered on defiance. Dani wasn't entirely sure what had got into him.

As soon as the door was closed, Bevan rang the number of the incident room in Crieff for an update. The fire had got hold very quickly and the heat was intense. The ground floor of the property had been virtually incinerated. There appeared to have been a room upstairs used by Sheldon as a study, where some of the items were undamaged. Dani just hoped they might yet be able to salvage something useful out of the debris.

Ronnie Sheldon had died from asphyxiation, as a result of inhaling poisonous fumes. His lungs and respiratory system had also suffered burns due to the heat of the smoke he'd breathed in. Mercifully, Ronnie would have been unconscious or dead by the time the fire itself reached his room. The pathologist was in no doubt that the act should be treated as murder. The accelerant used was so powerful it created an inferno that killed in a matter of minutes.

Dani thought through the implications of this. The arsonist had shown no consideration whatsoever for the life of Ronnie Sheldon. There was no way this could be viewed as a crime of passion. It was pre-meditated and utterly cruel. It many respects, it was quite unlike the murders of Joanna Endicott and

Daniel Goff. She wasn't sure why, but Dani got the feeling that this killing was in some way more personal. In this case, the murderer had set out to completely obliterate Sheldon and everything he held dear. The police unit in Crieff were examining Ronnie's arrest record and trying to eliminate the criminals he'd put away over the years as potential suspects. All lines of inquiry at this stage were valid. Dani suddenly had the sense that she should find Bill and Joy Hutchison. Bevan suspected the news of Sheldon's death was going to hit them hard.

She pulled on her rain jacket and headed out in the direction of the Carraig Hotel. Dark grey clouds were making the town gloomy, even though it was only mid-morning. Bevan entered the foyer and glanced about her. Bill and Joy were sitting, rigidly, on the sofa opposite the reception desk. They were both wearing waterproof jackets zipped up to the neck, even though it was very warm in there.

Bill stood up stiffly as she approached. 'I wanted to come and see you,' he announced, but I wasn't sure I'd be welcome.'

'Let's find somewhere quiet where we can talk.'

The residents' lounge was deserted. They chose a group of seats positioned behind a bookcase and Dani ordered morning coffee. 'Have you seen the news?' She asked.

'Yes,' Joy replied shakily. 'We haven't known what to do with ourselves since we found out.'

'Did you speak with Ronnie, before...,' Bill's words trailed away.

'Only very briefly, I'm sorry. I was due to meet up with him this afternoon. Look, Bill,' Dani leaned forward and lowered her voice. 'Did you mention to anyone that you'd asked me to get in contact with Ronnie?'

Bill considered this for a moment. 'Not directly,

but Joy and I were discussing it here in the hotel, last evening at dinner. The dining room was very full and noisy. I cannot imagine us being overheard. How about you, Detective Chief Inspector, did *you* inform anyone of your plans?'

Another detective might have taken exception to the impertinence of this question, but Dani was beginning to become accustomed to Bill's manner. 'I informed DC Calder, but I never announced it to the entire team. I was waiting to see if it resulted in a proper lead.'

Joy began to wring her hands, her brow furrowing in concern. 'What does it mean, DCI Bevan? Why would somebody want to kill poor Ronnie?'

Bill sat bolt upright and looked at his wife. 'Perhaps that's what your dream meant. It wasn't telling us to *contact* Ronnie Sheldon at all. It was a *warning* that his life was in imminent danger.'

'Hold on,' Dani said sternly. 'We need to stay rational about this. Somebody must have got wind of the fact I was about to interview Sheldon regarding the Ardyle case. They then set out to make sure this wouldn't be possible. Unless the event is entirely unconnected, and Ronnie was killed for another reason.'

Bill raised his eyebrows at this. 'I don't believe that's terribly likely, is it?'

'We've *got* to keep an open mind,' Dani replied with emphasis, trying to ensure she didn't get sucked into adopting the Hutchisons' world view without question. 'For the time being, I'd like you both to stay here in Ardyle. If there's somebody out there who doesn't want the past raking up again then you two might be potential targets. Keep your heads down and stay out of risky situations.'

'We could do some asking around the town, see

what folk can remember about the original investigation. It might not only have been Ronnie Sheldon who possessed information about the case. The locals might divulge more to us than they would the police. We lived here for a long time, Detective Chief Inspector.'

Dani let her eyes roll up towards the ceiling. 'Just for heaven's sakes be careful, there's a particularly nasty murderer out there. Don't make the mistake of underestimating him.'

Dani made her way across the marketplace towards the Town Hall. DC Kendal sprinted down the steps to intercept her path.

'Ma'am! I've been searching for you everywhere. I think I might have discovered something.'

Bevan followed the eager young man inside. He led her towards a trestle table which he had transformed into his work station. A couple of tiny lap-top computers sat open before him. 'I've been looking into the life Daniel Goff led when he was working abroad. I decided to try the same trick I'd used in Stirling and post messages on the Facebook pages of various colleges and universities in all the major European cities. A couple of hours ago, I got a result.'

Dani leant over and scanned his notes.

'I got a reply from my post on the home page of Estudio Toledo, which is a small language college in Madrid. It said that if information was required regarding Daniel Goff, then I should private message a specific Facebook account, which I did.' Kendal summoned an FB page up onto the screen. A photograph of a good-looking forty-something man smiling on a deserted beach stared back at them. 'His name is Gregory McAuliffe. He worked with Daniel Goff, teaching English at the college in

Madrid, in 2004. He's now back in the UK and lives with his wife and children in Oxford. I had a long phone conversation with him after the briefing this morning.'

Dani pulled up a chair.

'McAuliffe was newly married when he spent a year teaching in Madrid. His wife was a trainee doctor and working extremely long hours. McAuliffe had always wanted to spend time abroad, to polish up his language skills, so they both decided this was a good opportunity for him to do it. McAuliffe shared a flat in the city with Goff; the language school had arranged it for them. Greg said he found Goff quiet, clean living, and a perfectly good housemate. But then, one Friday evening, Goff persuaded Greg to come out with him for a drink. When they arrived at the bar, there were two young and very attractive Spanish girls there, who both seemed to know Goff. Greg wasn't totally comfortable with the situation, but he spent a pleasant enough evening with them.

After that point, Goff brought one of the girls, who was called Natalia, over to the apartment a lot. Gregory McAuliffe began a relationship with her. He knows it was stupid, but he was a long way from home and the temptation was too much. A month after it started, Goff confronted Greg in the kitchen of their flat. He produced photographs of him and Natalia together, some of which were extremely compromising. Goff asked McAuliffe for money. In total, Greg paid him several thousand pounds. He realised he'd been scammed and ended his fling with Natalia. Fairly soon afterwards, he returned to the UK, where he told his wife what happened. He knew he couldn't allow himself to be blackmailed indefinitely.

Greg and his first wife subsequently divorced. He is now happily married to somebody else. McAuliffe said he always felt guilty for not reporting Goff to the police, but he was embarrassed about the whole episode and wanted to leave it behind him. When he saw my post, he felt he wanted to warn me about what Daniel was like.'

'So that's how Daniel Goff made his money. We need to speak with Philippa Graves again, as soon as possible.'

Chapter Thirty Two

Philippa Graves was living back at home with her parents in Brentford, West London. It looked like it was a squeeze. The small terraced house had a cramped hallway which led into a sitting room at the rear. After letting Bevan and Calder in, Mr Graves left the three of them alone in this pleasant room to talk.

Philippa was wearing a track suit and her thin mousy hair was secured in a ponytail, as if she'd just returned from a trip to the gym. Mr Graves came in a few minutes later with a tray of teas and a plate filled with bourbon biscuits. He set it down in silence and slipped straight out.

'Have you found out who attacked Amit?' She enquired when her dad had gone.

'That isn't our case,' Dani explained. 'We are here to talk about Daniel.'

Philippa looked puzzled. 'Daniel Goff? What has he got to do with me?'

'When did you first meet Mr Goff?' Andy asked.

The woman crossed her legs and her eyes darted to and fro. 'He came to Jo's flat just over a year ago. They'd hooked up for the occasional drink since he'd been living in London. After that we met at parties.'

'And when did you and Goff decide on the plan to extort money from Amit Batra?'

Philippa flinched. 'What do you mean?'

'Well, the idea was that you would begin a relationship with Batra. Goff would take incriminating photographs of the two of you together, and then he would threaten to show them to Tanisha Batra if Amit didn't pay him. Or have we got that wrong, Ms Graves?' Andy kept his expression steely.

Philippa sat very still. Tears began to fill her large eyes and gradually escape onto her cheeks. 'Things hadn't got that far.'

'Then tell us how far they *had* got,' Dani demanded, her voice perfectly level and devoid of sympathy.

'Jo threw a party at the flat about three months ago. It was just a few drinks and nibbles. Daniel Goff was there and James had brought Amit along with him. Towards the end of the evening, Dan sidled up to me and made a joke about Amit obviously fancying me. I laughed it off. But the next time he visited the flat, Dan came to my room and knocked on the door. Jo had clearly told him that I was struggling to find work and was obliged to be flexible with my rent. He sat on the edge of my bed and asked me if I wanted to make some money. Dan said it would be easy for me. He would handle all the difficult stuff – the transactions and things.'

'All you needed to do was seduce Amit Batra,' Bevan stated.

Philippa nodded. 'He was already fairly keen. Life was very difficult for him at home. I genuinely liked Amit. The plan was that Dan would take the photos whilst we were staying in Scotland. It seemed like the perfect opportunity.'

'Had Daniel Goff confronted Amit with any photographs before you set out for Ben Lomond?'

'No, I really don't think so. The only shots Dan had by that stage were of Amit and me out together in restaurants, canoodling a bit. We planned to get some really incriminating ones whilst we were at the bothy. We'd not had the chance by then.' Philippa suddenly looked confused. 'But Amit did behave differently after he was rescued. He wasn't acting the same way with me as he had done before. Perhaps Dan did tell him something on that mountain, or showed him what was on his camera. It's impossible to know what went on when they were stuck up there on the hillside, lost and frightened. I'm just not sure any longer.'

'Did Joanna Endicott know about your blackmail scheme before the holiday to Scotland?'

'No, she didn't. I'm certain Daniel wouldn't have told her. He respected Jo, you see. Dan wouldn't have wanted her to know that's how he made his money.' Philippa looked sheepish and hung her head. 'I didn't really tell Jo about me and Amit either. I don't know why I said that. I suppose I wanted to show that she and I had been close. It wasn't only James bloody Irving who'd been her friend.'

Dani sat forward. 'Were James Irving and Joanna Endicott ever involved in a sexual relationship?'

Philippa glanced up again. She seemed surprised by the question. 'I wouldn't have said so. If they were then they never used our flat. Jo didn't treat the men she slept with very well, but she and James really got on. They were good mates.'

'We'll have to pass this information on to the Metropolitan Police team in charge of Amit Batra's murder inquiry,' Dani said.

'I had nothing to do with Amit's death – I swear. I was here at Mum and Dad's on the night he was killed. My brother was at home too. I wouldn't have hurt him, or Dan. What's going to happen to me now, DCI Bevan?' Philippa looked suddenly like a lost child.

'I'll have a word with the CPS. All you are guilty of right now is the intent to commit blackmail. I don't expect there's enough evidence to charge you. All I'm interested in is who murdered Daniel Goff, Joanna Endicott and Amit Batra, so if you can think of anything else that may be of use to us, call me straight away.'

Philippa took Dani's card. She appeared a little more relaxed.

Bevan glanced at her surroundings. 'Your parents have a nice home here, Philippa. Stay with them for a while and get yourself sorted out. Maybe teaching isn't the right career for you, but something else will be. Steer clear of people offering you easy money. Crime is crime. There isn't a more sanitised version of it. It's a dangerous business and people get hurt. You've been incredibly lucky to come out of this alive.'

Philippa started to cry again. 'I'm sorry, Detective Chief Inspector,' she sobbed. '*Please* don't tell my mum and dad. I promise I'll never do anything like this again.'

Chapter Thirty Three

'Daniel Goff sounds like the sort of chap whose luck was always going to run out eventually,' said DS Driscoll.

'I agree,' Dani Bevan added. 'He was bound to wind up either in prison or dead. But the question remains, who was it that finally caught up with him?'

'Amit Batra's got to be a prime suspect,' Andy suggested. 'Irving thinks that Batra had got hold of Goff's camera somewhere on that mountainside. If it held incriminating photographs of him and Graves, it gives Batra a motive to kill Goff, in order to get the camera off him and ensure his silence.'

'But what about Joanna Endicott, what would Batra's motive be for killing her?' Driscoll said.

'Perhaps she simply got in the way,' Dani chipped in. 'My main concern is who *else* wanted that camera. Batra took it back to Loughton with him and it looks as if he was battered to death for it.'

'So was Goff blackmailing another man?' Andy offered.

'It's certainly a possibility. I think we can rule out James Irving because he's unmarried and is free to have a relationship with anyone he chooses.'

Sammy Reid looked as if he might say something. Dani nodded in his direction to encourage him to contribute. 'Irving said in his statement that Goff had been snapping away with his camera during the climb. Maybe he photographed something inadvertently. Whatever else was stored on the camera may be unrelated to the blackmail.'

'We need to take all of these scenarios under advisement,' Dani announced. 'Meanwhile, I've decided to get myself kitted out and go for a wee walk.'

Bevan took the police 4x4 and drove down to the bothy. The owner told her there was an English family staying there for the half-term break, but that they didn't mind her parking outside and using the footpath behind the cottage.

There were no cars visible, so she assumed the family were out. Bevan took the opportunity to walk around the property and peer into each of the small, dilapidated outhouses which seemed to jut straight out from the hillside. It was sunny, with a fresh easterly breeze. Dani set off along the track that led to the Ptarmigan ridge. She had no intention of climbing Ben Lomond itself, but wanted to get a feel for the terrain.

Whatever was going on in the lives of Endicott, Goff, Batra, Irving and Graves, Dani was convinced that the key to the case lay in what happened out there on the hillside that day. As she fell into her stride, Bevan imagined the progress of the five tourists, each of them embarking on the climb for their own, very different reasons.

The DCI also thought about the schoolchildren, led in their separate groups across the National Park, collecting data and listening intently to the words of the teachers in charge. Her father had been Headmaster of a rural primary school for many years. On Colonsay, the staff and parents were always eager to take the children's lessons out into the glorious countryside that surrounded them. It would have seemed perverse not to. Was it simply a stroke of luck that no similar tragedy had befallen them? Bevan didn't think so.

Progressing past the gushing burn towards the top of the first ridge, Bevan's mind was drawn back to when she had first joined the wee school on Colonsay. It was such a small place that Dani was inevitably taught by her own father on many occasions. She'd certainly sat through umpteen of his assemblies; cross-legged and bored, in the hall which also accommodated every single wedding, christening and funeral party that the villagers threw.

Huw Bevan was strict but fair. Like all good schoolmasters of his generation, he was determined that his pupils should learn the basics of literacy and mathematics, while at the same time developing a strength of character that would serve them well throughout life. Many of his ex-students still wrote to him, explaining how they often referred to his old sayings in times of strife, finding them of great comfort.

If her father's dedicated staff ever took the children out on a trip, they all stayed close together. Huw Bevan wouldn't have dreamt of allowing any of the pupils to stray out of his sight. Ardyle School must have been slightly larger, but not by a huge margin. Dani wondered how those three weans: Katrina, William and Neil, could have become cut off from the rest. The weather must have been a factor, certainly, but something still didn't quite sit right with the detective about the events of that day.

Bevan took a deep breath as she reached the summit of the west ridge. It had been a strenuous climb. The views on this clear day were terrific, with the Arrochar Alps and Loch Lomond in the distance.

But conditions were starkly different on the afternoon that Endicott's group had been there. Visibility was very poor. Continuing along the ridge from this point would have been fraught with dangers. Meandering off the main path could have led a walker straight over the edge of a precipice. Dani strode on, confident that the weather would hold. She checked her smartphone. There was no reception, just like Irving and Graves had claimed. Turning a sharp bend in the ridge, the imposing silhouette of Ben Lomond suddenly appeared before her. She imagined how terrifying it would seem against a dark sky.

The path took her ever upwards. At one point, she had to ascend a small rock-face, placing her fingers carefully into the tiny, smooth hand-holes, shifting her weight onto the toes of one foot in order to hoist herself onto the next plateau. This was definitely not a route for the faint-hearted. She wasn't intending to, but Bevan continued on to the summit. The views across the National Park were breath-taking. It was the school holidays and the top of Ben Lomond was teeming with folk, though she'd seen no one on the Ptarmigan path.

Dani decided to follow the tourist route down the mountain, where she found herself overtaking family groups. Many weary dads had wee-ones secured in carriers to their backs. This track was much less arduous and clearly preferred by beginners. Dani felt it revealed much about Joanna Endicott's personality that she deliberately chose the more difficult path. It was almost as if she had wanted certain members of the group to be unable to complete the climb.

Dani consulted her map and cut across the heathland towards the bothy. Looking at her watch when she reached the jeep, Bevan noted she'd done the ascent in just over five hours; three hours up and two down. Dani saw smoke spiralling upwards from the chimney and a Land Rover Discovery sitting on the gravel next to the police truck. She decided to knock on the door and let the family know she was leaving. A plumpish middle-aged lady, with curly, silver-blond hair answered the door. A handsome Airedale terrier stood on guard by her side.

Bevan displayed her warrant card. 'My name is DCI Danielle Bevan. I wanted to let you know that I'm finished up here and about to head back to the station in Ardyle.'

'Do you have a moment, by any chance, Detective Chief Inspector, only my husband was hoping to have a word?' The woman inched backwards to allow Dani to enter.

The bothy had quite a different atmosphere from when she was last here. A young boy and girl, who Dani would place in their early teens, were lounging on the sofas in the sitting room. A tall, bearded man emerged from the kitchen and introduced himself. 'Do please come in and have a seat. I am Bruce Glasser, and this is my wife, Elaine.'

Dani sat at the kitchen table and repeated her own name and rank. 'What can I help you with, Mr Glasser?'

'It may be nothing at all, but when the owner said a police officer would be up here today, I thought I may as well mention it.'

Bevan nodded her encouragement, noticing out of the tiny windows how the light was rapidly fading and feeling the strains of the day's climb begin to make her limbs heavy.

'Two days ago, whilst Elaine was down in the village getting some supplies, the kids and I saw a man hanging around on the hillside. After twenty minutes or so, I walked over to ask him what he was doing. The chap had a bunch of flowers in his hand. He said he was looking for the memorial to the children who died on the mountain. The flowers were to be laid beneath it. He intimated it was an anniversary of some sort. There wasn't much I could say in response to that, but the fellow headed off along the mountain path soon after and I didn't spot him again. He must have returned by a different route. I wouldn't have thought much of it, but it just felt as if he was hanging around and watching the place. It was most disconcerting. We're actually fairly remote up here in the glen.'

'Would you be able to provide us with a description of this man?'

Bruce Glasser shrugged. 'I'll give it a try.'

'Then could I ask you to come down to the incident room in Ardyle tomorrow morning and provide us with a statement? A police car will be sent over to pick you up. This information might prove to be very important to my investigation.'

'Of course, Detective Chief Inspector. If you really think it will help, I shall be pleased to do my duty,' he replied.

Chapter Thirty Four

DC Kendal downloaded the e-fit software to one of his laptop computers. He carefully inputted the details that Bruce Glasser had supplied them with. When the profile was complete, Kendal printed off a copy and took it over to DCI Bevan.

Dani pinned the picture to a flip chart and gathered her team around it. Like all computer generated images, it was difficult to imagine this random patchwork of features in human, living form. Bevan had often wondered how useful they really were, beyond giving a general indication as to age and sex.

The face staring out at them was partially obscured by a woolly hat, pulled down to cover the ears. The man had dark eyes beneath bushy brows and a stubbly growth on his chin. There were no obviously distinguishing features.

'What age did Mr Glasser think the man was?' DS Driscoll asked.

'He suggested mid-forties. This chap was wearing walking gear and had a rucksack on his back, in addition to the flowers he was carrying. Glasser said he was of average height, possibly 5'10. His accent was Scottish.'

Andy squinted his eyes at the picture. 'Could it have been Bill Hutchison?'

'Well, Bill is in his late sixties for starters, but perhaps he could appear younger, if he covered his grey hair. There is a passing resemblance, I suppose.' She turned towards Sammy Reid. 'This man claimed he was visiting a memorial for the children who died in the Ardyle tragedy. Is there such a thing?'

DC Reid nodded. 'There is a commemorative cairn out on the heathland near Tom Eas. It is positioned equidistant from the points where the three children were found. The pupils at Ardyle Primary School each placed a stone to make up the cairn. There is a small plaque at the bottom. Every ten years since the event, the villagers have gone to lay flowers at the memorial. It happened in April of last year, for the thirtieth anniversary.'

'But there's been no significant anniversary within the last week or so?' Dani inquired.

'No, not that I'm aware of. Perhaps this man was referring to the birthday of one of the children. It certainly wasn't Katrina, she was born in May.'

'Thank you very much, Sammy. I think it might be a good time for me to have another chat with Bill and Joy.'

*

'It's a very powerful place, spiritually,' Joy Hutchison explained, stirring a sugar lump into her tea.

'But neither of us have been out there since the thirtieth anniversary ceremony last year,' Bill continued. 'We occasionally go to the cairn on Neil's birthday, but not always - his grave is in the churchyard, you see. That is where we go to lay our flowers, in the house of God.'

'When is Neil's birthday?' Bevan asked lightly.

'The 25th March,' Joy swiftly replied.

The Wallaces' enormous coffee machine began vibrating loudly and conversation was no longer possible for several minutes. Dani simply sipped her cappuccino in silence and watched Bill and Joy performing an obviously well-rehearsed ritual with their tea-for-two, sloshing in the milk and sharing out the last of the pot between them.

When the machine stopped, Bill leant forward and lowered his voice. 'We've been doing some asking around in the village,' he said in a theatrical whisper.

In spite of herself, Dani felt her interest pique. 'Did you discover anything useful?'

'You may not like what we found out, DCI Bevan,' Joy stated tentatively.

'Oh, yes?'

'We spoke to the landlord at the Rob Roy Bar. Joy and I have known him for years. He began complaining about the heavy-handed police presence in the town. He didn't mind the extra business, but he'd got angry with a group of officers who were in his pub on Friday night. Apparently, a policeman from 'out of town' was regaling the others with tales of how the locals claimed they'd seen visions in dreams and that his boss was actually taking it seriously.'

'Andy,' Dani muttered in disappointment. 'Did he mention any specifics?'

'The landlord couldn't recall, but obviously he was busy serving at the time. If DC Calder *did* let slip that you were going to speak with Ronnie Sheldon, then *anyone* in that pub could have overheard it.'

'And then repeated the tale to all their other kith and kin in Ardyle.' Dani sighed heavily. 'I'm very sorry for this. I believed I could rely on Andy Calder to be discreet. I would never have told him otherwise.'

'We know that Detective Chief Inspector,' Joy said gently, laying her hand on top of Dani's. 'But at least now we understand how the information got out. Don't be too hard on DC Calder. He didn't realise the implications of what he was saying.'

Bevan admired Joy's capacity for tolerance and forgiveness. She was not convinced she'd be able to match it. A man was dead because Andy had decided to mouth-off to his colleagues in the pub. It was incredibly out of character, but she couldn't let it go.

Dani stepped out of the Wallaces' coffee-shop with a heavy heart. She turned towards the Town Hall and began the short walk across the Market Square. Standing by the Celtic Cross, was a lady Dani recognised. She was dressed in high, shiny patent heels a long black woollen coat and looked incredibly out of place amidst the slightly shabby surroundings. The lady twisted her head as Bevan approached, her ruby red lips parting in a smile.

'DCI Bevan, I'm glad I caught you. Your colleagues said you wouldn't be long.'

'It's Sally, isn't it? James' sister?'

'That's right,' the elegant woman led Dani towards a bench on the edge of the square where they both took a seat.

As Dani glanced across at her companion, the penny suddenly dropped. 'You're Sally Irving-Bryant QC. I've seen you a few times at the High Court in Edinburgh. Sorry, I hadn't realised until now.'

She swept a gloved hand dismissively in front of her. 'Not to worry, sometimes it's best to leave our professional personas behind at family engagements. In your line of work, I'm sure you'd agree. My mother probably told you that James was too soft for the criminal bar. Well, that assessment doesn't apply to me.' Sally chuckled at what was obviously a long-standing family joke.

'Is this a social or a professional visit?'

'A bit of both. James was rather distressed after you performed your disappearing act at Dad's party the other night. He and I managed to drag out of

Mum what she'd said to make you so upset. James was really angry with her.'

'I wouldn't want him to be. Your mum was only giving her opinion. It simply made me realise I had no business becoming so friendly with a witness in a murder case.'

'That is what I'm here to talk about. James is rather hopeless at defending himself, but I wanted to clarify whether or not my brother is a suspect in the murder of Joanna Endicott. Do you actually believe he was her lover at the time she died?' Sally subjected Dani to her piercing, advocate's gaze.

'If James would like to come back into the station and amend his original statement, it could clear the matter up once and for all.'

Sally sighed. 'After we dragged out of Mum what she'd said to you, I questioned my brother about his relationship with Joanna. I told him in no uncertain terms that it was not a game. He could not go lying to the police in a murder inquiry, men had gone to jail for less.'

Dani felt her heartbeat quicken.

'James had a very brief fling with Joanna Endicott. It *was* when they took the holiday to Madeira last year, but it was short-lived. They got on extremely well, were both attractive people and one evening, when they were out together for dinner, they decided to see if it might work if they became more than just friends. So James booked the holiday. It was a romantic hotel, they had the bridal suite, but my brother said they spent the entire week in a fit of giggles. The whole scenario just didn't work for them. They had a glorious time anyway, lazing by the pool and drinking cocktails into the early hours, but only as *friends* Detective Chief Inspector.'

'And James wasn't jealous of the men in Joanna's life after that point?'

'He swears that he wasn't. James said Joanna was very high maintenance as a girlfriend. He could not have sustained a long-term relationship with her. Tell me DCI Bevan, is my brother likely to be charged?'

'I really don't believe James killed Joanna or Daniel Goff. As long as he remains in the country, he can rest easy.'

Sally's body relaxed. 'Thank you.'

Dani stood up. 'I really need to get back.'

'Of course.' The woman seemed to hesitate. 'Dani, just for the record, James really doesn't often bring girls home to meet us. In fact, you're the first. I know he lied, but I expect it was because he didn't want to lose your respect. Once this case is over, perhaps you could contact him again?'

Dani could tell this hadn't been an easy speech for the QC to make, so she smiled broadly. 'I will be sure to do that Sally. I liked him very much too.'

Chapter Thirty Five

Bevan asked DC Calder to meet her for a drink in the hotel bar. Once she'd bought him a glass of wine, she confronted her friend with what Joy and Bill had told her in the café.

Andy put a hand up to his forehead and rubbed vigorously at his temples. 'The boys and I were enjoying some banter, but I honestly don't remember saying that.'

'Had you been drinking?'

'I treated myself to a second pint, because it was a Friday night. I felt okay, but perhaps my tolerance for alcohol has reduced more than I'd realised.'

'So you don't recall exactly what information you might have divulged that evening?'

He shook his head. 'Christ, do you think that's why Ronnie Sheldon is dead?'

'I'm not sure. I'll definitely need a list of all the folk who were in the Rob Roy Bar last Friday. I'll get Driscoll to go in and get a statement from the landlord tomorrow morning.' Dani sipped her drink.

'Maybe he's got CCTV cameras out front, so we can see who went in and out.' Andy made the proposal half-heartedly. 'I'm really sorry, Ma'am.'

'You weren't to know that my decision to meet with Sheldon would provoke this kind of reaction. Don't beat yourself up. If the suggestion hadn't come from Joy Hutchison's dream, I wouldn't have kept the thing quiet.'

'Thanks, Dani, you're a good boss.' Andy shoved his glass aside, obviously having second thoughts now about the wine.

'Look Andy, I really wish you hadn't got such a downer on the Hutchisons. Of course I welcome alternative points of view, but your animosity towards Bill is beginning to undermine me in meetings. I'd even go as far as to say it's starting to affect your judgement. I know you don't have any time for all the spiritualist stuff they come out with, but the couple mean well. They're a great source of information and let's face it, in this case, we need all the help we can get.'

Andy had agreed to give Bill Hutchison the benefit of the doubt in future. Not long after, he retired to his room. Dani ordered a hot chocolate and decided to drink it downstairs. The fire was crackling in the hearth and it was interesting for her to observe the other residents coming and going after dinner.

Within a few minutes, she had company. Bill and Joy entered the bar area, looking furtively about them until their eyes finally alighted upon Dani, seated at her table in the corner.

'I'm glad we've caught you alone,' Bill said conspiratorially. 'May we sit down?'

Dani pulled across a couple of stools. 'Of course.'

Joy's expression looked almost mischievous in the dancing firelight. 'We walked up to the Cairn this afternoon,' she said. 'Bill and I found the flowers.'

Dani raised her eyebrows.

'It was the bunch that the man hanging around the rental bothy must have placed there a few days ago,' Bill explained.

'Where are they now?' The detective sat bolt upright.

'In our room,' Joy continued. 'We thought it best not to bring them down here into the bar.'

'Very wise. Was there any kind of note or message with them?'

'It was obvious the bunch had been there a little while because the blooms were very much the worse for wear. There was a card tucked inside. It was completely blank except for the letter 'M'.' Bill gestured to the waitress and ordered them some brandies. Dani politely declined, saying she would stick to her hot chocolate.

'I'll need to bring over an evidence bag and get the bouquet sealed up first thing in the morning. Did you both touch the flowers?'

'We handled them as little as possible and wore gloves, Detective Chief Inspector. We didn't touch the card at all.' Joy seemed rather pleased with herself.

'And we replaced the flowers with a bunch we'd brought along ourselves. Otherwise it wouldn't have felt right to remove them.'

'Thank you both, it was an enterprising idea.'

'Being back by the memorial reminded us of what an unsettling aura the place has. There is a great deal of negative energy there. It is why we don't visit very often.' Bill gratefully received their drinks, immediately taking a swig of his.

'But we did have a good look around today, in case the man had left anything else behind. About half a mile away from the Cairn, is a ruined bothy. The police must have searched it when they were looking for Daniel Goff. It's completely dilapidated now and there's no roof, but Bill and I recalled it was lived in at one stage. Someone from the village owned it but we can't for the life of us remember who it was. It might be something worth looking into. The dwelling is so close to where the children were found.'

Dani felt she should probably end their discussion at this point, before she got her arm twisted into promising too much. The detective told the couple she would be paying them a call first thing in the morning and then promptly retired to her room, where she had quite a lot to think about.

Bevan lay on top of the duvet and crossed her arms over her chest.

The man who visited the memorial had laid flowers for someone with the initial 'M'. They couldn't have been for any of the children: Katrina Reid, Neil Hutchison or William Sanderson. None of the three had birthdays around this time either, she'd already checked.

But the greatest conundrum of all for Dani was what the Ardyle tragedy had to do with the deaths of Joanna Endicott and Daniel Goff, if anything at all. It was with this question circling around in her head that the detective finally fell into a deep and dreamless sleep.

Chapter Thirty Six

DC Andy Calder was doing his best to be helpful. He'd carefully bagged the bedraggled bunch of cheap carnations, was preparing to print the labels, and poised to send them off to the forensic lab in Glasgow.

'There's nothing distinctive about the flowers at all. It's not as if they've even come from a florist. I'd put money on them having been purchased from a supermarket foyer or a petrol station.'

Dani agreed. They looked like a last minute attempt at appeasement from a tight-arsed errant husband rather than a symbol of remembrance. 'It's the card that interests me. What is significant about the letter 'M'?' Bevan turned and waved DC Sammy Reid over to join them. 'Did Katrina or any of the other children have a nickname?'

'Katrina certainly didn't. She even hated people calling her 'Kat'. I couldn't really say for the other two. They might easily have been called by a pet name at home. We'd need to talk to the parents to find out for sure.'

'That's what I'm trying to avoid,' Dani replied dryly. 'I don't want the press getting hold of the idea there's a connection between the two investigations. There'd be an immediate feeding frenzy. The pictures of those poor children would be plastered over the front pages of all the nationals, just like they were thirty years ago.'

'My mum would be in pieces if that happened,' Sammy responded with feeling. 'She has dealt with things quite differently from the Hutchisons. Mum doesn't like the tragedy to be mentioned at all.'

'I can completely understand,' Bevan said, thinking that she'd adopted a similar strategy to deal her mother's death. A psychologist might take issue with the approach, but it had certainly worked for her, as it must have done for Mrs Reid.

Dani had arranged to borrow one of DC Kendal's laptops. She took it with her into the office and sat down at her desk. The first person she was keen to look up, was Samuel McAlister, who had been Headmaster of the Ardyle Primary School in 1983. It turned out he retired from his position in 1991, continuing to live in the area until his death in 2003. His wife had died in 2006. The couple were survived by two children, who would now be aged in their late forties or early fifties. Dani decided to look into their son and daughters' whereabouts more closely, if it proved necessary at a later stage.

Jack Ford, the teacher who had led the group of children that got lost on the mountain, was 41 years old in 1983. He'd worked at the school for 8 years when the Ardyle tragedy occurred, mostly in charge of Physical Education classes. He and his wife had lived in a cottage in the town. They had two children; a boy called Michael, who was 13, and a girl called Jennifer, who was 9 at the time the children died.

Dani observed how Ford's youngest was lucky not to have been one of the pupils out on the hillside that day. Presumably, she had been in the year below and her brother attending the High School in Callander. Ford was now in his early 70s and still lived in Ardyle. Bevan made a note of his address and returned to the main hall.

DS Driscoll was back from interviewing the landlord of the Rob Roy Bar. He was holding a shiny disk in his hand.

'Is that the footage from the pub's CCTV camera,

Dave?' She called across to the officer.

'Aye, I'm about to ask young Ian Kendal to have a look through it. Between him and Sammy Reid, they should be able to identify most of the local folk coming in and out. The landlord's given me a list of the people he could recall serving, but he was very vague, Ma'am. I got the sense they were busy on Friday night.'

'That's enough to be getting on with. There's not a great deal we can do with the information as it is, except cross-check it with any names that come up in the Crieff inquiry. Thanks, Dave.' Dani approached Sammy Reid, wanting to pick his brains before he became ensconced in the Rob Roy's CCTV recordings. 'I'm going to pay Jack Ford a visit. Is there anything I should be aware of before speaking to him?'

Reid made a face. 'He's not terribly communicative at the best of times, Ma'am. If you ask him questions about the Ardyle tragedy, I don't expect it'll improve his mood much. But Jack's a decent man, his bark's worse than his bite.'

Dani felt she had a reasonable idea of what kind of man Jack Ford would be. As she reached the front door of his well-maintained little cottage and pressed on the door-bell, Dani discovered her preconceptions had been largely accurate. Jack was tall, lean and taciturn. Bevan would have said he was in his early sixties, if she didn't know any different; his white hair was still interspersed with numerous dark strands.

'How can I help you?' He asked in a thick local accent, making the question sound as unfriendly as possible.

'My name is Detective Chief Inspector Dani Bevan. I'd like to come in and talk to you if I may.' She hoped he would be cooperative. Bevan didn't have the authority to compel him to speak with her.

He stepped back resignedly, grizzling under his breath, 'I've only got ten minutes.'

'I won't keep you long,' Dani responded brightly, stepping into a hallway with polished wooden floorboards and a grand staircase stretching straight up to the second storey. Ford led her into the kitchen at the rear of the property, which was small but had room for a circular table and a couple of chairs. She pulled one out and sat on it. 'This is a lovely house.'

'I've spent the last five years restoring it. The place was practically falling down when I bought it.' Jack filled a kettle and placed it onto the little stove.

'Have you lived in Ardyle all your life?'

The man turned his dark eyes to rest upon her suspiciously. 'I moved here with my family when I got the teaching job at the school. Been in Ardyle ever since, mind.'

'And now you're here alone?'

'My wife died fifteen years ago.'

'I'm very sorry to hear that.'

'She had cancer, it happened very quickly. My daughter helped me through it. She lives in Stirling now with her husband and kids.' Jack took a matching pair of mugs down from a shelf and laid them out carefully on the worktop, deliberately avoiding Dani's gaze. 'Are you here to question me about the man and woman who died up on Ben Lomond?'

'Why do you ask that?' Bevan was surprised by the question.

Jack Ford spun around and rested his weight on the counter, his expression one of sadness and resignation. 'Well, this is the second time there have been deaths up on that mountain. I was involved on both occasions, so I suppose that might make me a suspect of sorts. I was certainly treated that way by the police when the schoolchildren died. You'd have thought I'd murdered them if you'd heard the way DI Sheldon spoke to me.' The kettle began whistling merrily and Ford turned back to his task.

'In what way were you involved in the deaths of Joanna Endicott and Daniel Goff?' Dani asked carefully, shifting forward in her seat.

'Well, I wasn't, obviously. But I helped out in the search. I used to be a volunteer with the Ben Lomond Mountain Rescue. For as long as I'm fit enough, I'll always be willing to help out when a walker's got into trouble. This town is really switched on to mountain safety. We prided ourselves on not having had a single death in the National Park for over thirty years. We can't make that claim any longer, sadly.'

'Which part of the mountain did you search?' Dani took a cup of coffee from him and placed it on the table in front of her.

'I was up on the north-west side of Ben Lomond, following the course of the Cailness Burn. We've had walkers wander out that far in the past. They just completely lose their bearings if they don't have the right equipment. There's an old abandoned farm at Cailness, which folk often head to for shelter. We found a group of lost teenagers taking refuge in one of the outhouses there once, a couple of years back.'

'So you didn't see Goff or Endicott while you were out on the hillside?'

'No. Our search leader received the news they'd located two of the climbers at about mid-morning, but that there was still one chap missing. We carried on looking until late afternoon. We found nothing. At that point, I had no idea one of the climbers was dead.' Jack cradled his mug to his chest.

'Have you heard about the death of Ronnie

Sheldon?'

The man shifted from one foot to the other. 'Aye, it was on the Scottish news.'

'Have you had any contact with Sheldon since the Ardyle investigation of 1983?'

'I didn't much like the man, Detective Chief Inspector. When Sheldon finally left the town, it lifted a heavy burden from me and my wife. I would certainly never have sought him out.' Jack hung his head and mumbled, 'but I'd not have wished that fate on the man either.'

'All Sheldon's files relating to the case were destroyed by the fire. We have very little evidence left of what happened to the children on that night in 1983, Mr Ford. Why do you think those three youngsters got separated from the rest of the group?'

Jack looked uncomfortable. His cheeks flushed pink. 'Is this going to start up all over again!' He blurted out angrily and then proceeded to take several deep breaths, deliberately calming himself down. 'I had six children in my group. I'd sent them out in pairs to collect soil samples from the heathland. Suddenly, the mist descended on us and it was as dark as night. I called out to the students and three came straight back to me. Then, all of us set out to locate the others. The wind was getting up and it was becoming increasingly cold, so I sent the pupils back with Miss Harris to the schoolhouse and carried on looking for the missing children alone. I was out there all night. I never stopped searching until we discovered their poor wee bodies. I don't know why they'd strayed so far from the rest of us. I could never understand it. I was sorry then and I'm sorry now. But it's not going to bring them back, is it?' Tears had escaped onto his lined cheeks.

'Who was Miss Harris? I haven't heard her name mentioned before.'

Ford wiped his damp face with a handkerchief. 'She was a trainee teacher who'd been with us for a few weeks before the tragedy occurred. She wasn't much more than a child herself. I think the Headmaster knew her family and had offered the girl a placement at the school. Kathleen Harris was on the trip to help with the children. She was collecting samples with a couple of them when the weather changed. If Kathleen hadn't been there, I wouldn't have been able to go off and look for the lost bairns. I needed her to lead the other students back to the village. She was a Godsend.'

Dani stood up and placed her mug on the draining board. 'Okay, thank you for talking to me. I know it wasn't easy for you.'

The old man followed her to the front door. 'The incident made me lose my nerve. I was never able to take youngsters out on the mountain again. I couldn't trust myself. I didn't want another child to get hurt.'

Dani laid her hand on his arm. 'I know, Mr Ford, I know.'

Chapter Thirty Seven

Bevan slipped into the seat next to DCs Reid and Kendal, pulling across one of the laptops and logging on. 'How are you progressing with the CCTV?' She asked, keeping her eyes on the screen.

'It looks as if pretty much the entire male population of Ardyle were in the Rob Roy on Friday night and half of the females too. There was a big Rangers' match on.' DC Reid sighed.

'Just make a note of the names Detective, then we'll pass them onto Crieff.'

'For the record Ma'am,' DC Kendal chipped in, 'I never heard DC Calder mouthing off about the Hutchisons in the pub. I was with him for most of the night.'

'Thank you Ian, I'll tell Andy that. He'll appreciate it.'

Dani focused her attention towards the search engines of the Police Scotland database. No one by the name of Kathleen Harris appeared on their system. She tried the drivers' file first and then the property file. Neither made reference to a Kathleen Harris matching the age that the girl would be now. *Crimint* and *Holmes 2* also drew a blank, which Bevan was expecting. She didn't imagine the woman had any criminal convictions. At some point, Kathleen must have got married and changed her surname. Bevan would have to search the genealogy sites to find out any more.

She turned towards Reid. 'Do you recall a girl by the name of Kathleen Harris? According to Jack Ford, she was a trainee teacher assisting the staff out on Ben Lomond when the children went missing.'

Reid stopped what he was doing and considered this for a moment. 'I'm sorry, Ma'am. The name doesn't ring a bell. She can't have been at the school for very long. I was only in the infants back then. I'm not really sure that I would have remembered.'

'Of course, not to worry. I'll put someone on the task of checking her out properly.'

'I'll do it, Ma'am,' Kendal announced. 'We're just about done here.'

Bevan returned to the hotel for dinner. Andy Calder wanted to stay on and assist DC Clark to plough through the mammoth list of Scottish motorists they had identified as having entered London in the days before Batra's murder. Dani hoped Andy wasn't beating himself up too much. Tomorrow she would order him to slow down.

The Hutchisons were seated by the window. Dani was hoping she might see them. It looked as if they'd only just ordered. 'May I join you?'

'Of course.' Bill stood up and made a space for Dani at the table.

'Any news on the flowers, Detective Chief Inspector?' Joy enquired, as soon as Bevan had sat down.

'Not yet I'm afraid,' Dani smiled to herself. 'It takes a few days at least to get any results back from the forensic lab in Glasgow.'

While Dani relayed her order to the waitress, Bill poured her a glass of red wine.

'Just a small one, please,' she said with haste.

The man nodded knowingly.

'I paid a visit to Jack Ford this morning.'

'Oh. How is he?' Joy asked politely.

'He seemed very well. The man is extremely fit for

his age.'

'Jack still walks regularly, I hear. He's also been doing up that old house. Keeping himself busy I expect,' Bill commented.

'Jack's been on his own since Mary passed away,' Joy added. 'It can't be easy for him.'

'The Fords had a son and daughter though, didn't they?' Dani sipped her wine.

'Yes, Jenny was a lovely girl. Michael was similar to his father, quiet and sensitive, but he was a good lad just the same. I think that Jack and Mary struggled to get over the schoolchildren's deaths - a bit like us, really.' Joy looked thoughtful.

'When Mary Ford was diagnosed with cancer, she slipped away very quickly. Almost as if it was the excuse she'd been looking for to give up.' Bill sat back to allow the waitress to set down their food.

'It's very sad,' Dani said. 'Jack suggested that he and his wife hadn't got on very well with DI Sheldon.'

'Ronnie was simply doing his job. He had to question the Fords a great deal in the aftermath of the tragedy. Understandably, the parents were very keen to find out exactly what had happened. Sadly, Jack was the only one who could really tell us. It put the couple under a considerable amount of strain, I believe.'

'But Jack said there was somebody else out on the hillside with him. A young student teacher called Kathleen Harris?' Dani leaned forward, putting down her knife and fork.

'From what I can recall, Kathleen wasn't more than a child herself. She was 18 years old and young-looking with it. The girl helped the investigation as much as she was able. Ronnie took a statement from her at the time.'

'Do you know what became of Miss Harris? Jack thought her parents might have been friends of

Samuel McAlister.'

Joy crinkled up her face in concentration. 'I believe she left Ardyle soon after. The girl must have been traumatised, poor lamb. The McAlisters knew a lot of the local families. They were on the dinner-party circuit. It wouldn't surprise me if that's how she'd got the placement.'

Dani decided to end their discussion and concentrate on the food instead, which was lovely. She allowed Bill to top up her glass just a little and when Dani returned to her room an hour later, she felt relaxed and contented.

It wasn't late, so Dani kicked off her shoes and lay back on the bed, flicking through the television channels. She tutted loudly as the mobile phone next to her started to vibrate. It was an unknown number.

'Hello, DCI Bevan.'

'Hi, Dani? It's Sally Irving-Bryant here. Sorry to bother you in the evening. James gave me your number. I hope you don't mind.'

'Not at all, how can I help?' Dani sat up straight at the sound of the woman's commanding voice.

'When I came to see you in Ardyle the other day, I saw a man walking across the market square that I recognised. It took me a few days to place him, but when I did, I checked back through some of my old case files. I thought I'd better let you know what it threw up.'

'Yes, I'd like to hear it.' Dani felt her heart beat faster.

'This chap was a witness for the prosecution in a case I was defending about ten years ago, before I made silk. The defendant was a fairly unpleasant fellow, with a record of misdemeanours as long as your arm. On this occasion, he was accused of having grabbed a young girl outside a newsagent and then trying to bundle her into a van. Compared to the guy's previous record of petty thieving, it seemed a bit out of character. The girl was too upset to testify, so the entire case revolved around the evidence of this one witness. He stood up in court and described how my client had offered the girl sweets. When she refused one, he'd taken her roughly by the arm. The girl began to struggle with him and our witness ran over to intervene. At this point, the witness claimed my client was dragging the child towards the back of his van. As the witness approached, the defendant took off, jumping into his vehicle and speeding away. The witness wrote down the registration number, reported the incident to the police, and the court case duly followed.'

'It sounds as if this chap was acting as a good, responsible citizen. What's the problem?'

'Well, as was my job, I looked into this chap's background. It turned out the man had been receiving psychological treatment for some months. At one stage, he'd needed to be sectioned. When I challenged him on this in open court, he broke down admitting he'd made the whole thing up.

Apparently, he'd lost his son several years before, suffering a series of nervous breakdowns since. Taking this into account, the Judge recommended the issuing of a police caution and that the man should cover the court fees. He was not prosecuted for perjury. For some reason, the case has always stuck in my mind, probably because the chap was so believable.'

'What was the name of the witness?'

'William Harold Hutchison,' Sally said.

'But what about the little girl? *Something* must have happened outside the shop.'

'The girl eventually admitted that she'd stolen a packet of sweets from the newsagent. My client had been having a cigarette outside and saw her do it. His brother-in-law was the manager of the place, so he reached over to take them off her as she ran out of the door. This is what Hutchison had witnessed. To his addled brain, it was some kind of abduction attempt. The stuff about him dragging her towards a van was pure fantasy. I'll fax you through the details.'

'Thank you Sally. That would be helpful.'

The woman grunted an acknowledgement and promptly ended the call.

Dani lay back, with the mobile resting on her stomach. 'Oh Bill,' she lamented quietly. 'What on earth have you done?'

Chapter Thirty Eight

Bevan had an early night and slipped out of the Carraig Hotel at the crack of dawn, hoping to avoid the Hutchisons. It was a drizzly, dull morning and the detective stopped at the Wallaces' café to buy herself a cappuccino and a Danish. She needed cheering up after last night's revelation.

Dani felt desperately sorry for Bill. She genuinely liked him, but was now unsure if anything the man had ever said was true. To her surprise, Andy Calder and Rick Clark were already at the Town Hall when she arrived.

'Don't tell me you two pulled an all-nighter on that traffic evidence?' Dani was incredulous.

Andy chuckled. 'No fear, Ma'am. Rick's place is just around the corner, we worked late and Rick's wife offered to make us dinner. I ended up staying over in their spare room. I hate hotels.'

'I appreciate the hours that you've both put in. Have you come up with anything?'

DC Clark approached his boss with a lengthy print-out. 'We've got fifty names that fit the criteria we applied. They're all men and women who drove from Scotland to London on the days in question, and have links either to Stirling or the Loch Lomond area. We're currently trying to narrow it down even further.'

'Can I have a look?' Dani laid the papers out flat on the table and scanned the list. A name struck her as familiar. She tapped her finger on the page. 'This one, Micky Ford, what do we know about him?'

Clark went back to find his notes. 'Okay, Michael Alan Ford, 44 years old and a delivery van driver from Crianlarich. He had a legitimate reason to be visiting London. He had a consignment of electrical goods for a warehouse in Docklands, his employers verified his movements. The van's got GPS tracking. I was about to remove his name from the list.'

'Well don't for the time being. Unless I'm mistaken, this man is Jack Ford's son – the teacher in charge of the kids who died in the Ardyle tragedy. Have we got an address for him?'

'Aye, it's here somewhere.'

'Right, Andy and I will pay him a visit.'

Crianlarich was an attractive village six miles northeast of the head of Loch Lomond. The drive was a stunning one, taking them past a number of impressive Munro peaks.

'This place must be heaven for hillwalkers,' Andy commented cheerfully, as they navigated their way through the narrow streets.

'Dad and I stayed here for a night when we walked the West Highland Way. It's really geared up for tourists.'

The address they were looking for was up a farm track a mile or so outside of the village. Micky Ford's place was a cottage set on the edge of what looked like a large estate. Snow-capped hills flanked them on three sides and a gang of floppy-haired Highland cattle eyed the detectives with blatant hostility from the adjacent field. The stone building was whitewashed and had newly fitted windows. Bevan noticed a spiral of smoke escaping from the chimney. An unmarked grey van sat on the driveway. 'I think he's in,' she remarked.

Andy hammered on the door. The man who answered was a younger version of Jack Ford, except with a thicker set frame. His upper body bulk was accentuated by the cable-knit sweater he was wearing. Muddy walking boots sat on the doorstep and Micky stood in the hallway in his socks.

'What do you want?' He growled.

Andy produced his warrant card. 'We're from Strathclyde Police. Could we have a word?'

'I suppose so, come in.'

The man shuffled into the sitting room. It was dark except for the light being produced by a fire in the open grate. Micky switched on a table lamp, which didn't do much to alleviate the gloom.

The room was messy, with magazines and books piled up in corners. It smelt of mildew and wet-dog. 'Can I make you a cuppa?' He said.

Dani swiftly refused, before Andy had a chance to agree.

'Sit down, Mr Ford. We need to ask you a few questions.'

The man lowered himself onto the arm of the tatty sofa. 'I'm not sure what this is all about.'

Andy made a point of flipping through his notebook. 'You made a delivery of electrical equipment to a warehouse in Docklands, East London, on the 24th of this month, is that correct?'

'Yes. I do that trip every six weeks. My boss has got all my receipts from the journey.'

'Did you stay in London overnight?'

'Of course. I've got a mate in East Ham I always bunk down with. He's called Jimmy Cavanagh. I can give you his number if you want?'

Dani noted how helpful the man was being.

'And what time did you get to Mr Cavanagh's house on the 24th?'

Micky thought about this. 'About five o'clock. Jim was only just back from work. After we'd both had a wash, we went down to The Rising Sun on the High Street. We stayed there 'till closing and picked up a pie and chips on the way home.'

'Did you spend the entire night at your friend's house?'

Micky looked bemused. 'Of course I did. I was bloody knackered after driving all the way down from Scotland. I did'ne go dancin'!' The man laughed. 'Now, what's this all about, eh?'

'Do you live here alone, Mr Ford?' Dani asked.

'Aye, I've never married. Not a law against it that I know of,' he attempted a smile but it appeared forced.

'But you grew up in Ardyle,' she stated.

Micky's expression darkened. 'Aye,' he said warily. 'What's that got to do with anything?'

'Do you know a man called Amit Batra?' Andy chipped in. Worried the interview might get side-tracked.

'Nope. Indian chap, is he? There's plenty of them in East Ham. Both of Jimmy's neighbours are from Bangladesh. Quiet folk.' Micky crossed his arms.

'Mr Batra lived in Loughton, A few miles away from East Ham. He's dead now though. His house was broken into in the early hours of the 25th October. The man was battered to death while his wife and children were hiding upstairs.' Andy allowed his words to settle between them.

'What the hell has that got to do wi' me?' Micky seemed genuinely shocked.

'Mr Batra had been involved in an incident not far from here, a few days before he was murdered. He was part of a group of climbers who became lost on Ben Lomond in bad weather. Batra was rescued, but the other two were found dead. You must have heard about it? Your father took part in the search.'

Dani watched the man closely.

'Yes, I did hear about it, but I'm not likely to remember their names, am I?'

'It just seems a coincidence, Mr Ford, that you were travelling to London on the same day that Mr Batra was killed.'

Micky leant forward. 'Well the last I heard, a man couldn't be arrested because of a coincidence.'

'You're absolutely correct. But if you could just give us the name and address of Mr Cavanagh, we'll have a word with him to double-check that's where you were.'

Micky walked over to a cabinet which sat against an exposed stone wall. He opened a drawer and retrieved an address book. He began to copy out the details onto a scrap of paper. 'You know my van has built in GPS? If you check with my boss, he'll be able to tell you exactly where I was during that trip. It sends me spare most of the time. It's like travelling with big brother.'

'Oh, we've already done that, thank you. But it was extremely thoughtful of you to point it out.' Bevan gave the man a broad smile, plucking the address from his hand and leading Andy Calder out of the front door.

Chapter Thirty Nine

It was beginning to get dark as the two detectives drove parallel to the banks of Loch Katrine. The surrounding hills looked ominous in the encroaching gloom. When Dani was last here, she'd taken a very pleasant boat trip with her father on the SS Sir Walter Scott, alongside a gaggle of excitable American tourists. The landscape appeared quite different now. It was suddenly clear how quickly this mountain range could become a place of danger and threat. The sheer vastness of it made Bevan feel small and a little frightened.

'There's not enough evidence to get a warrant to search his cottage,' Dani said.

'He was very quick to tell us what he'd got up to during his trip to London.'

'It was almost as if he'd planned to use the GPS in his vehicle to provide him with an alibi. He was rather keen to remind us to check it out. Of course, it only tells us where his *van* was, not him.'

'But if this pal of his backs up the story, there's not much we can do.' Andy sighed heavily.

'We'd need forensic evidence from the Batras' house to link Micky Ford to the scene in order to get a warrant for his place. Although, now he knows we're onto him, Ford will undoubtedly dump the camera and the mobile phone, if he hasn't done so already.' Dani stared out into the darkness.

'I'll call DI Long first thing in the morning and fill him in on our progress. So, you think this Micky Ford could be our man?' Andy glanced across at Dani.

'Oh yes, I certainly do.'

When they got back to Ardyle, Andy Calder decided to go into the Town Hall to finish off some paperwork. Dani returned to the hotel alone. As she passed the desk, Bevan noticed Joy Hutchison talking to the receptionist. She loitered for a moment, intercepting the woman as she headed towards the lift.

'Joy.' She touched her arm. 'Could I speak with you?'

The lady looked surprised. 'Bill has gone to bed. He was feeling under the weather.'

'That's okay. It was you I wanted to talk to.' Bevan hooked her arm through Joy's and led the woman purposefully towards the residents' lounge. They sat at a table by the fire. Dani leant forward. 'I received a phone call yesterday evening, after we had dinner. A friend of mine works at the law courts in Edinburgh. She had some information for me about a case that was heard there ten years ago.'

Joy's cheeks flushed a deep scarlet. 'You mean the incident with the little girl.'

Dani nodded, waiting for her to elaborate.

'Bill wasn't very well back then.'

'He was receiving psychiatric treatment?'

'His mental health deteriorated when we moved to Falkirk. We thought it would make things better, but it didn't. Neil seemed to dominate Bill's thoughts during that period. After a few months, he suffered a complete nervous breakdown.'

'It's perfectly understandable.'

'I was very worried about him. He was ranting and raving about the things Neil and the other children were telling him. The voices never stopped, even at night. Poor Bill couldn't sleep. Eventually, I asked the GP to section him. I was frightened he might do something silly.' Joy's bottom lip began to wobble.

Dani reached forward and took her hand. 'You did the right thing,' she insisted. 'I only wish somebody had done the same for my Mum. Then she would probably still be alive.'

Joy nodded weakly. 'It certainly helped. Bill was put in a nice place with a lovely garden. After six months he was so much better. They sent him home then. But this incident with the girl happened not long after. Bill was trying to make small trips on his own. The doctor had recommended it. On this occasion, he went to the parade of shops about half a mile from our house to buy a pint of milk and the papers. As he was approaching the newsagents, he saw the man grab the girl. Bill said he began dragging her towards the curb, where an unmarked van was parked. Of course, Bill ran forward to try and stop him.'

'But my friend told me Bill admitted in court he'd imagined that bit. All the accused did was to try and apprehend the girl. Then he took back the sweets she'd stolen.'

Joy shook her head. 'The barrister for the defence was very fierce. When she questioned Bill, she told the court all about his breakdown. She made it sound as if he was totally unreliable and a fantasist. Bill became very upset. He began to doubt what he'd seen. He no longer felt sure about it, the lawyer had worn him down. Bill finally admitted he could no longer be certain. My husband was the only witness and the case collapsed. There were some very unpleasant news reports in the press about it afterwards. Bill was made out to be a time-wasting crackpot. Thankfully, our friends and family remained supportive throughout.'

'So Bill never said he'd fabricated the entire incident?'

'It was more that his testimony was completely discredited. Then the girl confessed to stealing the bag of sweets and this seemed to satisfy the judge that Bill had misinterpreted what he'd seen, as a result if his mind being unbalanced.' Joy tutted irritably.

'But you don't believe he did make a mistake about what he'd witnessed?'

'I know my husband has his eccentricities and for a long while he was very ill. But he's also an extremely observant and perceptive man, Detective Chief Inspector. I've no doubt at all that his account of what happened outside the shop was perfectly true.'

'How interesting,' Dani replied.

Dani stood in front of the flip-chart and addressed her team. 'Michael Alan Ford is 44 years old. He is the eldest child of Jack and Mary Ford, Jack being the teacher embroiled in the Ardyle tragedy. Micky grew up here, attending the Primary School and then the High School in Callander. Does anyone know him or the family?'

A number of the officers shook their heads.

'He's a decade older than most of us local lads, Ma'am. I vaguely recall his sister. She used to work in one of the cafés on a Saturday,' Sammy Reid offered.

'Well, he now rents a cottage on an estate outside of Crianlarich.' Dani turned and pointed to the e-fit of the man seen hanging around the bothy. 'It's possible that this man is Micky. The age and build certainly correspond. Did anyone matching this description go into the Rob Roy bar on Friday night?' She looked towards Reid.

'No, I don't think so, but Jack Ford was in there.

He was one of the first locals I recognised from the CCTV.'

'Okay, well that might provide us with a link to the death of Ronnie Sheldon, but the flowers are a far stronger lead.'

'His name begins with an 'M',' DS Driscoll chipped in.

'But he wouldn't be laying flowers for himself,' Andy responded, with a note of incredulity to his voice.

'What about his mother? Her name is Mary,' Driscoll continued, not allowing Andy's negativity to put him off.

'Good point Dave. And Mary Ford passed away fifteen years ago from cancer.'

'But why put flowers for *her* on a memorial commemorating the children who died in the Ardyle tragedy?' Andy stated.

'It indicates that Micky thinks there is some kind of connection between his mother's death and what happened on that mountainside thirty years ago,' Reid suggested.

'How did you get on with checking Ford's alibi for Batra's murder, Andy?'

'Jimmy Cavanagh confirmed the guy's version of events. He said they went to the pub at about half past five, stayed until closing and got chips on the way home. Micky went to bed in his spare room and remained there until they shared a cooked breakfast the next morning. But when I described the details of the attack on Amit Batra, Jimmy faltered a little. I reckon that if DI Long brings the fella into the station and lets him stew in an interview room for a while, his story will begin to fall apart.'

'But we'd still need forensics to tie Micky to the scene. DI Long says they've lifted nothing conclusive from the Batras' property. The perpetrator was thoroughly gloved up. The only one who saw him was Batra, who is now dead.'

'And we've still got the issue of motive. We don't know why Micky Ford might have wanted to kill Batra,' Driscoll added. 'We assume it was for the camera Amit had taken from Goff, but we've no idea what was on it. Was there some kind of connection between Ford and Goff that we don't know about?'

DC Kendal stepped forward. 'I've carried out a bit of research on Kathleen Harris, Ma'am.'

'Great, share it with us, Ian.'

'Kathleen Amanda Harris grew up in Aberfoyle. She was the youngest of three children. It seems her mother was a cousin of the Ardyle Primary School's Headmaster, Samuel McAllister. We have to assume that's how she got the placement at the School. It can't have been a formal arrangement, because she doesn't appear on any of the staff lists from that time. The first evidence of employment I found for Kathleen was as an entertainer on a cruise liner. She was a cabaret singer for a couple of years on the Atlantic route from Southampton to New York. I haven't been able to trace her whereabouts since then. I'm assuming she got married, but I've not tracked down the certificate yet.'

'It's a bit of a career change from primary school teacher to cabaret act!' Andy remarked.

'Perhaps she wanted to do something totally different. The deaths of those children must have really shaken the young girl. It seems perfectly natural to me that she'd want to get as far away from Ardyle as possible.'

'It is almost as if she chose to adopt a completely new life,' Kendal added, and the room fell momentarily silent, as the officers contemplated this scenario.

Chapter Forty

Bevan scanned the shelves of her little office in the Ardyle Town Hall. Amongst the accounting books and self-published histories of the town, was a pile of maps. She picked up one of Loch Lomond, turning it over to examine the broader view of central Scotland printed on the back.

Bevan estimated that it would take Micky Ford less than an hour to drive from his cottage in Crianlarich to Crieff along the A85. She had no evidence which connected Jack Ford's son with the death of Ronnie Sheldon, but if he'd discovered that Dani was about to interview the ex-detective, it wouldn't have taken Micky long to act upon that information.

He certainly had the opportunity. It was motive she was lacking.

Her thoughts were interrupted by a knock at the door. 'Come in!' She called out, not bothering to look up.

The old door creaked on its hinges.

'And who says that women can't read maps?'

Dani's head jolted upwards. 'Sam!'

The American detective was dressed casually in cords and a thick woollen jumper. He dropped a large soft bag down by his feet. 'Don't I get a proper hello?'

Dani manoeuvred her way around the desk, allowing herself to be enveloped in an enthusiastic bear-hug. She planted a kiss on his stubbly cheek.

'How lovely to see you. At the risk of sounding rude, what the hell are you doing here?'

Sam laughed. 'I had some leave owing, so in the

great tradition of American tourism, I've come to visit the homeland.'

Dani found to her surprise that she was genuinely pleased to see him. 'Well I'm glad you did.'

Sam's face became more serious. 'Plus, I didn't want to leave you carrying the can over all the gutter press stuff. I know I was acting like an SOB after the trial. I do realise it wasn't actually your fault.'

She nodded. 'Look, with the investigation and everything, it might not be such a good idea for you to stay with me at the hotel.'

Sam put his hands up in the air. 'I've booked myself into a B&B in the town for a couple of nights. Then I'm off to see Stirling Castle. You'll barely even know I'm here.'

Bevan arranged to meet Sam Sharpe for dinner at a local restaurant later. Before that, she wanted to check something on the police database. Dani commandeered Kendal's laptop once again and logged onto their *Holmes 2* software. Joy had given her the name of the man Bill accused of grabbing a little girl outside the newsagent in 2003.

Dani put his name into the system. A long list of offences sprang onto the screen. Sally Irving-Bryant was right; many of his early crimes were acts of petty theft and minor drug misdemeanours. But as Dani scrolled further through the information, she lingered over the details of his more recent convictions. These were of an entirely different nature.

In 2006, he was cautioned for loitering outside a primary school in Kilsyth. Then, in March 2008, he was convicted of the serious sexual assault of a minor. He dragged a young schoolgirl into the back of his van and drove it to a piece of waste-ground. He assaulted her in the vehicle and then deposited the girl back at the same place he'd picked her up. The man had served four years of an eight year sentence and was currently out on licence. His name had been added to the Child Sex Offenders Register.

Dani logged off and sat back in her seat. 'Well I'll be damned,' she muttered. 'Bill was absolutely right.'

Sam had chosen a quiet little pub that served food. They sat at a table in the corner which was lit by a small candle in a jar. Dani was still in her work clothes but Sam had donned a smart, light blue shirt which he wore open at the neck. She noticed he was wearing a new watch that appeared to be a designer brand. His sandy blond hair had been neatly tamed. Dani thought the guy looked rather handsome.

'What do you fancy eating?' Sam flashed the smile that had won Dani over in the first place. She felt her stomach flip.

'I'm just going to have the risotto. I've done a lot of eating out in the past few weeks. I can't manage anything too heavy.'

'But you won't mind if I have a burger?'

Dani grinned. 'Of course not.'

'And I'm going back to my B&B later, so there's no need to lay off the onions.'

Dani laughed. 'I'm not convinced you've ever been that considerate, Detective Sharpe.'

'No, I probably haven't.'

'How are your lads?' Dani suddenly asked, feeling that perhaps she hadn't shown enough interest in them in the past, 'and your ex?' She added for good measure.

'They're doing really well.' He seemed surprised by the question. 'Jake's trying out for his High School soccer team. That's all he's talking about right now. Janie's got a boyfriend. The boys appear to like him. They're talking about marriage, maybe.'

Dani hadn't heard Sam discuss his family like this before, but then she'd probably never really inquired about that side of his life. 'How do you feel about the prospect?'

'I'm really happy for Janie. It's just tough to imagine another guy playing dad to your kids, especially with them being up in Canada and me in Virginia.'

'But you're still very close to them. I've heard you on the phone.'

'Yeah, I'll survive. Hey, Dani, you never told me what went on with your Mom. I'm really sorry.'

'How did you find out?'

'The West Virginia Post did a follow up piece on you. They must have taken their information from the Scottish broadsheets.' Sam lifted a beer mat and twirled it between his fingers. 'You could have shared it with me. I would have understood.'

'I just wasn't sure we had that kind of relationship.' Dani stood up. 'I'll go and place our order. What would you like to drink?'

Chapter Forty One

Sam walked Dani back to the Carraig, a short stroll across the market square.

'You know what I'm going to say.' Dani smiled and raised an eyebrow. 'I don't really need escorting home, I am a DCI.'

'And I don't know what guys you're used to having dinner with, but in my book, you walk the gal home.' Sam took her hand and gave it a squeeze.

'You're the second person who's said that to me in the last couple of weeks.'

The American turned to her, with a puzzled expression on his face.

'Andy suggested I'd been going out with the wrong kinds of men. He was only joking of course, but it made me think.'

'How is Andy?' Sam asked this with genuine concern.

'He's doing a great job, but his behaviour is a little unpredictable. There are times when he can be downright insubordinate. He keeps contradicting my DS, who happens to be an excellent detective.'

'It's still very soon after his heart attack. I'm amazed he's even back on active service, to be honest.'

Dani made a face. 'That's because I vouched for him. I told the DCS he was ready. I knew how desperate he was to get back into the field.'

'Well there you go. You're just going to have to put up with him acting out of sorts for a while. As far as your DS goes, Andy's trying to prove he could have done a better job. If it hadn't been for his hospitalisation, Andy would be the DS now, right?'

Dani nodded slowly. 'I hadn't considered that. Andy's resentful of DS Driscoll. It simply hadn't occurred to me. It's like having to handle the moods of a teenager.'

'Which I have more experience at than you,' Sam added with a grin. 'You've just gotta ride it out sweetheart.'

They'd arrived at the entrance to the Carriag Hotel. It was before 10pm and several couples were exiting through the glass doors. 'I meant what I said,' Dani stated quietly. 'You can't stay here with me.'

'I know,' he replied, his eyes twinkling mischievously in the light emanating from the lobby. Sam leant over and placed a kiss on her lips. 'I do miss you when we're apart. I may not have made that completely clear up until now, but it's true.'

Dani was momentarily taken aback. She wasn't expecting this kind of declaration. It really complicated things. Before she had a chance to respond, their conversation was interrupted. A figure was hurrying down the steps towards them. The lady's face was in shadow, but as she grew nearer, Dani could see it was Joy Hutchison.

'Thank goodness you're back, DCI Bevan. Please come quickly, Bill has got himself into a bit of a predicament.'

The three of them rushed towards the entrance. As Joy led them through the lobby she explained, 'there's a group of rowdy men in the restaurant this evening. They've been drinking a lot and causing a disturbance to the other guests. One of the men began making lewd comments to that lovely young waitress from Inveraray. Bill decided to intervene.'

When they entered the dining room, Dani could immediately see the predicament that Bill Hutchison had got himself into. A heavily built chap with a closely shaved head was squaring up to him. Bill was standing his ground, but was clearly way out of his depth. The hotel manager was loitering uselessly beside them.

Dani got out her warrant card. She and Sam strode towards the table. 'Is there a problem here?' She demanded.

'Ah, Detective Chief Inspector,' said Bill, his voice a little shaky. 'These gentlemen have been causing a disturbance and intimidating the waitresses. I have simply asked them to moderate their behaviour.'

The burly man puffed up his chest and took another step towards Bill. 'We're paying customers, too. It's my mate's birthday and we're just having a good time. This fellow,' he poked Bill hard in the chest with one of his thick digits, 'doesn't know how to have fun.'

Dani automatically swept the man's arm away from Bill and yanked it behind his back. 'And that,' she said forcefully, 'was common assault. So I suggest that if you don't want to spend the night in a cell, you'll sit back down like a good little boy and when the waitress comes back to the table, you're going to apologise, alright?'

The man nodded, obviously in pain.

Dani released her grip and turned towards the manager. 'No more drinks for this lot, unless you want to lose your licence. And in future, when you've got a group of this kind in, don't put your youngest waitress on the table. If you want their money, serve them yourself.'

Bevan promptly hustled Bill out of the room. They made their way in the direction of the residents' lounge. Joy helped her husband into one of the soft seats.

'Are you okay?' Dani asked.

Bill nodded. 'I'm sorry you had to bail me out. I

thought I had the situation under control.'

'Don't worry,' Sam chipped in, 'they were a bunch of assholes. I'd have been tempted to take them on myself.'

'But it wasn't very wise,' Dani added pointedly, looking daggers at the American. 'You could have ended up getting badly hurt, Bill. For some of these men, picking a fight is an essential part of a good night out. You should have spoken to the manager, and if you'd got no joy from him, called the police.'

'I realise that. I was too hot-headed. Sometimes I find it difficult to take a step back from these situations.'

Sam patted him on the shoulder. 'Don't beat yourself up. No harm done.'

Bill turned in Sam's direction. 'You must be Detective Sharpe. I'm very pleased to meet you.' He put out his hand.

Sam was surprised. 'That's right.'

'This is Joy and Bill Hutchison. They have a connection to the case I'm investigating.'

'I followed the trial of Richard Erskine very closely. You and DCI Bevan did a great job to catch him. It's just a shame the so-called British justice system wasn't able to finish the job.'

Sam's expression became serious. 'We have the same problem in the States. Lawyers can discredit just about any evidence these days. The more smoke and mirrors they produce in the courtroom, the less likely we are to secure a conviction.'

'Very well put. The way these barristers set out to destroy the reputation of witnesses and victims is quite scandalous.'

Before the discussion had a chance to go any further Dani interrupted, 'this is all very fascinating, but I really must retire to my bed. I've got an early start and Detective Sharpe needs to return to his guesthouse.'

The couple stood up, taking their leave of Bill and Joy.

'He's an interesting guy,' Sam said, as they reached the entrance lobby.

'Oh, you don't even know the half of it,' Dani chuckled. 'I'll tell you the whole story when we've got more time.'

Sam brushed his lips against her cheek. He smelt very faintly of soap and wood smoke. 'See you tomorrow?'

'Yeah, of course. Just come along to the incident room whenever you feel like it in the morning. I could actually do with your input on this investigation. I'll ask DCS Nicholson if you can advise DC Kendal on a lead he's chasing up which has a connection to the United States. That'll give me a legitimate reason to involve you in the inquiry.'

Sam beamed. 'Great. I was beginning to think you'd never ask.'

Chapter Forty Two

Detective Sharpe had dressed smartly. He wore a crisp white, open-necked shirt and dark chinos. His bulky form had a little more definition to it. Dani wondered if he'd been working out.

'So, you've not got enough evidence to search this guy's place. How about surveillance? Can you sit a couple of plain clothed detectives outside his house?' Sam directed his questions to the officers gathered around the flip chart in the centre of the Town Hall.

'Ford's cottage is so remote he'd be onto us straight away. But we're keeping in contact with his employer. Micky is carrying out his regular deliveries. Thanks to the company's GPS system, we know where he is most of the time,' Dani responded.

'It's what he's getting up to in the evenings that would really be of interest to us though. He could be disposing of evidence and all sorts. It's obvious he's already had bonfires in his back garden,' Andy commented irritably.

'But you don't have the authority to find that out yet. So you need to focus on what *can* be done,' Sam said this forcefully and Dani thought she saw the flicker of a smile cross DS Driscoll's face. 'If you put an unauthorised surveillance on his cottage and the suspect clocks it, the case will collapse if it comes to court.'

'I'm keen to see if it's possible to make a connection between Micky Ford and the arson attack on Ronnie Sheldon's property,' Dani continued. 'Ford lives less than an hour's drive away. Jack Ford claimed that Sheldon made the lives of him and his wife a misery back during the Ardyle investigation in

'83. If we can ascertain a forensic link between Micky and the fire, we might just have enough to arrest him and get a search warrant. There were no forensic traces left at the Batras' property, but in this case, we may finally strike lucky.'

'So Bill and Joy's son died in the original Ardyle tragedy,' Sam reiterated, as he sat in the passenger seat of Dani's car. The mountainous landscape rolled past the windows as they headed north-east to Crieff.

'Aye. Neither Bill nor Joy dealt very well with their grief. Bill had a serious nervous breakdown about fifteen years ago. Since then, he's been hell bent on bringing the bad guys to justice, in whatever form he encounters them.'

'Was there anyone to blame for the tragedy then? The Fiscal ruled it as death by misadventure, didn't he?'

'That's correct, but the more connections that develop between the deaths of Endicott, Goff and Batra and the events of thirty years ago, the more I'm beginning to wonder if the incident can have been as straightforward as it appeared.'

'Perhaps Ronnie Sheldon was onto something back then. That's why he wound up dead.'

'But why did the information never come out in the intervening years?'

Sam shrugged his shoulders. 'Because it was too sensitive or there wasn't enough evidence to make a proper case? You and I have both been involved in investigations like that in our time. We know darned well what went on, but we just can't prove it.'

The market town of Crieff possessed a rather attractive main street, lined with dark-stoned, slightly austere buildings and with a pleasant church in the centre. Dani had arranged to meet the officer in charge of the arson inquiry at the remains of Ronnie Sheldon's house on Aberfeldy Road.

The place they were looking for was impossible to miss. There was a conspicuous gap in the pattern of the semi-detached Victorian villas which comprised this long street. The property adjacent to the void looked as if it had suffered a violent amputation. A smoke-stained wall dropped down to the ground on one side of it and piles of rubble lay beneath. Dani pulled the car up to the curb. She and Sam got out and surveyed the scene.

'The structural damage must have been too severe to save the building,' Sam explained. 'The neighbours were lucky their house didn't have to come down as well.'

'It reminds me of photographs taken during the Blitz,' Dani commented. 'I suppose because the housing stock is Victorian.'

As they cast their eyes across the detritus, Dani could identify small sections of floral wallpaper and the occasional charred item of furniture. Whilst they performed a solemn examination of what remained of the Sheldons' lives, a car drove up fast behind Dani's, screeching to a halt.

A man in his thirties jumped out, slamming the door shut behind him. 'DCI Bevan?' He called across.

'Yes, you must be DI Barr?'

They shook hands and Dani introduced Detective Sharpe.

'Sorry I'm late. We're short-handed at the station.'

'Not a problem. Can you fill us in on where you're up to with the investigation?'

DI Ewan Barr stood with his legs slightly apart

and began to recount the evidence, like he was reading out a shopping list. 'Ronnie was asleep in the bedroom at the upstairs rear of the house when the fire broke out. The techies now believe the blaze was started in the kitchen. The appliances and cupboards were doused in petrol and a lighted match tossed onto it. The assailant fled out through the back door. The flames took hold within minutes. Ronnie had a smoke alarm in the hallway but he'd taken out the batteries. We don't know why.'

'Perhaps it kept going off randomly, mine does that. I'm often tempted to take it down.'

'Aye, maybe so. The fire started at about 2am. The pathologist reckons Ronnie was dead from the fumes by 2.45am. The neighbours raised the alarm at 3.15, when one of the householders saw smoke billowing past their bedroom window. The Fire Brigade and ambulance were outside by 3.30. The house was engulfed by then. Fire officers needed to get the blaze under control before anyone could enter the building. Ronnie's body wasn't brought out until nearly five. Obviously, he was long gone by then.'

'Did you know Ronnie Sheldon?' Dani suddenly asked, observing the man's woeful expression.

'I'm just about the only serving officer at my station who didn't. Ronnie played golf with the majority of Crieff CID. His wife was well-known in the town before she died, too. Judy ran fund-raising events for the Police Veterans' Society. This case has been extremely sensitive for us.'

'Any leads?' Dani prompted.

'Not much in terms of forensics. We found a petrol can dumped in the waste ground a half mile over the back there. A couple of prints were visible, but they didn't match anyone on the database.'

'That could be useful when you do get a suspect,'

Dani suggested, glancing at Sam.

'Yes, that's right. We also have a witness who saw an unmarked silver-grey van parked in a layby next to the woods in the early hours of that morning. It's not far from where the petrol container was dropped, so we believe this may be the attacker's vehicle. It certainly matches with our theory that the man made his escape across the waste ground that these houses back onto, then through the wood and out onto the road.'

'An unmarked van, you said? Is this witness reliable – have you got a signed statement?' Dani took a step forward.

Ewan Barr smiled at her eagerness. 'Yes to both questions. The chap who reported seeing the van is a salesman who lives in Crieff. He was headed home from a trip to Oban, having reached that section of the road at roughly 1.45am. He'd never noticed a vehicle parked in the layby before. It made him suspicious. When we ran an appeal on local radio and T.V after the fire, he came forward directly.'

'Good. His testimony may be crucial.' Dani explained their suspicions about Micky Ford.

'Like you, we've been struggling to identify a motive. If this Micky Ford had a grudge against Sheldon, it might just provide the breakthrough we need,' Ewan responded hopefully.

'But we're still no closer to understanding why Ford would want to prevent Sheldon from speaking with me. Did you recover anything at all from the house after the fire?' Dani held her breath, hardly daring to hope that any object had survived the inferno.

Ewan broke into a grin. 'I've got something for you in the car, hang on.' The man jogged back to his vehicle and lifted a file from the backseat. 'It's really not much, but a few papers blew around the garden when the house was being pulled down. One of the neighbours kindly gathered them up a few hours later. He handed the pile to one of our DCs, when she was performing the house-to-house enquiries.'

Dani took the bundle with trepidation, as if she were being handed a newborn baby. 'Does it contain anything significant?'

'I'm not sure Ma'am. I've had a good look through it, but it didn't mean terribly much to me or my officers.'

'Thank you, DI Barr. We'll take it back to Ardyle with us.'

'And I'll fax you the statement about the vehicle. Our witness even provided a partial number plate. See if you can get a warrant issued on the strength of it. We'd want to search the van too, and if we could get Ford's fingerprints thrown in, it would really make my day.'

Chapter Forty Three

Dani made Sam hold the file on his lap for the entire journey back to Ardyle. 'I'm not sure what you think might happen to it, if we simply placed it on the back seat.'

Bevan chuckled. 'I'm not taking any chances. It's a miracle those papers survived the fire.'

The DCI had already been on the hands-free to Andy, telling him to watch out for the fax from Crieff and to get Driscoll to phone through to Pitt Street with their request for a warrant, as soon as they received the witness statement from DI Barr.

'I'm just honoured that you entrusted me with it.' Sam attempted a formal bow, as if he were being presented to royalty.

'Och, stop horsing around, you'll bend the file!' Dani said, giggling. 'Just read the details out to me then and have done with it.'

Sam put on the latex gloves Dani kept in the glove compartment and gently removed the sheets from their folder. Some of them were burnt in places and discoloured, making the papers extremely delicate to handle.

'Okay, this first sheet is part of a letter. It's from The Association of Police Counsellors, confirming Judith Sheldon's membership. It is dated July, 1982.'

'Fine, nothing significant there.' Dani felt her heart sink with disappointment. She was crazy to have ever got her hopes up in the first place. Dani drove the car parallel to Loch Arklet, which was shimmering in the lowering afternoon sun.

Sam scanned the next piece of paper in silence.

'What's that one about?' Bevan prompted impatiently.

'Hang on. I'm just trying to make some sense of it.'

Dani sighed with frustration. 'Well, if you read it aloud I might be able to assist you there.'

'Okay, okay. Does the name Kathleen Harris ring a bell?'

'Yes, she was the student teacher who was with the children on the mountain when they got separated from Jack Ford. She took the other students back to the school. We haven't been able to trace her current whereabouts, but I'm working on it.'

'Well, these two pages seem to be from Judy Sheldon's counselling notes, but they've been ripped out of a book at some point. She's put Kathleen's name at the top of the page. Would Ronnie's wife have had reason to counsel her?'

'Judy counselled all the parents of the children who died. I suppose she could have seen Kathleen during that period too. The girl would have been pretty traumatised after the tragedy.'

'The comments are hand written, so it's tricky to read. The weird thing is, they don't appear to be discussing the Ardyle tragedy at all. The subject of their sessions was babies.'

Dani glanced across at the American. '*Babies?*'

'Yeah, like the pros and cons of adoption versus termination, that kind of thing.'

'Is there a date on those pages anywhere?'

Sam examined the thinly spaced lines closely. 'At the beginning of the third sheet, Judy had marked the start of a new session. She'd added the date numerically at the head of the page: 03/05/83 - that's the 5th of March 1983, a month before the

Ardyle tragedy.'

Dani considered this and shook her head. 'No, in Britain we put the month second, meaning it was the 3rd of May; *after* the children had died.' The detective fell silent, trying to work out the significance of this information.

Sam continued sifting through the pile. 'The rest of this data applies to other police cases. Judy must have counselled the families involved in a multiple road traffic accident on the M8 in 1986. There are lots of entries concerned with that. But certainly nothing which could be related to your current investigation.'

Dani nodded, concentrating on her driving. She said very little else before they reached Ardyle, by which time, it was nearly dark. The two detectives entered the incident room to find DS Driscoll and Andy Calder still hard at work.

'Any news on the warrant?' Dani asked, removing her coat and laying it on a desk.

'I've sent off the statement along with the evidence we'd already gathered on Micky Ford. I'm still waiting to hear back from Head Office,' Driscoll explained.

Andy moved forward, perching on the edge of a table. 'Did you get any more leads from the Ronnie Sheldon investigation?'

Dani ran through the contents of the papers recovered from Sheldon's house. 'If Kathleen Harris was expecting a baby at the time of the Ardyle tragedy, does it have a bearing on the case? I've been thinking through the facts in my head on the way back from Crieff. It sounds as if Kathleen was considering adoption or perhaps a termination, so this pregnancy was unwanted. It's possible the baby was never born.'

'How old was Kathleen at the time?' Sam asked.

'She was eighteen years old. But Jack Ford and Joy Hutchison both described her as 'childlike',' Dani said.

'Would Ronnie Sheldon have known that Kathleen was pregnant?' Andy suddenly put in, 'I mean, what is the protocol in these situations? Did Judy have to keep the subject of her counselling sessions a secret from her husband?'

Dave Driscoll stepped forward. 'I've been to a training seminar on this. From what I can recall, everything discussed with the police counsellor remains strictly confidential. The same rules apply as in any therapy session. I suppose it complicates matters when the counsellor is married to the chief investigating officer.'

Dani looked thoughtful. 'Do we think that Judy told Ronnie what went on in those meetings – off the record, perhaps?'

Sam nodded. 'I'd say so, wouldn't you? Maybe they had an understanding that Ronnie couldn't use the details gained from her therapy sessions overtly in his investigation, but I can't believe they never discussed it.'

'So is this the information that Micky Ford wanted to stop us finding out – that Kathleen Harris was expecting a baby at the time of the Ardyle tragedy?' Dani looked at each of her officers in turn.

'If it was,' Andy stated. 'Then the question we should really be asking is who was the father?'

Chapter Forty Four

Bevan's phone bleeped her awake at 6.30am with the news that the warrant had been granted. She promptly texted the team, hoping they might be able to surprise Micky Ford with an early morning visit. Dani decided to leave Sam out of this one. She didn't want a wrong move on her part placing a question mark over their use of correct procedure.

An hour later, she and Andy Calder were on the road, with a couple of squad cars following close behind. It was a sunny morning, but bitterly cold. A hoar frost had welded itself to the windscreens of the police vehicles. It had taken a good ten minutes to scrape off. As the sun rose steadily higher, Dani watched the last of the tiny clusters of ice sliding down the glass into a watery mush.

'Did you have time to produce a search schedule?' Andy asked.

'Yep, I e-mailed it to the whole team. It's based on the floor-plans I received from Stirling Council. Micky doesn't own a dog or a gun licence. There shouldn't be any nasty surprises waiting for us when we get inside.'

'Has Ford got any deliveries booked in for today?'

'Not until this afternoon, and it's local. I really hope the van's there. DI Barr wants it searched too.'

The journey took them less than an hour, the country roads being fairly empty at this time of day. There would be no way to hide their arrival. Micky's cottage sat on high ground and the incoming track was visible for miles into the distance. Nevertheless, Andy slowed his speed right down and approached the cottage as inconspicuously as possible.

Micky Ford's silver-grey transit was parked in front of a set of dilapidated garages. Dani gestured for the other officers to remain in their vehicles whilst she and Andy advanced towards the front door. Calder knocked loudly. 'Mr Ford! It's the police!'

There was no response for several minutes. Dani began hammering hard on the old panels. 'We don't want him disposing of evidence whilst we're standing on the doorstep for Christ's sake.'

Then the door opened. Micky Ford looked as if he had only just got out of bed. 'What's going on?'

Dani held up both the court order and her identification card. 'We have a warrant to search these premises, Mr Ford. May we come in?'

Andy was already striding past the man, not waiting to receive a proper reply. Dani turned and gave her colleagues the signal to enter. Micky stumbled backwards into the sitting room, looking shell-shocked. The house vibrated with the pounding onslaught of heavy, police regulation boots.

'Can we have the keys to your van, Mr Ford, and any outhouses that you have access to on the property?'

Micky walked zombie-like into the dirty kitchen and took a key ring off a hook. 'This longer one is for the outhouse with the lock on the door. It's the only building out there that's serviceable.'

Dani handed the set of keys to DC Clark and nodded towards the vehicle outside. 'You aren't under arrest at this stage, but I would ask if you could provide me with your fingerprints and a swab of your DNA for my records. It would be in your interests to be seen to cooperate with our investigation.'

Micky rubbed at his eyes, like a toddler waking from a nap, giving himself some thinking time. 'But I don't *need* to provide you with that stuff, if you haven't arrested me?'

'That is correct.'

'Then I'd rather not, until I've spoken with a solicitor and found out what my rights are.'

'Fine, it's your prerogative to decline.' Inwardly, the DCI was cursing. 'How long have you lived in this property, Mr Ford?'

'About five years. I was in Ardyle before that.' Micky looked her straight in the eye. Now he'd got over the shock of their arrival that flash of defiance was back.

'Did you live with your father before?'

'On and off, then he bought his current place and started doing it up. It was time for me to move on. I've helped him with some of the work on the house, mind you. I laid the paving stones front and back.'

'Are you close to your father?' Dani observed the man carefully. He was manipulating the cord of his pyjama trousers with his fingers, as if miming the preparation of a roll-up.

'Of course. I haven't moved very far away. He knows he can call on me whenever he needs to.'

'Do you remember a girl called Kathleen Harris? She was a student teacher at the primary school in Ardyle, when your father was working there.'

Micky shook his head slowly. 'I'm hardly likely to recall the lassie after all these years now, am I?'

'But she was out on the hillside with your dad on the day the schoolchildren died. You may remember her for that reason?'

'I was at the secondary school in Callander back then. I was never home until after dark.' Micky turned and pottered around the kitchen, filling a filthy kettle with water.

'But perhaps at weekends you might have seen her in the town. Kathleen wasn't all that much older than you. I'm sure some of your pals would have known her.'

'Why on earth are you so interested in this woman? What's it got to do with you searching my house? If you want to ask me any more questions, then I want my solicitor present.' Micky banged the kettle hard on the worktop.

Dani put up her hands in a conciliatory manner. 'That's okay, Mr Ford. You don't have to talk about anything you don't want to. I promise not to mention Kathleen again, especially if it's upsetting for you.'

Micky's cheeks flushed red. 'I didn't say it was bloody upsetting. I said I didn't know the lassie, alright?'

Andy stomped down the stairs, looking for his boss. Dani stepped into the corridor to speak with him. 'There's nothing in the house, Ma'am.'

'Go outside and help Clark and Driscoll with the van. It may be our only hope. Whilst you're there, try all the outhouses and garages.'

Andy nodded and disappeared through the front door.

Dani ignored Micky and followed Andy into the front garden. She wandered across the lawn to the side of the house and into the untamed wilderness that lay at the rear of the property. A rusty metal brazier was positioned in one corner of the plot. Dani walked up to it and looked closely at the ash that lay in a heap at the bottom. She found a long stick and poked about in the cinders. This was more than your average bonfire, she thought to herself. The heat had been so intense that whatever had been thrown onto it was reduced to dust. But then she saw something glinting in that fierce autumn sun.

Dani reached into her pocket and pulled out a pair of plastic gloves and an evidence bag. She squatted down on her haunches and delved into the pile of ashes, lifting out the molten remains of a brilliantly shiny object. Dani dropped it into the bag and set off back to the car, with just the hint of a self-satisfied smile on her face.

Chapter Forty Five

The scant amount of evidence they'd managed to lift from Micky Ford's cottage had been labelled and sent off by mid-afternoon. Bevan was prepared to pay a premium to get what remained of the camera processed quickly by the forensic laboratory in Glasgow.

Dani gathered the team together, having sent out for proper coffees and pastries from the Wallaces' café. Five minutes later, a couple of their young waitresses delivered the order to the Town Hall, informing Bevan that a few extra cream cakes had been added for free. Dani made a mental note to drop in and thank Charlotte when she had a spare moment.

Bevan smiled as she watched the lads tuck in. They'd had an early start and no time for lunch. Dani reached for a huge, spiralling Danish pastry herself, as hunger finally caught up with her. The sight of a perfectly cut quarter of strawberry gateau, carefully wrapped in grease-proof paper, made Dani automatically think of James Irving, and their meeting in Jenner's tea-room. She recalled his kindness and consideration on that occasion and had to almost physically shake her thoughts back to the present.

'I'm just praying there's something that can still be lifted from the camera's memory card,' Bevan began, her mouth full of cinnamon custard.

'Are you sure it's the same device that was taken from Amit Batra's house on the night of the break-in?' DS Driscoll enquired.

'I'm absolutely positive, even if we can't prove it

forensically. At least we can now be certain we've got our man.'

'The casing looked like it was made from some kind of highly reflective metal. It was probably that case which saved it from the fire,' DC Kendal added. 'I've never seen anything like it before in this country, and I fully confess to being a bit of a gadget nerd.'

'Maybe Daniel Goff had bought it when he lived abroad,' Andy suggested. 'It might be worth having photographs of it taken and circulated in the press both here and in Europe. With something that unusual and distinctive, we might find a retailer who remembers selling it to Goff.'

'That's a great idea, Andy. Ring the techies at Pitt Street. Ask them to take some shots of the camera case and send them to us. Even if we can't get anything off the memory card, we might be able to identify the camera itself.'

'There were definitely traces of petrol in the back of Micky Ford's van. The carpet reeked of it. But it's purely circumstantial. He could easily claim he used the stuff on his bonfires. I don't think it's enough to tie him to the Ronnie Sheldon murder,' DS Clark added.

'The registration number that DI Barr's witness provided us with matches the transit van's minus about two digits. I reckon it's enough for Crieff CID to haul the guy in for questioning,' DS Driscoll said positively.

'I agree. If we get something back on the camera that links it to Batra or Goff then we've got grounds for an arrest,' Dani responded.

Andy Calder creased up his face. 'Micky Ford is clever. He's left almost no forensic evidence behind in any of these murders, assuming they're all down to him, of course. I think we need more. The guy's got far too much wriggle room if this ever gets to court. We need to find a new angle, keep digging into the 1983 Ardyle case; because there's something here we're missing. There's no way on earth Ford is going to confess, he isn't the type. So we're going to have to nail him.'

Bevan sent a text to Sam, asking him to meet her at the Wallaces' café. It was late afternoon when she got there and the place was almost empty. Charlotte was behind the counter, polishing the enormous coffee machine, trying to get a perfect shine from its myriad pipes and spouts.

'Thank you for the cream cakes,' Dani said quietly, perching on one of the tall stools.

Charlotte spun around. 'Och, that's no problem at all. You and your men have provided me with an awful lot of business in the last couple of weeks. Now, can I get you something?'

'A couple of Americanos please. I'm expecting a friend to join me.'

Charlotte turned back to her machine, gently manipulating its levers and dials. The door to the café opened. Dani watched Sam approach, taking in his broad smile and reassuringly burly physique. He sat beside her and placed his hand briefly on the small of her back. She liked the subtlety of the gesture; he was deliberately trying not to place her under any pressure.

'Busy day?' He asked casually, removing his padded jacket.

Dani filled him in on the results of the search of Micky Ford's cottage, pausing when Charlotte set down their drinks. 'I didn't think it would be wise for you to come along,' she concluded.

'Sure, you're quite right. No need to attract the

attention of the Scottish press again. Actually, I had quite an eventful day myself.' Sam raised an eyebrow playfully.

'Oh yes?' Dani was intrigued.

'I hooked up with Bill and Joy in the town. They offered to drive me up to Loch Arklet. We took a walk through the glen, the landscape is stunning. It's kinda like a miniature version of the Great Lakes. I loved it.'

'I'm glad you're managing to see the sights. It wouldn't be much of a holiday otherwise.' Dani sipped the coffee, appreciating the deep, almost nutty flavour.

'At the risk of sounding cheesy, you were the only sight I came to see.'

Dani shifted about awkwardly, keeping her vision fixed on the cup her hands were cradling. She was unsure where Sam was going with this.

'Dani, I've got something to tell you. I want you to stay calm and not flip out, okay?'

Bevan twisted around on her stool, giving the American a puzzled look.

'About a week ago, I got a call in the States from Andy Calder. He told me I had some competition; that you'd been seeing this guy who he thought was bad news. Andy said he was giving me a friendly warning and I could do whatever I liked with the information.'

Dani's mouth dropped open. Anger and embarrassment, in equal measure, crept through her entire body, making her cheeks flush crimson.

Sam laid a hand on her arm. 'It was my decision to come here. I'd never made my intentions towards you clear, that was a mistake.'

'You don't need to say anymore,' she interrupted in a croaky whisper. 'We're fine.'

'No, I really do. I'm not far off reaching my 25

years of service. This gives me options. All I can say for the moment is that while my boys are growing up, I need to be living on the same continental land mass as them. But as time goes on, there's a possibility we could be together, which is a scenario I'm very keen on. It's probably not enough to offer somebody like you, but it's all I got.'

Dani leant forwards and placed a kiss on his lips. She wasn't quite sure how to reply to him, so for now this felt like the most appropriate course of action. Sam slipped his arm around her waist and pulled her close.

'Do I get to come back to your hotel yet? 'cause I gotta say, trying to be a good boy these last few days has been killing me,' he whispered softly into her ear.

She smiled, scattering some coins on the counter next to their half-drunk coffees and leading Sam out of the café by the hand.

*

Chapter Forty Six

Andy Calder had spent the previous night back at home with Carol and Amy. Dani wasn't expecting him at the Incident Room until midday. Sam had urged her at breakfast not to be too hasty to confront him. He suggested she take a few days to consider things first. Sam was convinced that Andy had meant well and was trying to look out for her best interests.

This may have been true, but Dani felt his actions were so inappropriate she wasn't sure she could continue working with him. He'd interfered in her private life in a way that Bevan hadn't thought the man capable of. But then, it was Dani herself who'd dragged her personal relationships into the workplace, so could she really blame Andy for thinking he could stick his oar in? Suddenly, Dani recalled the fortune teller at the Irving's party, telling her she had problems separating private from professional and seeming to be aware of what had happened to her mother. Bevan didn't like all these people appearing to know so much about her, she didn't like it one little bit.

As Dani entered the Town Hall, DC Kendal leapt up from his seat and jogged towards her. 'I've got something interesting on Kathleen Harris, Ma'am.'

Bevan took the chair next to the young detective whilst he summoned up a screen on one of his laptops.

'After she began working on the cruise ships, I found her impossible to trace. For a while, I thought she might have emigrated to the United States; meeting an American on board one of the ships and marrying him, perhaps. But the official US databases I tried, with Detective Sharpe's assistance, didn't have any record of her doing this. The last movements I'd pinpointed for Kathleen were in 1984. So I applied a little lateral thinking. Harris is a very common surname so it took me a while, but eventually I had the idea that maybe Kathleen had started using her middle name, which was Amanda. 'Kathleen' struck me as quite old fashioned for a woman of her age, even back in the 80s. I reckoned maybe it wasn't very cool for a cabaret singer.'

Dani nodded, impressed by the lad's logic.

'I tried Amanda Harris first, but drew a blank with the women I checked out; they didn't quite fit the evidence we had. Then I had a go with Mandy Harris. My cousin calls herself Mandy. She cringes if anyone refers to her as Amanda.'

'And?' Bevan prompted.

'Here, look,' Kendal swivelled round the laptop. A marriage certificate was displayed on the screen. Kathleen officially changed her name to 'Mandy' in 1985, but I suspect she'd been using it ever since starting work on the cruise ships. 'Mandy Harris, aged 23, married Charles Oliver Endicott, aged 34, at St Giles Church, Buckinghamshire on 24th August 1988.'

Dani stared at the document, the information taking a while to compute. 'Oh my God. Kathleen Harris was Joanna Endicott's mother.'

Within a few minutes, the entire team were gathered around Ian Kendal's workstation. 'Why didn't we know this already?' Dani demanded.

'Well, we knew that Joanna's mother and father

were dead. Mandy Endicott died of ovarian cancer in 2009 and Charles passed away in 2011. DS Driscoll ran police checks on them both. They were completely clean,' Ian explained. 'It didn't seem necessary to carry out a detailed background investigation. Even if we had, I'm not sure we would have made the connection.'

'Hang on, when was Joanna born?'

'October 1983,' Dave Driscoll called out, the details of the case imprinted on his brain.

'But Harris married Charles Endicott in 1988. Joanna would already have been five years old. So, was Charles actually her father? Has anyone looked at Joanna Endicott's birth certificate?' Dani glanced around the room and then she stopped dead still. 'Shit,' she muttered darkly. 'Joanna was the baby.'

'What do you mean, Ma'am?' DC Clark asked tentatively.

Sammy Reid pushed himself forward. 'If Joanna was born to Kathleen Harris in October '83, then Kathleen must have been two months pregnant at the time of the Ardyle tragedy. *Joanna* was the baby that Kathleen was discussing in her therapy sessions with Judy Sheldon.'

'So Kathleen *did* have the baby and she kept her,' Dani added. 'When did the woman start working on the cruise liners?'

'The first indication she was employed on a cruise ship was in the summer of '84 and the last evidence I found was in '86,' Kendal explained.

'Can you take a child with you if you work on one of those vessels? Sammy, can you find that out for me?'

The young man nodded and scuttled off to make a start.

'What if Kathleen, now calling herself Mandy, met Charles Endicott on board a cruise ship? He had money and was older than her. Perhaps he was prepared to take Joanna on as his own child. Mandy certainly married into a wealthy family to end up living in a two million pound home in Chiswick.'

DS Driscoll looked thoughtful. 'So why did Joanna come back here to Ardyle all these years later? Was she aware of her mother's connection to the place?'

Dani tapped a pen on the desk. 'I think she must have done. James Irving said Joanna was the brains behind their decision to take the holiday in Ardyle. He intimated that she was the driving force behind everything. Joanna Endicott undoubtedly had a purpose for returning to Loch Lomond.'

'She would have been back here searching for her real father,' declared a voice from the centre of the hall. Dani turned to see Andy Calder standing there, his hands on his hips. In all the excitement, they had completely missed him come in.

Bevan texted Sam and asked him to join them. She wanted to hear as many ideas on this new development as possible. The American arrived within twenty minutes.

DS Reid was the first to provide Bevan with his input. 'Joanna's birth certificate lists her father as unknown and her birthplace as Queen Elizabeth Hospital, Birmingham.'

'What was Kathleen doing there?' Dani exclaimed.

'Perhaps she went to stay with a relative for the birth. Her family may have wanted her to remain away from home for a few months, so there wasn't any gossip,' Reid suggested.

'It sounds like the 1880s not the 1980s,' Dani muttered incredulously, 'carry on please, Sammy.'

'Joanna was officially adopted by Charles

Endicott in 1988 and took on his surname. Before that time, Kathleen worked for Royal Atlantic Cruises from the spring of '84 to the summer of '86. She sang with a troupe of other girls. According to the man I spoke to at Royal Atlantic, a couple of them had young children. He told me the company has always been progressive about its working conditions. There was a crèche on board both the liners Kathleen had been employed on. The women in the cabaret often worked it out between them so that there was someone free to watch the kiddies during performances. He said it was actually a great environment for the little ones to grow up in, but the women usually had to leave when their children reached school age.'

'Joanna was three years old when her mother stopped working on the cruises. We assume she'd met Charles Endicott by then and had begun a relationship with him,' Dani contributed.

'Aye, the Endicott family had a huge old pile in Buckinghamshire, which is where Charles and Mandy got hitched. A few years later, Charles was working in London and they bought the property in Chiswick.'

'So what prompted Joanna to go looking for her real dad?' Sam Sharpe pitched in.

Dani considered this. 'Perhaps she'd started digging into it after her adopted father died in 2011. It may have taken her all that time to make the connection with Ardyle. As soon as Joanna knew her mother had been living up here when she was pregnant, the lawyer made plans to come for a holiday.'

DS Driscoll paced across the room to join them. 'I've just been on the phone to Joanna Endicott's maternal aunt. She was one of the relatives DC Clark and I interviewed. Vera Mortimer told me she'd lived in Solihull at the time Kathleen was expecting Joanna. Kathleen's parents sent her down to stay with her aunt for the birth.'

'Why didn't she tell you this in the first place?' Dani proclaimed.

'She says we never asked her. Also, Kathleen's parents wanted the whole thing kept on the quiet. After Kathleen started referring to herself as Mandy and married Charles, the family decided never to mention the fact that Joanna was illegitimate. It didn't seem to matter once Charles had adopted her.'

'Do you know what?' Dani said in exasperation. 'That actually makes a lot of sense.'

Chapter Forty Seven

'We need to take this right back to the day the walkers set out to climb Ben Lomond,' said Andy. 'But this time, we bear in mind that Joanna Endicott was in Ardyle to find out who her biological father was and perhaps to make contact with him.'

'This entire case revolves around who had got Kathleen Harris pregnant,' Dani stated.

'Micky Ford refused to give us a DNA sample, which could be significant,' Driscoll added.

'Micky would only have been thirteen or fourteen back in 1983, could he really have been having a relationship with Kathleen?'

'If the boy was sexually mature, then you betcha,' Sam responded. 'We have cases in Richmond of juveniles fathering kids pretty much every day of the week.'

Dani rose to her feet, as if she'd suddenly made her mind up about something. 'I'm going to have another conversation with Jack Ford.'

Andy Calder grabbed his jacket, 'I'll come to.'

'No,' Dani automatically replied. 'I'll take Driscoll. Andy, you can chase up forensics about that camera.'

Sam Sharpe visibly cringed. Andy shot him a suspicious glance, but not another word was said.

Jack Ford appeared to be deeply unsettled by their visit. This time, Bevan and Driscoll sat in the front room of the little terraced house. A small wood burning stove had been installed in here and the floorboards recently polished. A film of dust created by the process was still discernible along the windowsill.

Jack carried in a tray of teas. The colour of the liquid was the same deep, chestnut brown as the logs piled next to the stove. 'My son says you've been harassing him.'

'That isn't the case, Mr Ford. We received a court order to search his premises based on strong evidence linking him to two major crimes.'

'Then why haven't you arrested him, eh?'

'Because our enquiries are still ongoing. New evidence is coming to light all the time.'

Jack didn't look happy to hear this. 'What kind of new evidence?' The man clasped his hands tightly in his lap. Dani saw beads of sweat spring to his forehead, although to her, the room was freezing.

'We spoke about Kathleen Harris before, the student teacher who accompanied you and the children out on the mountainside. How well did she know Micky?' Dani sat forward in her seat.

Jack frowned. 'She didn't know Micky at all. I don't think they ever met. My son was at the Secondary School, their paths never crossed.'

'That's what Micky said too. But they may well have seen each other in town occasionally. Ardyle is a small place.'

'But Kathleen was only at the school for a short period of time. Her parents were very protective. She went straight back home to them whenever she wasn't at the primary.'

'You seem to know a lot about her comings and goings back then Jack. I don't see how you can be so certain Kathleen never came into contact with your son.'

The old man looked confused. 'I just know. Micky was a quiet boy, he didn't go out much.'

'Were you aware Kathleen Harris was two months pregnant at the time of the Ardyle tragedy?' Driscoll asked.

Jack shook his head. 'She was only a little girl herself, that can't be right.'

'I'm afraid it is true. Kathleen gave birth to a baby girl in the October of 1983. She called her Joanna.'

Jack gazed down at his knees. 'No, there was no baby.'

'Joanna was adopted by the chap Kathleen married in 1988, when she was five years old. But she came back here a couple of weeks ago, to try and find her real father.' Dani leant right down, as if she were whispering into the ear of the man slumped in the chair before her.

He whipped his head up. 'What are you telling me?' His voice was filled with horror. 'It wasn't that girl who died on the mountain, please say it wasn't!'

Dani took Jack's hands in hers, 'I'm so sorry. Joanna Endicott was Kathleen Harris' daughter. She must have come back to Ardyle looking for answers.'

Tears were dripping from his face. 'I didn't know Kath had the child. Judy Sheldon told us she was going to get rid of it. Why on earth didn't she?' He looked at Dani with a plaintive expression on his face.

'Because the baby was her little girl, Mr Ford, Kathleen wanted to keep her.'

Driscoll escorted Jack Ford to the local police station where he could conduct a proper, taped interview. Dani walked into the Town Hall, watching the team at work. Andy was on his mobile phone, talking animatedly and jotting down notes. She smiled at Sam, who came over to stand next to her.

'You look relieved,' he said.

'I think we're finally getting somewhere,' she replied.

A few officers glanced up from their tasks and

noticed Bevan's presence in the building. One by one, they drifted over to the centre of the hall, instinctively forming a tight semi-circle around their boss.

'Jack Ford is currently at the Ardyle Police Station providing Dave Driscoll with a formal statement.' Dani immediately glimpsed the expectant face of Sammy Reid, standing behind DC Clark. She wondered how he would take the news. 'Ford has admitted to being the father of Kathleen Harris's baby.'

A few gasps went up from the men.

'Are we sure he isn't just covering up for his son?' Andy asked levelly.

'He has agreed to take a DNA test, but I take your point, we should keep an open mind on this. However, his story fits with what I had already imagined may have gone on during the day the schoolchildren went missing in April 1983.

Jack alleges that Kathleen had set her sights on him soon after arriving at Ardyle Primary. She was a young, very pretty girl and Jack described her as 'precocious'. Because she was a relative of the Headmaster, Samuel McAllister, Kathleen had a certain air about her; as if she could do whatever she pleased. According to Jack Ford's version of events, the girl seduced him. They began a sexual relationship in the January of 1983. Their liaisons took place mostly in his car, which Jack drove up to a lover's lane near Loch Arklet. Then, in February of that year, Jack got hold of the keys to a wee bothy which was positioned on the heathland just south-west of the Ptarmigan ridge.'

'It's in ruins now, but it's very close to the place where my sister died,' Sammy Reid added, in a cold and emotionless voice.

'That's right. The Hutchisons noticed it when

they went up to the Memorial Cairn to look for the flowers. Bill said he thought someone local had owned it, but he couldn't recall who. In fact, it was one of Jack's fellow teachers at the primary school. He lent Jack the key so he could store his walking gear in there and use the kitchen when he was out hiking. Of course, Jack Ford realised he could use it for a quite different purpose. He began meeting Kathleen there, during the times when he knew it would be empty.'

'Were the two of them in the bothy on the afternoon the children went missing?' DC Reid had edged himself out of the group and was standing almost directly in front of Dani. His face was a mask of disbelief and horror.

Bevan addressed her words only to him. 'The school trip must have seemed like a golden opportunity for them. They didn't get the chance to meet often. The weather had been very fine when they first reached the hillside. The pupils were happy to wander off and collect their samples without much supervision. Jack said it was Kathleen who had the idea to use the bothy. While the children were busily occupied, she led him by the hand to the old cottage. He claims they were only in there for half an hour – forty five minutes at the most.

When they were done, they both got quickly dressed. As soon as he stepped out of the door, Jack could see the weather had closed in. There was a mist hanging low over the heathland and it was terribly cold. He and Kathleen set out to find the children. They ran up and down the glen calling their names. The pair quickly located most of them, but three remained missing. The rest of the story is exactly as Jack told it to the authorities; Kathleen took the pupils back to the school and raised the alarm, while Ford searched all night for the others.

They only found their poor, frozen wee bodies the following day.' Dani had her arms around Reid by this point and his head was buried into her shoulder. 'I'm really sorry Sammy.'

'What happened afterwards?' prompted Andy.

'Jack and Kathleen agreed not to mention they'd left the children. Jack didn't want his wife to find out and Kathleen's parents were very strict. It seemed to them to be the only option. But as the investigation intensified, the pair felt under increasing pressure. During this time, Kathleen discovered she was pregnant. The girl was in a terrible state. She told Judy Sheldon about her condition in one of their counselling sessions. Kathleen subsequently told Judy all the details of her affair with Jack.'

'It must have put Judy Sheldon in an awful position, knowing she had this information whilst trying to counsel the victims' parents at the same time.' Sam Sharpe drew in a breath.

'Yes, it was an awful strain. In the end, Judy couldn't keep it to herself. She told her husband about Kathleen and Jack's relationship.'

'So Ronnie Sheldon knew? But he took no action,' Andy interjected.

'He didn't know for certain the pair of them had been in the bothy when they should have been looking after the children, but I'm pretty sure he guessed. The problem for Ronnie was that he couldn't use the information. Judy's sessions were supposed to be confidential. She would have lost her job. DI Sheldon put a great deal of pressure on Jack Ford in the aftermath of the tragedy, hoping he might confess to what he'd done without the need for Judy's evidence, but he never did.'

'How did Jack find out that Kathleen was expecting his baby?' Kendal enquired.

'Judy was racked with guilt about the

information she had on Jack Ford. Mrs Sheldon was very reluctant to allow him to go unpunished, or to continue teaching youngsters. So, she finally decided to tell Mary Ford what she knew. Judy turned up at their house one day and knocked on the door. She was invited in for a coffee and without warning, Judy Sheldon told Mary everything. Jack's wife confronted him later, when he returned from work. He couldn't deny it; there would have been no point. Judy had reassured Mary that Kathleen was determined not to go through with the pregnancy. If the girl didn't end up opting for a termination, then she was going to have the baby adopted. This was the last Jack Ford heard on the subject.'

'So Mary forgave her husband?' Sam stated quietly.

'Yes, but the knowledge of what he'd done took a terrible toll on her. When she was diagnosed with cancer in the late nineties, the poor woman simply gave up. Mary hadn't the strength to fight it. The illness was a blessed release from her misery.'

'How much did Micky Ford know of all this?' Andy piped up.

'Not very much, according to his father. He said Micky knew nothing about the affair or the pregnancy.'

Andy took a decisive step forward. 'Well at some point, he sure as hell found out.'

Chapter Forty Eight

It was late by the time Dani had finished at the incident room. She'd wanted to read carefully again through Jack Ford's statement, just to ensure he wasn't shifting from the story he'd given her and Driscoll that afternoon.

She locked up the doors and sighed as she made her way down the stone steps. When Dani reached the bottom, Sam Sharpe emerged from the shadows.

'How long have you been waiting there?'

'About an hour or so.'

Dani slipped her arm through his. 'You really don't have to give yourself pneumonia in order to prove you're committed to me.'

'I know, but I wanted to see you. It's been a tough day.'

'It's only going to get tougher.'

'How do you mean?'

'I've got to tell Bill and Joy what we found out about the Ardyle tragedy. I don't know how they're going to take it.'

'I'll come with you.'

Dani leant her head against the American's thickly padded shoulder and they walked arm-in-arm towards the Carraig Hotel. The Hutchisons were still seated in the residents' lounge when they arrived. Both had brandies placed on the table in front of them, almost as if they were preparing to receive bad news. Sam and Dani removed their coats and took the sofa opposite.

'Good evening, DCI Bevan, Detective Sharpe.' Bill nodded to each of them, rather formally.

'Were you expecting us?' Dani said, half-joking.

'In a way, yes we were,' Joy explained. 'We had a visit from Maggie Reid this afternoon. Her Sammy told his mum all about what happened today.'

'I'm very sorry. I wanted to break the news to you in person.' Dani felt a lump forming in her throat.

Bill shuffled forwards in his seat conspiratorially. There was a mischievous smile on his face. Bevan thought he appeared decades younger than when she'd last seen him. 'Would you like to know something fascinating? Joy and I went for a walk this afternoon through the glen. At about a quarter past two, I felt this extraordinary sensation; it was as if a physical weight was being lifted from my shoulders. I turned to Joy and I knew by the look on her face she'd experienced the same thing.'

'We stared at one another for a good minute and had a sort of epiphany. I said to Bill, "she's done it; our DCI Bevan has found out the truth. Those children are free. They've gone. I can feel them flying away from us. The wee ones can finally rest in peace."'

To her great surprise, Dani felt tears escaping onto her cheeks. 'Oh, I sincerely hope that's true.'

*

'They sure are an unusual couple,' Sam said flatly, as they lay in bed together, with Dani's head resting on his chest and an arm tucked under his waist.

She chuckled. 'You can say that again.'

'I wouldn't have had you down as the type of gal who believes in angels and that type of hokum.'

'I don't, but the Hutchisons had created a kind of fantasy world after Neil died and in some weird way it gave them both comfort. Plus, the pair are extraordinarily convincing. Bill has this razor-sharp instinct that could easily be mistaken for something supernatural.'

'Give me an example.'

Dani described Bill's experience ten years ago as a witness in the High Court in Edinburgh.

'So you didn't tell Bill and Joy that he'd been right all along about that guy?' Sam said, when she'd finished her tale.

Dani raised herself up to look him in the eye. 'It would have broken Bill's heart to find out that lowlife creep went on to abuse another child. Knowing he was right all along wouldn't have given him any solace. Bill is only interested in stopping the bad guys, not in proving himself correct.'

Sam shifted down so that he could place a kiss on her lips. 'I think I'm starting to quite like you, DCI Bevan.'

Dani folded her body into his, rubbing her cheek against the stubble on his chin. 'And I might just be warming to you, too.'

Andy Calder had a determined look on his face. He intercepted Dani as soon as she entered the incident room. 'Ma'am. I've heard back from forensics in Glasgow.' He led her towards a computer on one of the desks. 'They've sent me some images they lifted from the digital camera.'

Dani stared hard at the screen. The techies had obviously done their best to enhance the pictures, but they were still very unclear.

Andy clicked through the bank of photos. 'There's a good number showing Amit Batra with Philippa Graves. They'd been deleted from the device, but the techs managed to retrieve them from the memory. Most of those are fairly innocent; the pair are having dinner or holding hands. But they're enough to prove an affair.'

'So that's why Amit wanted it. The question still

remains, at what point did he take the camera from Goff? Was the man alive or dead at that stage?'

'It's these shots which are of greatest interest, Ma'am.' Andy enlarged a couple of the photographs. They were part of the set Goff must have taken as they climbed the Ptarmigan ridge. But these two were not your regular tourist snapshots. They were a little blurry and seemed to have been taken whilst the photographer was on the move.

'That's Joanna Endicott,' Dani stated, peering at the woman in the picture, who appeared to be remonstrating with a man. He was tall and bulky, dressed in hiking gear and with thick, dark hair. 'Is that Micky Ford?'

Andy nodded. 'I'm pretty certain of it. Judging by the fine weather in that shot and the position of the sun, I'd say it was early morning.'

Dani perched on the edge of the desk and starting thinking. She ran through the details of the case in her head, including the timeline of events on the day that Joanna's group set out to climb Ben Lomond.

Bevan turned to Andy and laid a hand on his shoulder. 'Micky told me that he was still there for his father, even though he'd moved out. He said he was always on the other end of the phone. What if Jack Ford called him when he heard there were walkers missing on the mountain? They needed as many volunteers as possible to assist in the search.'

'It would have been perfectly natural for Jack to ask his son to help out too. So Micky Ford was one of the volunteers who searched Ben Lomond that morning. He was amongst dozens of others from Ardyle and wouldn't have been conspicuous. It isn't a long drive from Crianlarich.'

Dani shifted her vision back to the photograph Daniel Goff had taken on his shiny camera. 'Micky

Ford discovered Joanna and Daniel on the mountainside. But he got more than he bargained for. Joanna must have recognised him. Somehow, she knew who Micky was. Perhaps she'd already been investigating her mother's life in Ardyle and knew her connection to the Fords. Maybe Micky told her his name and it was familiar to her. Either way, Joanna confronted Jack's son on that hillside and told him exactly who she was.'

'Joanna Endicott was a clever woman and a lawyer. She would undoubtedly have done her homework before the holiday. I expect Joanna knew exactly who she was searching for. But Micky had no idea at all. He didn't know about his dad's affair or about the baby. All he knew was how his mum changed after the Ardyle tragedy, how she became unhappy and withdrawn, eventually to simply give up and die.'

'Joanna must have been jubilant to discover Micky on that mountain. I can almost imagine her clipped English vowels confidently informing Jack's son how his father had bedded her mother, when she was no more than a child. The pieces must have all slotted into place for Micky; how guilty his father was about the deaths of the schoolchildren and how there'd been something unspoken and sorrowful between his parents after that time.'

'Micky grabbed for her throat - probably wanting to choke those wicked words out of her mouth. The shock and anger must have been all consuming. He kept squeezing, until Joanna couldn't tell him anymore. I bet she didn't even get to the point of informing him that she was his sister.' Andy sighed.

'And Daniel Goff did nothing. All he could manage was to snap some photos as he ran away. But Micky must have chased him. Ford knew Daniel was a witness and he had that camera.' Dani suddenly looked up towards the ceiling and slapped a hand on her thigh. 'I know what Goff did! He threw the camera away, into the heathland. Most likely, he thought that Micky would go after the camera and not him. It would give him a chance to get away. But Micky decided to go for Goff first and then return for the camera later.'

'Micky caught up with Daniel Goff in those woods. The men were of a similar height but Micky was the stronger. They might have fought, or Micky may simply have lifted a branch or log and brought it down hard on the back of Goff's head. Then he shifted the body to the banks of the loch and threw it into the water. There wasn't time to dispose of Goff properly. Micky had to get back to retrieve the camera and appear to be participating in the search.'

'But it was Amit Batra who found the camera. He either saw Goff toss it into the undergrowth or he spotted the casing, glinting in the sunlight. Batra knew the significance of the photographs that were on it. Goff must have already threatened Amit with blackmail, as Philippa suspected by the change in his behaviour, so he decided to pocket it. Amit grabbed the device and not long afterwards, he was rescued. I reckon that Micky Ford wasn't far away when the mountain rescue boys picked Batra up. I think he saw the camera in Amit's hand. He resolved in that moment to get it back.'

'First, Micky tried to break into the bothy for it, but I stopped him. After that, we had officers guarding the place and then we allowed Irving, Batra and Graves to return to London. Micky's task became much more difficult. He was going to have to get the camera from Batra's home in Loughton.'

'But Micky is a delivery driver and he often made runs down to Docklands. This would provide him with his cover. All he needed to do was leave his pal's house in East Ham in the early hours of the morning and make his way to the Batra place. Micky is an experienced hiker, he may have trekked there through Epping Forest. Ford broke in, knowing exactly what he was looking for. It was easy to find the camera. He pocketed some other stuff as well, to make the robbery appear genuine.'

'Batra came down and confronted him. He probably knew exactly who it was. Batra may even have witnessed Joanna's murder; he was certainly twitchy enough after he was rescued. Micky would have overpowered Batra with ease; the guy was very unfit and probably terrified. I believe Ford beat him about the head deliberately. He needed to ensure Batra's silence. It looked like a burglary gone wrong, but it was cold blooded murder, just like the others.'

'At this point, Micky most likely thought he was safe. He'd left no forensic evidence at the Batra place and we were still searching for Goff, seeing him as our prime suspect for the Joanna Endicott murder.'

'Then things began to unravel. With Bill Hutchison's help, we found Goff's body. This meant we were beginning to look for a suspect who was closer to home.'

'I sounded off in the pub about you digging into the Ardyle case and the fact you were about to question Ronnie Sheldon.'

'There were plenty of folk in the Rob Roy that night who could have heard it, but I reckon it was Jack who mentioned it to his son. He was probably worried sick about the prospect himself. Joanna must have told Micky that Judy Sheldon was her mother's confidante. All of the sordid details of his father's affair were to be found in the notes and papers at the Sheldon house. What better way to get rid of all that evidence than to set fire to it.'

'We've finally got our motive,' Andy said with

feeling. 'Now all we need to do is prove it.'

Chapter Forty Nine

Bevan and Calder were in the process of discussing with DS Driscoll whether the photographs were enough to justify arresting Micky Ford, when Dani's mobile phone began buzzing in her pocket.

The DCI formed her face into a frown when she saw the caller was Sally Irving-Bryant. 'Sally?' She answered warily.

'Hello Dani, I'm sorry to bother you again.'

The woman sounded unsettled. 'Not a problem, how can I help?'

'I'm really not sure. It's James. We haven't heard from him for a couple of days.'

'Is that unusual?'

'Not necessarily. But he was planning to take some time off work. He'd mentioned coming to visit us for a weekend. Then Mum and Dad heard nothing more. Radio silence, as it were. The thing is, I told James something the other day that perhaps I shouldn't have.'

Dani felt her heart begin the race. 'What was it?'

'I had spoken to a judge friend of mine who said he'd recently issued a warrant to search a property in connection with the Joanna Endicott case – a cottage up in Crianlarich owned by someone called Michael Ford. I mentioned it to James, I don't really know why, I suppose to reassure him that progress was being made in the investigation. Now I just have this awful feeling my brother may have decided to do something foolish, although it would be incredibly out of character if he did.'

'Thank you for letting me know, Sally, can you ring me as soon as you or your parents hear from

James, okay?' Dani swiftly ended the call. She turned back to her colleagues. 'I think we may have a problem.'

The wind was blowing a gale. Andy pulled the police 4X4 up onto the side of the track leading to Micky Ford's cottage. They were still about half a mile away and not visible from the house. Dani zipped her puffa jacket right up to the neck and tried ringing James Irving's mobile number one more time.

'Still no reply,' she stated.

There were several squad cars and a van positioned in the village itself, waiting for Dani's signal to move in.

'Let's go the rest of the way on foot,' Andy suggested. 'We don't want to alarm Micky, if he has got James in there.'

Dani nodded, slotting a walkie-talkie into her pocket. She took a deep breath. 'We do this entirely by the book. We've got an arrest warrant for Ford, but our main priority is to ensure James Irving's safety, although if we can use the situation to gain more evidence against Ford, then let's take advantage of it.'

'Got that, Ma'am.'

The two detectives climbed out of the vehicle and proceeded cautiously along the track. After a quarter of a mile, they came across a BMW sports hatchback, parked at the edge of the road, jammed up against the hedgerow.

'That's James' car. What the hell is he playing at?' Dani muttered.

'He thinks this guy may have brutally murdered his two best friends in the world. James wants some answers,' Andy responded levelly.

'But it's not in his nature to go all Dirty Harry on us.'

'He's upset.'

'Not as much as he will be when I get my hands on him,' she fumed.

As they approached the run-down cottage, Dani saw the dark profile of Micky Ford in the back garden. He was chopping wood with an axe. The sight made Bevan feel sick. The man turned as they marched closer. Dani stepped over the low stone wall, scanning the cottage and outbuildings as she passed.

'To what do I owe this pleasure?' Micky called across, laying the axe down on the grass.

'Have you seen a man by the name of James Irving?' Dani asked calmly.

'Nope.' Micky gave a sly smile. 'I don't get many visitors out here.'

'Mr Irving's car is parked just up the road. Where else would he have gone?' Dani was beginning to lose her patience.

'Maybe he went for a walk in the hills, although I wouldn't recommend it from this glen. There are too many steep drops.'

Dani could stomach the man no longer. 'Then you won't mind if I take a look around?'

Micky shook his head but he appeared uneasy.

Bevan entered the house through the kitchen door and swept up the stairs, checking each room. Nothing. 'James!' She cried out.

Dani pounded back down to the hallway, glancing into the grubby living room, looking for any signs of James having been there. Maybe they were too late, she thought desperately.

Then she heard a noise. It was very faint, but it sounded like a pipe being tapped. Dani whirled around the ground floor, opening cupboards and kicking against panels. She started shifting the stack of bags and shoes that were piled up at the bottom of the stairs. Behind them all was a small doorway. Bevan wrenched it open.

The DCI had to crouch down low to get inside. But once through the narrow frame, the space beyond it was slightly larger. She saw his feet first. His legs were bent round into an unnatural position. There was blood seeping from a wound on his head. Every so often, the prone form before her was making the monumental effort to jolt his body, so that his boots knocked against the metal pipe he was tethered to.

Dani reached out and touched him. 'I'm here. You don't need to do that anymore. I heard you.'

The body slumped down in relief.

She released the tape from James' mouth and made sure he could breathe properly. 'I'm coming back for you, I promise. But I've got to make sure we can nail this bastard, for everything.'

James nodded. 'Do what you have to do,' he croaked.

Dani crawled backwards out of the cramped chamber. As soon as she emerged into the hallway, the DCI got onto the walkie-talkie and demanded immediate back-up and an ambulance. She jogged out into the garden, where Andy was keeping an eye on Micky. Dani scoured the ground for the axe, which she kicked out of reach with her boot. Then she got out her cuffs and firmly secured Micky's hands behind his back. 'Michael Alan Ford, I am arresting you for the assault and unlawful imprisonment of James Irving and the murder of Joanna Endicott, Daniel Goff, Amit Batra and Ronnie Sheldon.'

Whilst Dani continued reading Micky his rights, Andy rushed back into the cottage, following the trail of discarded rubbish bags to the cupboard under the stairs. 'James?'

'I'm in here,' the man hollered in reply.

Within moments, the back-up team arrived. Andy and Ian Kendal shifted James carefully out of his cubby hole and rested him on the filthy sofa until the ambulance got there. But Dani and Driscoll had already guided Micky Ford straight into the back of a van, whisking him away to the nearest police station.

Chapter Fifty

James Irving was recuperating in a very pleasant private room at the Edinburgh Royal Infirmary. Dani waited until he was fully awake before she entered.

His handsome face was badly bruised and a bandage secured tightly around his forehead, obscuring his left eye.

'What on earth did you think you were doing?' Dani sat gently on the edge of his bed.

'Is this part of my official questioning?'

'No, it's the shocked disbelief of a friend.'

James smiled and then winced. 'When Sally told me there was a suspect - who he was and where he lived, something sort of clicked in my head. This incredible rage took over. I'm not the brave type, as you know, but I felt I needed to confront this fellow. For the sake of Jo and Amit.'

'I do understand. But you could easily have been killed. Micky Ford has murdered four people. He's extremely dangerous. You could have called me to find out how the investigation was progressing.'

'I didn't think we were still on speaking terms.'

Dani sighed, realising how her irresponsible behaviour had put a civilian at risk.

'Andy told me all the details in the ambulance. This Micky Ford sounds like a clever guy. I don't think I would have approached him if I'd known how well he'd covered his tracks. I thought he was just some mindless thug. He was keeping me in the cupboard under the stairs until it was dark enough to take me out into the hills. The plan was to march me up one of the mountains and push me off a precipice. When he told me what was to be my fate, his voice was almost gleeful.' James shivered.

'What did you say to him when you arrived at the cottage?'

'I'd formed this sort of crazy plan on the way up from London. I told Ford I'd witnessed him killing Jo and Daniel. I had a Dictaphone in my pocket and my idea was that he would begin confessing everything to me and I'd catch it on tape.'

'Just before he murdered you and then destroyed the tape,' Dani responded dryly.

'Yes, I can see now that it wasn't a very good plan.'

'But it would have shaken him up, just the same. Do you still have the recording?'

'I think so, the guy never knew it was in my pocket, he was too busy beating me about the head and tying me up.'

'Did he actually say anything incriminating?'

'I'm not sure I recall. I was too busy being absolutely bloody terrified.'

'Well, we'll take a listen back at the station. It might make an interesting addition to the evidence we've already got on him.' Dani sounded philosophical.

'You *have* got enough to nail him, haven't you?' James shifted himself up slightly.

'You can never be totally certain. I had cast iron forensic evidence in my last case and the guy got off. I'm not counting my chickens.'

'Well, that's bloody depressing.'

'Oh, we'll get a conviction for his assault on you and most likely for the murder of Ronnie Sheldon. It's the other three where I think he's got a chance of an acquittal. Micky Ford has been extremely smart.'

'But he had Goff's camera in his possession. He'd tried to incinerate it, for heaven's sake.'

'It's good, but it's circumstantial. The best hope

we have is the statement from Jack Ford. He's prepared to testify that he informed his son I was about to question Ronnie Sheldon, the evening before the fire was started. He's also willing to tell the jury all about his affair with Kathleen Harris in 1983. I don't think the man wants to be a party to any more deaths. He is devastated that Joanna is dead. He genuinely didn't know Kathleen had gone on to have his baby.'

'Does Micky know yet that Joanna was his half-sister?'

'I'm honestly not sure. I think he must have worked it out and that was why he refused to give me a DNA sample. But Andy is going to spring it on Micky during the interviews, see if it rattles him enough to confess.'

'I don't reckon he'll tell you anything. That guy's a hard bastard. No remorse at all.'

Dani nodded sadly, she was inclined to agree.

James lifted his hand and placed it gently on top of hers. 'Are we still friends?'

'Of course,' she replied. 'But wait for me to call you next time. It's a bit melodramatic to get yourself kidnapped just so I can come and rescue you. It's actually a little kinky.'

James started the chuckle and then reached for his ribs. 'Oh, don't make me laugh; I'm in bloody agony here.'

Dani squeezed his hand and stood up. 'Don't worry I'm leaving. Make sure you get some rest.'

Dani Bevan observed her team closely. They looked absolutely exhausted. Now that Micky Ford was on remand, with no chance of being bailed, the adrenaline they'd been running on for the past couple of weeks had dissipated. She herself was fighting the fug of fatigue. But there was still more to do. Dani wanted all the evidence ready and in place.

'There's no hope of getting a confession out of him, Ma'am,' Andy began. 'Micky didn't even flinch when I told him Joanna was his sister.'

'We knew it was a long shot. I still think we've got enough. Micky took part in a line-up and Bruce Glasser identified him as the man who took the flowers up to the memorial. Then we've got the photographs, the witness's description of Micky's van parked up in Crieff and James Irving's testimony relating to the assault, with taped proof of the entire incident on Irving's work Dictaphone. The forensic team are currently working on the prints from the petrol can found near the Sheldon house. They believe Micky may have left his fingerprints on it when he handled the container back at his place, before he put the gloves on.'

'Jimmy Cavanagh has also withdrawn the alibi he provided for Micky when he was staying at his place in London. When he found out Ford was in the frame for three other murders, he admitted that after they got back from the pub, Jimmy was so out of it he had no idea if Micky left the house again that night,' Andy said.

'So the flowers,' Dave Driscoll put in, 'the 'M' on the card was for his mother, Mary, is that right? Our Micky *can* be sentimental about some things then.'

'Yes, once Micky had found out the truth from Joanna, he realised that his mother's life had been effectively ended on the day the children died. She was as much a victim of the Ardyle tragedy as they were. The poor woman was never happy again.'

'Perhaps Micky should have blamed his father for that, not all these other poor people,' Sammy Reid stated firmly. 'I refuse to feel sorry for the man, or any member of his family. The only innocent victims in all of this were Katrina, Neil and William. May they rest in peace.'

'Come on,' Dani suddenly announced. 'I'll buy you each a pint at the pub. Then we can all drink to that.'

Bevan had texted Sam Sharpe to invite him along. They deliberately avoided The Rob Roy, opting instead for a quaint little pub on the Market Square. When the officers had all piled inside there was barely a spare table remaining. Dani left a handful of notes with the landlord, who smiled gratefully at the unexpected business.

Dave Driscoll began to take orders. Dani found herself squashed up beside Andy Calder at the bar. 'Perhaps I'd better stick to the cokes, after my track record in the pubs of Ardyle,' he said lightly, flashing his boss a cautious glance.

'We're celebrating, Andy. Allow yourself a half at least.'

He chuckled. 'Look, Dani, I know Sam told you I called him in the States. I had absolutely no idea he was going to come to Scotland. I thought he might just send you a bunch of flowers. It was out of order, I'm sorry.'

Dani turned towards her friend. 'You could have placed me in a really awkward position. Just imagine what you would have thought if I'd contacted Carol about something you'd done.'

The man nodded. 'Aye, I'm not sure what came over me. It just seemed clear that you were making a colossal mistake getting involved with that Irving bloke. He's a smooth-talking, public school, lawyer-type. He's not one of us, like Sam.'

'Carol isn't a police officer either, she's a nursery nurse. I've never said she's not right for you. It's a double-standard, Andy.'

'But my phone call encouraged Sam to step up to the plate – or am I wrong?' Driscoll handed Calder a half of 70 shilling.

Dani said nothing. She couldn't disagree.

The detectives glanced towards the door, where Sam Sharpe was entering the pub, followed by Bill and Joy Hutchison. Andy leaned closer and murmured into her ear, 'I happen to think that the guy is good for you. He's uncomplicated and decent. You've had enough difficulties in your life without having to deal with a man who doesn't know what he really wants.'

Bevan beamed broadly as the trio approached. Sam placed an arm around her and landed a kiss firmly on her mouth. The rest of the team let up a hearty cheer and a few wolf whistles. Once the bevvies were in, the police officers drifted off to their own individual tables. Dani found herself in a foursome with Sam, Joy and Bill.

'I met these two in the town,' Sam explained, 'so I dragged the pair in for a quick drink. I couldn't allow them to slope off without saying goodbye.'

'When are you heading back to Falkirk?' Dani asked the couple.

'We check out first thing in the morning,' Joy explained. 'It's time for us to return to the house.'

'Poor Rita will wonder what on earth has happened to us,' Bill chipped in.

'Will you be in touch with Louise after you get back?' Dani asked tentatively.

'Oh yes,' Joy added with enthusiasm. 'I thought it might be a good idea to offer to have the boys for a weekend, so Louise and Fergus can have a few days away together. They haven't done that for a while.'

'I think it's a wonderful idea. There are so many great attractions to take kids to now. I'm sure they'd love Edinburgh Castle.'

Sam looked at Dani in surprise. He'd not heard her speak in this way before.

'It occurred to me that I should bring Neil's train set down from the loft. I'm not sure why it's been hidden away up there for so long. Ben and Jamie would get plenty of use out of it.'

Dani grinned stupidly at the sound of this, slipping her arm around Sam's waist and taking a healthy swig of red wine.

Joy and Bill finished their brandies and stood up.

'Are you going so soon?' Dani was genuinely disappointed.

'We must leave you and your team to celebrate properly. We've an early start in the morning.'

Bevan left Sam at the table and escorted the older couple to the door. Joy kissed her on the cheek and Bill briefly took her hand.

'Keep in touch,' the DCI said quietly, embarrassed to find that tears were welling up in her eyes.

'Oh, of course we will.' Bill seemed to hesitate for a moment on the threshold. Then he turned back and said, 'have you been following the case up in Stonehaven?'

'It's a long way outside my jurisdiction, Bill. I've not seen any of the details.'

'A young man was found murdered in a boat shed. His throat had been cut and he was carefully placed. He'd been seated in a chair with his hands laid palm up on his lap.'

Dani stood very still and blinked.

'It's him, DCI Bevan. Richard Erskine has killed again. This time, you need to stop the man.'

And with that, Bill and Joy were gone.

Dani turned and looked back into the room. She saw Sam chatting animatedly to young Ian Kendal by the bar and Dave Driscoll deep in conversation with Andy, a hand resting on his shoulder. The detective took a deep breath and smiled. She'd deal with Bill's words tomorrow. Tonight, they needed to celebrate.

*

DCI Bevan will return...

If you enjoyed this novel, please take a few moments to write a brief review. Reviews really help to introduce new readers to my books and this allows me to keep on writing.
Many thanks,

Katherine.

If you would like to find out more about my books and read my reviews and articles then please visit my blog, TheRetroReview at:

www.KatherinePathak.wordpress.com

To find out about new releases and special offers follow me on Twitter:

@KatherinePathak

© Katherine Pathak, 2014

φ

The Garansay Press

Printed in Great Britain
by Amazon.co.uk, Ltd.,
Marston Gate.